A Rum Do

By Dave Cheadle

A Rum Do
Dave Cheadle

Cover Illustration Raphilena Bonito

ISBN 9781912821945

A CIP catalogue record for this book
is available from the British Library
Published 2021 Tricorn Books
131 High Street, Portsmouth,
PO1 2HW

Printed & bound in the UK

A Rum Do

Contents

Foreword

A 17-year-old boy from a Wiltshire farming village joins the Royal Navy in 1961. With little knowledge of life outside the village, this is a story of how he plots and manipulates his way safely as a junior.

After training, he joins a frigate that sails to the Mediterranean. He witnesses the very strict rum culture that governs the lower deck. The living conditions on the small ship are a shock to him.

From the amusing run-ins with the Gunnery Officer to the very funny runs ashore in Gibraltar and Malta.

Then out to a small island in Hong Kong harbour where he witnesses hordes of Chinese refugees swarming over the border. On the lighter side, he sees The Beatles live just after their first LP. The hilarious day at the Navy swimming gala will be long remembered.

Finally, during his last months on Stonecutters Island, the worst typhoon Hong Kong has seen for many a year arrives. The 20 men fight 140-mile winds to keep the radio station running as well as having to rescue two families whose houses are surrounded by the sea.

On landing in Singapore on the way home, he is press-ganged into helping the Navy win the war that was not a war with Indonesia.

Interweaved with all these adventures is the worrying disappearance of two young girls associated with his close friends.

The boy

I sat on the wall just across from Swindon railway station watching the recruiting Petty Officer gather the lads as they arrived by car and bus. I had said goodbye to my mum, dad and sisters. They do not have a phone at home and I have never written a letter in my life. So it would be ten weeks before I could make any contact. Even though my father and I had signed documents to agree I would be in the Navy for nine years, I was undecided whether to cross the road and join the gathering.

I am just 17, having spent my life in a little farming village in deep Wiltshire. Over those years we had moved from a temporary bungalow to a new council estate in the village. The bungalows were put up early in the war to house workers at the Spitfire factory four miles away. Dad was removed from the Fleet Air Arm after a few weeks and sent to the Vickers's factory near Swindon to help build planes. He was a first-generation electrical and electronics engineer, not quite a boffin but his skills were essential to the war effort at home. To do his bit on the home front he spent the war in the Home Guard. He excelled and during the six war-torn years he rose from seventh in line for a rifle to second in line. He always claimed he would have been given a rifle if he had been born and bred in the village. Coming from Fulham and supporting Chelsea did not help. To be fair, he did help make hundreds of Spitfires and before that was a member of the Schneider Trophy

9

winning team in 1931. They won the world air speed record with the modified aircraft that was to become the very successful Spitfire.

Our new house was on the flightpath of the nearby American base so every evening after the war I would lie in bed and listen to the biggest bombers in the world rattle our windows. This was in the fifties when the strategic air force flew 24 hours a day carrying nuclear bombs over Russia. I remember wondering as they came into land if they still had their bombs. The noise they made, I was always surprised and relieved when they thundered overhead and nothing dropped off. When the monies were short you could visit the American office in the village with broken glass and get cash. With three engines on each wing, the B39 broke a lot of windows, though probably not as many as the villagers claimed.

The Americans brought fridges, cigars and cheap fuel to the village. Father usually came home from the pub with fat cigars and was very happy. Father was not so pleased when my sister wanted to go to the dance at the base.

As a child, we used to head up to London to visit my grandparents. Although I was a country boy, my dad and mum came from Fulham. Nearly every month in the summer we would stay with my granny in Munster Road for a weekend. Granny controlled her large family and if she said there was to be a gathering, then all the family did as they were told and gathered!

She had a house with three floors and further rooms up

in the roof space. As far as I can remember, as many as seven different families or more would gather over the weekend. Some staying at 194 Munster Road and the rest coming from all around London.

My bedroom was up in the roof. I shared it with other kids and a big water tank. Lying in bed late at night I listened to my father playing the piano and twenty odd drunks singing at the top of their voices. The only interruption was the tank topping itself up after someone had used one of the six toilets spread around the house. We soon got fed up and sneaked down the floors to witness all goings on around the house. Card games went on through the night where fortunes were won and lost. Arguments and fights would break out and Granny would drive the culprits into the road waving her big stick. It amazed me how she could not walk without the stick but during a fight she could wade in and bash people over the head with it. Dancing would be in one room, which was mainly full of women, any man dragged in by his wife was shouted and jeered at.

On Saturday afternoon all the men and boys went to see Chelsea. In the fifties all small boys were passed down over the crowd to seats at the side of the pitch. There were also men in wheelchairs, most of them wore their medals received fighting Hitler. Whilst we waited at the end of the game to be picked up by Dad, we chatted with the ex-servicemen about the game. Roy Bentley was my idol and he scored lots of goals. Peter Sillett and Ron Greenwood were also very good.

I hardly ever saw my parents throughout the two days of

partying. Before he got married my dad was the resident pianist at the Durell Arms Pub on the corner of Munster Road and Fulham Road. So all the men would drag him down there at night and again before Sunday lunch.

My favourite time was Sunday morning. Granny would prepare a Sunday roast for forty or fifty people. The great hunks of lamb or beef would be placed in the massive oven. All the veg and puddings were prepared by Granny and the kids. Before the grown-ups arrived in the main dining room, us kids would eat around the kitchen table. We would have the pick of the crispiest roast potatoes and specially made Yorkshire puddings followed by jellies and ice cream. Every child would receive a wrapped present at the end of the meal. The older children would then take us off to play whilst the mums and dads had what was usually a four- or five-hour lunch. At the end of the lunch we all headed to our homes. For us it was on the train to Swindon and then change for the village train. My mum and dad slept for the whole journey.

At school, my academic achievements were very strange. I was top in maths and pathetic in every other subject. I soon found out that mental arithmetic was where I really excelled.

My main achievements were outside of school where, from a young age, I had business savvy. I worked as a milkman's assistant to the guy who also ran the village pub. I added eggs and papers to the milk round and made serious money. Driving around the area in a milk van in the early hours of the morning was fun. Arthur the landlord always took the wheel when we delivered the milk to the police. I used to get up at 4.30 and my last delivery was just before nine. This was to my school with crates containing small bottles of milk for us kids.

A new school was built in the village. I was 13 and in the oldest year to start at the school. The first six months were chaos, with teachers joining and leaving and the buildings being finished. My friend and I suggested to the Head that we could run a tuck shop. This we did. The Head left soon after. We ran that tuck shop for two years without the new Head knowing that it was our business and did not belong to the school. Nobody ever asked! We did cringe whenever anyone said what a great job we were doing. At this time, I was probably earning as much as my father.

The new school had three tennis courts. My class had never played before but we fell in love with the game. Four of us started taking it seriously and it was the PE teacher's favourite game. We were all very good and left school with talk of us playing for the county. Not that Wiltshire had a reputation for providing England with players. To the best of my knowledge, all of my three rivals never bothered after leaving. The game went on to give me much pleasure.

End of school was approaching and so now, what to do? Career opportunities in the village amounted to farming or factories. I knew most of the local farmers from my milk round and through the pub landlord. I got a job at one of the farms just outside the village.

Farms around the village have very large fields and ploughing with large tractors and very noisy engines made it extremely boring. However, falling asleep and waking up with the tractor and plough embedded in a hedge was not a pleasant experience. In Wiltshire we plough very deep so all the equipment is firmly stuck in the hedge when you crash into it at speed. The only way to get it out was to run across the fields, grab another tractor and drive it back to the accident as fast as you could. Then hook up a chain to pull your tractor free from the hedge and drive like mad back across the fields. After which the second tractor needs to be returned. Followed by a sprint back to the rig and pretend nothing has happened. After four or five times of thinking I got away with it, I decided farm labourer was not for me. The owner did not disagree as he had watched a few of my adventures. I think his wife and kids enjoyed a fair few as well.

I considered farm management, however my local college said that if my family did not own any land I would really always be a lowly paid farm labourer. This would be true even if I was promoted to manage somebody else's farm. I had lived amongst local farmers long enough to realise the truth in that statement. With my farm labourer credibility ruined in the Wiltshire farming community I contemplated my next move. I had O levels in maths and technical drawing, so apart from a draftsman apprenticeship at Vickers, options were limited. I did not want to follow in my father's footsteps.

I found myself outside the recruiting offices of the Army, Navy and Airforce. They were all next to each other in Swindon. I didn't know if my gift of the gab and entrepreneurial spirit would be of any use in the services. My first priority was to get out of the village. Making money would have to wait.

The Army would be full of shouting and running here and running there. Although I was fascinated by aircraft, had been watching them as a boy soar overhead and my father was connected with the industry, I thought the Airforce had an air of snobbery. I knew it would be full of oiks who fixed things for the fighter pilots who would all be Hooray Henries.

I had seen the sort gathering in our market square for the weekly hunt. Mounted on fine horses with glass in hand shouting posh welcomes to each other. Henrietta, Cynthia and Reginald would leave us to pick up the horse shit as they happily trotted off to gallop through their vast lands.

I finally chose the Navy. The Navy promised travel and the prospect of getting far away from village life.

I went through the recruitment process and was selected to be an artificer but then failed the medical, as I had something wrong with my ear. When the recruiting office called me, I was very upset, however he told me I could still join as junior radio electrical mechanic. He quickly said I should pass the medical for a junior mechanic as it can be completed by your local GP. He provided the forms which I presented to my village doctor. When we got to the ear section, he put his head under the table and whispered. I just about heard what he said and repeated it. He stayed down and gave me three or four more words and I passed with flying colours.

On the wall just across from Swindon railway station, I thought about the options and figured what had I got to lose. So, I jumped off the wall, crossed the road and joined the throng.

I had left the village and my first ever long train journey was enjoyable. Chatting to my new friends and enjoying the West Country as it sped by kept my mind away from thoughts of family and friends. My new life was ahead and luckily I found going into the unknown very exciting.

In the early sixties, communication was by post, only businesses and well-off people had phones. If any urgent message was needed to be sent, you went to the Post Office and sent a telegram. Buses, trains and motorbikes were the only form of transport for most of the population. The radio and national newspapers were the only way most people got to hear the news. TV was just beginning to spread across the country. As far as my family was concerned, I would be off grid.

We arrive at Plymouth Station and climb into the back of the first of many RN lorries in my career. The canvas roof only just keeps out the rain and certainly not the cold. The last seat on each side was the only place you could see out properly and they were taken by the two Navy guys giving the orders.

1960's Royal Navy

Little did I know that in 1960 the Royal Navy was still barely out of officers buying their own commissions and also depended on the Henries from the country estates to provide their Naval Officers.

At the time I joined the Navy it still had a very old-fashioned system. The Naval Officer was god and could not be approached. You could only complain to the next up in seniority. The gap between the lower deck (Chief Petty Officer and below) and upper deck (Naval Officers) was very large. Each rank soared above the basic junior ratings. Approaching and talking to any Naval Officer, or even Petty Officer, was just not possible.

The Navy increasingly needed intelligent young recruits to be trained in navigation radar, gunnery radar, computers and sophisticated communication systems. The lower deck was being filled with intelligence and not the labourer it used to require. This meant fitness and muscles were now being replaced by men of a more delicate nature. Over the next ten years the electrical and electronics sections would become close to 50% of the manpower on a ship.

A Gunnery Officer could no longer scream, flay and lash his ratings to throw more shells into the guns. Now he had to ask politely (OK, forget politely) how soon the radar or computer would be fixed. It was a strange time to be joining the Navy. It would take quite a few years before the Navy realised that its officers should be studying the up-and-coming technology.

Over hundreds of years, the Navy had developed and perfected a way of replacing the recruit's way of life. The Navy was their new family. Gradually each recruit would realise that he could not do anything without permission. The food, accommodation and medical needs would be decided for them. They would be told where and when to go, when to sleep and when to wake up.

For the next nine years there was no escape. In this era, nine years was fixed in stone. Many of the ratings joining would spend their years trying to wriggle out and escape, few succeeded.

The new class of joining recruits was to be taught how to become a matelot in ten weeks. A class consisted of about 25 boys aged between 17 and 23. In the beginning there would be all trades mixed together. The main problem with this was the variety of different sizes and intelligence. The course was mainly physical with the onus on strength and fitness. The idea was to keep adding pressure until each student broke. This was still a time when the wooden stick was carried by all teaching staff and could be used when no one was looking.

HMS Raleigh

We finally stopped in amongst many wooden huts apparently in the middle of HMS Raleigh, the Navy Training School. We are told to form into three lines. With a Petty Officer (PO) and a Leading Hand (LH) marching back and forth in front of us shouting orders or statements, not sure which. The fact that they tried to teach us how to stand to attention and march in civilian clothes within the first ten minutes of being in the Navy was strange but to shout at us for getting it wrong was hilarious. Anyway, we walked, tripped, stumbled and ambled to our wooden hut.

The hut was a long thin room with lots of windows on both sides. Below each window was a bed and small cupboard. At one end there was a door that led to a long wide passage, straight across the passage was the toilet and washrooms for 25 of us. At the other end of the hut on the left was a single bedroom and, on the right, a small office. These were the living quarters of the Leading Hand (LH) which is the navy's equivalent of an Army corporal. Leading Seaman Adam Yelton was the man who would be in charge of us over the next ten weeks.

So we each settle down at the bedside with our name on. Next to me sat a strange looking lad whose name was James Hickingbottom. This I know because I read it on his bedside name tally. We were speaking to each other but he was foreign and I could not understand a word he said. It took time, but gradually we could just make out a few words each of us said. He pointed at a map and I realised that he was from 'something bridge' near Wakefield. Speaking slowly, I made what I thought was a funny quote. He replied 'gee oar thaas codding'. The deep Wiltshire yokel and the deep Yorkshire man eventually became friends but never fully understood each other. Even today after any quip I say 'only codding'.

Before I had chance to understand what anyone else was saying the door at the end of the cabin flew open. In walked three large Navy guys. Banging their sticks on the end of each bed they passed, they finally stopped in the centre of the room. 'Everybody shut the fuck up,' screeched the leader of the three. 'I am Leading Seaman Adam Yelton and for the next ten weeks I am in charge of you all. This mess deck will be immaculate at all times. You will rise at six, be in bed exhausted by ten. If you are lucky, in two weeks you will be allowed down the NAAFI [social club on base] for two hours for a pint.' I will not bore you with his hour-long rant of all that he will do to us if we failed to obey his orders. The two other LHs were from the huts either side of us and were obviously close friends. All three were probably six foot three and looked like the front row of any good rugby unit. They finished most rants with shouts of 'no poofters' and would swing round and stare into the face of whoever was nearest and shout 'what do we want?'. 'No poofters' would need to be shouted back.

When they left, we all looked shocked and stunned, some guys even frightened.

Jim in the next bed said, 'I thought they wanted us in

their Navy? What's the point of killing us before we get to a ship?!' Some other guy shouted, 'We should name the bastard "Screech". With a name like Yelton it's perfect, he does not yell he screeches!' So our leader was named Screech.

One of the lads asked, 'What do you call them in sheep shagger country, Dave?' Most didn't have a clue what 'no poofters' meant, myself included. My parents never told me any of the facts of life so I had a lot of learning to do. In our village we had enough coping with girls, especially during the potato picking, when all the village would gather. It would be five or more weeks before I found out what they really meant and how it was illegal in the Navy and the rest of the country. So for now I listened carefully whenever the subject came up and dutifully said 'no poofters' as soon as Screech's face lunged at me with that question.

Next day we were marched to the galley for our first breakfast. As I approached the serving table there was a chef in a greasy whiteish jacket waving a metal slice. 'What do you want?' he demanded.

'What are those?' I said pointing to a large tray of flat whitey-yellow things floating on grease. Once again, I was the laughingstock.

'EGGS idiot!' shouted the chef. In Wiltshire, an egg has a yolk which has a ¾-inch dome and is orange; these were flat and a very light yellow colour. I then pointed to what looked like stew on fried bread. 'What's this?' And he said, 'Shit on a raft!' I arrived at the end of the queue with spam in batter and baked beans on my plate.

After surviving the breakfast embarrassment, Screech marches us off to the hairdresser. Although it was only a haircut, Screech could not wait to reduce us all to convicts. It would soon become obvious that embarrassing us, or inflicting any other punishment, would make his day. So, my blond locks and Cliff Richard cut was soon on the floor.

Then on to the clothes store. The fact that the RN felt the need to force us to wear their brand of underpants and vests I found very strange. They were like 1920's woollen swimming trunks. Most of the clothes were thrown at us and getting the right size was impossible.

We assumed we could change them later after the rush. No, it seemed they preferred to ridicule us over the next ten weeks. Each parade or occasion would require us to dress in certain clothes. Once we stood in line, Screech would walk down, check each of us and burst out laughing at whoever had a garment too big or small. The offender would then have to step out, do a twirl and report to stores.

Any other instructor would have told us to forget everything else and just concentrate on getting the right fitting for their boots. Instead, Screech threw roughly sized boots at everyone and refused to allow any exchanges. Marching and running many miles with heavy packs in the wrong boots did not make a man of you and was not funny. However, think of the fun he would have when he scraped us off the road.

I will not bore you with the day-to-day tasks we had to do to get fit and used to the Navy way of life. I expect all armed forces would have had a similar experience to the one we endured.

Many evenings we would be locked in when Screech and his two pals would roar off into the night on their motor bikes. They each had a large Norton Dominator and when not out would spend the other nights taking them apart. They often came back drunk and into our room to shout abuse and to rattle their sticks along the beds. Sometimes they would be in one of the other rooms either side of us. We would hear them and be grateful some other classes were getting it instead of us.

The 25 of us found lads of like minds and tended to mix together. I spent most of my time with the three London lads. They were funny and very streetwise, at the same time nice guys who got along with everybody. All three are about six feet tall and good looking in their different ways. Danny Smith has light brown hair and is slim with broad shoulders. Mick McDonald is stocky and has large hands and impressive muscles in his arms and legs. Gino Mancini is just a standard six-footer with tight black curly hair and a Mediterranean tan gained by way of his Italian parents.

The London lads could open all the doors, including the office and Screech's bedroom. Even his filing cabinet was opened for us to explore. The telephone in the office could be used but it had to be used sparingly, as getting an outside line could get Screech in trouble and he would guess we had used it.

When the lads first got into the office, Gino was in there studying the report sheets that were laid out. 'It looks like Screech fills these reports out and then puts them in the out tray. So the plan is we change the marks if anyone is struggling once they are ready to be sent to the main office.' Danny and Mick nodded and I just shrugged my shoulders.

The boys' trade would be able seaman and they would go on to fire guns and missiles whilst performing day-to-day seaman duties. From their whispers I got the feeling a judge had let them off a small prison sentence if they joined the Navy. Still, they were a joy to be with, always making me laugh and looking for trouble.

One day they were talking about two guys who seemed to spend lots of time together. Both were always immaculately dressed, with never a hair out of place. Danny said, 'I think Philip and Robert are rather fond of each other.'

'We need to look out for them,' said Mick. 'If Screech susses them, he will inflict pain and anguish and leave them bruised before he reports them.'

'I will have a quiet word with them and tell them we have their back,' said Danny.

'Hey careful what you promise,' laughed Mickey.

'What the hell are you lot talking about?' I asked. I got a full explanation and they followed it with, 'Those guys have a life to live and they do not deserve any agro. It's how they are and they cannot do anything about it and should be left on their own. We have seen at close hand in our streets in London, they suffer terrible beatings by coppers and ignorant drunks. They are used as snouts, or if they have money or are famous they are blackmailed or exposed to the press. As it is illegal the law is not on their side so they have to live underground.'

Our first pay day arrives, an event every two weeks for the foreseeable future. To ensure we all smoke, the Navy give us 300 cigarettes free of charge on a shore base and 600 at sea. This first pay ritual is made all the more amusing as we have to march forward, come to a halt, salute, give our name and stick out our pay book. The officer returns the salute and a PO peers round from behind the officer and sticks a few pound notes on the pay book and a bundle of cartons of cigarettes in the arm of the recipient. The PO then shouts 'right turn, quick march!' Ninety per cent of the guys on turning right throw the cigarettes into the air. The first few march on, leaving their ciggies on the floor. The rest of us were told to pick them up at the time. Would you believe Screech had us practising for two hours on how to right turn and not drop any cartons?

Today we are being introduced to our gas mask. First we are led into a room filled with new masks. Unlike the rest of our clothing, the team issuing our new mask took a lot of attention into making sure we had the right size and helped us adjust them to fit our face. The Petty Officer Gunnery Instructor (GI) explained that later in the day we will be sent into a gas chamber, which would be filled with gas. We immediately paid attention to every word he said. He went on that if your mask leaked you would find it hard to breath and would not enjoy the experience. Finally he said in the last few minutes of our time in the chamber, we would be told to take off the mask to ensure we would always take gas seriously.

We fell in and marched over to the gas chamber. Outside in three rows we were facing the GI. With Screech stood beside him he explained that in certain circumstances we may have to spend days in the masks. It is very important that we learn to eat and drink whilst keeping the masks in place. He pointed to a table which was stacked with rolls. 'Each of you go over and select a roll and come back and fall in.' The choice was a hot dog with mustard and tomato sauce or salad and mayonnaise. Later I wondered if the chefs who added sauces knew the exercise we were about to try. They may even have been hiding behind the hut, to watch us make fools of ourselves.

We were all told to put on our masks, this included Screech and the GI. The GI now started shouting through his mask. It was very muffled and difficult to understand. Eventually we understood that Screech was going to demonstrate when the GI shouted 'Eat!'.

He duly shouted 'Eat!' and Screech broke off a bit of hot dog roll, lifted his mask under his chin and quickly threw the food in and sealed the mask again. From an initial silence the muted laughs began to rise. Screech had a piece of bread in one eye and a hint of red and brown slime in the other eyepiece. The GI, who could not see Screech's achievement, shouted for silence in the ranks. Screech was shaking his head up and down and side to side trying to get the bread down to his mouth.

The GI then screamed for us to copy Screech and shouted, 'Troops eat!' We all copied and some of the guys' artistic creations were unbelievable. The one with a bit of sausage in an eyepiece was beaten by the one with a slice of tomato and the other with a cucumber slice. The GI held his hand up and took off his mask and, looking at Screech, who still had his bit of roll in his eye, started to laugh loudly. Even Screech saw the funny side of it, looking at all the class having achieved some part of food in an eyepiece. To punish us, the GI then proceeded to lecture on how the marines and army spent days in the trenches wearing their masks in the last war. We had to keep our masks on and finish our food throughout the lecture. Towards the end, the GI found it hard to concentrate with all the waggling of heads, trying to get at the last remnants of food stuck in their eyes.

Now to the gas chamber. Suddenly we were not so cocky, tightening the straps and worrying we would have a leak. The 27 of us were herded into the small room and watching the GI prepare the gas. The plan was to stay in the room for 30 minutes and then on the GI's order remove the masks and run out as soon as the door was opened. The gas started to produce a cloud and soon we had a hard job seeing across the room. After about ten minutes one of the guys started coughing and holding his mask, he went over to the door and banged on it. As they let him out another guy rushed past us and left with him. Eventually the GI took his mask off and shouted for us to do the same. We did, and immediately started coughing and pushing towards the door. It finally opened and we all rushed out and fell on the ground gasping for breath. To be fair, the GI was last to leave and didn't seem to need to fall on the ground dramatically like we did. The lad who rushed out behind the guy with a leak was taken back into the room and had to spend another 30 minutes to enable him to pass the test.

The day of our NAAFI trip arrived and we were allowed to go down to the bar from seven until ten-thirty. We sat in large groups swigging pints as fast as we could. By the time we were thrown out we were all singing and hanging around outside. Slowly, gangs of us drifted off along the paths back to our hut. As the four of us turned a corner we looked down a side path, and in the moonlight there were two people in each other's arms. They had their hoods up so we could not see who they were. Next minute we heard a shout of 'No poofters!'. 'Screech,' said Mick. We rushed down the path to find three blokes in civvies raining punches on the two people.

One of them broke away and ran. Two of the blokes in civvies ran after him. Mick and Danny followed the lad and the two civvies as they ran round the corner. Gino and I were left with the third civvy who was throwing punches and berating the lad. It was dark but Gino was struggling with pulling the attacker away. All I could think of was the old trick we played at school. So, I went on my hands and knees behind him, looked up through his legs and shouted 'Push him!'. Gino gave him a big shove and he fell backwards over my body and tumbled into a ditch. We grabbed the guy and ran. Once we had got a good distance away, we stopped and took the hood off the guy and it was Robert, one of the guys who we said we would protect.

'Get back to the hut and get into bed pronto,' said Gino.

'That civilian was Screech, wasn't it?' I asked.

'Yes and that makes the other two Cotton and King, Screech's two mates,' Gino replied.

Gino and I ran back to find Danny and Mick. Just as we were about to hare round a corner we heard shouting, so we stopped and peaked round the bend. The Naval Patrol had apprehended both our two guys and Screech's mates. Throughout the night the camp was guarded by the Naval Patrol, mainly around the perimeter fence.

We assumed the guy that escaped was our other friend Philip and he seemed to have got away. All we could do was get back to the hut and get into bed. Fifteen minutes after we got back, Philip rushed in.

'Did they recognise you?' we asked him.

He looked across at Robert with a smile and said, 'No I don't think so, how about you Robert?' Robert shook his head and we all waited to see who would come through the door next. Mickey and Danny crept in 20 minutes later and Mickey told the following tale.

We rushed after the two civvies (the other two Leading Hands) and came upon them holding the guy and punching him in the gut. Each of us grabbed one from behind and ripped them from him. At the same time there was a loud shout and sharp whistles. We looked up and running towards us was a Naval Patrol consisting of a Petty Officer and four guys waving night sticks. As they approached, we whispered 'Run!' to the lad and he was off into the trees. The PO took charge and demanded to know what was going on. Danny got in first and said we were going back to our dormitory when we saw these two civilians attacking a young lad. We shouted but they did not stop hitting him so we jumped on them. 'What more could we do?' said Mick.

The PO asked the two civvies who they were and they gave their names as Leading Hands Cotton and King from the training group. 'ID cards!' the PO demanded looking at them, he said, 'Take those two out of earshot as they are junior to these two.' There followed much discussion and finally the PO came over and said to us, 'We know who you are, so go back to your hut.'

As we left he asked if we knew who the LHs were. We said not at first, we were just trying to rescue a fellow sailor being done over by two civilians and it was dark. After you stopped us, we realised they were Leading Hands from our training huts.

'What were they doing? it was very nasty,' we said.
'We saw,' said the PO, 'and who was the lad who ran off?'

'Didn't get a look at him,' we replied.

So we were left not having a clue what was happening.

'Where is Screech?' asked Danny.

'Last time we saw him he was down in a ditch,' I said. Gino explained how he pushed him over me and we ran.

'What if he is still lying there?' asked Mickey.

'Let's hope it rains,' I said.

'Very hard,' said Gino.
'They must have been out on the town,' said Mickey. 'Why wear civvies if they were staying on camp?' Nothing more happened that night and we all drifted off to sleep.

Next morning there was no shout of 'Hands off cocks, Hands on socks!' and no Screech striding down the aisle banging on the beds. I am sure we were all ready to cry a 'No poofters' reply when leered at. However, all we awoke to was silence.

We dressed like lost sheep realising without Screech telling us what to do we were lost. At last, dare I say it, a sheepish looking Screech strolled into the room with a slight limp. His face and hands were covered in bloodied scratches with a plaster on his nose! We were all crossing our legs, biting our lips and turning our heads away. The first one to smile, grin or giggle would be dead and thank god no one did. We got our orders for the day, fell in outside the hut and were marched away to our first lesson. Once settled in the classroom, the instructor said today's lesson was first aid and dressing war wounds. You could not make it up!

Nothing more was heard about the incident but the four of us were being picked on. Any nasty job that came up, Screech would look round and almost apologetically select one of us. Gino said he would nip in the office every now and again and make sure we got the marks we deserved. It was agreed they did not know it was Philip or Robert that they attacked or they would have been in the firing line. Screech and his pals were probably too drunk and could barely remember how they got into such a snarling rage. We now visited the bar in the social club regularly and whilst the four of us sat round chatting it was decided we needed some insurance in case Screech found a way of getting back to us. Rumour had it that he was going away the next weekend, so the plan was to break in (not really necessary as Mickey had made himself a key). We planned to tear his place and office apart to see if he had any secrets.

Friday came and at the end of the day Screech roared away on his Norton. I suggested we go in at midnight and the other three just looked at me in distain. 'Why don't we do it on Saturday morning?' they asked. I shrugged. 'He has his curtains closed,' they added. Then it dawned, we could inspect the place without needing lights. If anyone came in through our room, we could go outside by the back door and vice versa. One of us lay on the bed nearest to Screech's room and one of us played football outside his door. Cotton and King were nowhere to be seen but we could not find out where they had gone. Finally, the duty PO would do rounds on an ad hoc basis but we would see him coming and none of the three had any reason to go into Screech's room.

We already knew where he kept everything as we had a casual search before just as a laugh. However, it was now important we find something juicy. My new pals were good at this and my job was mainly lying on the bed or playing football. At last, Danny had an exciting find and they came out with two large bags of stuff. We went over to the empty football fields and sat in a small crowd stand. There were books, photos, letters, knickers, shoes and a handbag. The subject was just teenage girls. I had never seen anything like it, the theme was violence and pain. It was disgusting!

Danny said, 'This geezer is not into beating up men, that's just his way of diverting attention away from what he really likes, and that's hurting teenage girls. These letters are about arranging and trapping girls and leaving them in a mess. They are also boasting about ones they each have performed on in a one-on-one situation.'

'The objects could be mementoes, I have read about such things,' Mike said. 'The problem is that all the letters are typed and there are no addresses or envelopes, also the names are no doubt false. As they were hidden under the floorboards in the ground we cannot prove that he knew about them. Even the photos are distorted and it would be hard to recognise any of them. They could be Eastern European. Screech could say he knew nothing about them and he had never even thought of lifting floorboards. He must pick his mail up in one of those shops that keeps mail for you. I expect lots of matelots in Plymouth use them.'

Mick suggested that we put it all back and come up with a plan. Admitting we broke into Screech's office was not an option, sending an anonymous letter was, but needed a lot more thought.

During most evenings we spent an hour or two in the social club, all of us enjoyed flirting with a gorgeous young girl called Patty. She just collected and cleaned the glasses as she was too young to serve drinks. We learnt her dad was a Chief Petty Officer and was not happy with this being her first job. He met her at the main gate every evening and if she was late he came straight into the camp to look for her. 'No chance of me walking you home then?' said Danny.

'What trade is he?' I asked.

'Stoker,' she replied.

'Chief Stoker! Christ does he come in the camp waving a big spanner?' laughed Mickey.

The next three days saw us on the water. We spent a day rowing large sea boats and got back to our hut absolutely knackered. Sat outside on the grass we were joined by some of the boys from the class in front of ours. They asked if we had done the day on the sailing ship yet? When we said it was in two days' time they told us what to expect.

The Captain of the boat is a retired Lt Commander war hero. He was badly injured in the war. His behaviour was weird and apparently we were in for an interesting day. The main warning we were given was that, if it was a nice day, he would make all the class jump in the water. The problem was he would insist that all the boys took their clothes off. His point was that he did not want wet clothes on board. There was a shower down below and he would send the guys down four at a time. However, he would send the smallest quietest guy down last on his own. He would then go down below and try to join him in the shower.

We told Screech about the strange skipper of the yacht. He said, 'I have heard about him, it's been going on for years, it's just a bit of harmless fun.' Walking away he turned round and said, 'I have always fancied a trip on that fancy yacht, I will ask if I can go with you to make sure you behave.' Then walked off chuckling.

The day arrived. It was a magnificent boat, the high-gloss varnish gleaming in the sunlight. The boat had been grabbed by the Navy from a high-ranking German minister at the end of the war. The yacht was old and had no engines so needed a very experienced sailor to navigate it out of the marina.

Here he was in all his glory, Lt Commander Retired Barkley Bertram Brown. He was a rotund bear of a man, ugly barely described him.

With a wide grin he cried, 'Welcome, welcome, all my young sailors fall in and I will explain your tasks. You are my crew and you must obey my every command. This fantastic yacht is a beast, fast and nasty, without engines we can easily get into trouble. We have a good breeze today and at full speed and leaning over at 40 degrees you will all have to be on your toes.' He welcomed Screech and said, 'They tell me you begged to accompany your men as you love sailing, so you will take the wheel while I show everyone the ropes [shrieking with laughter at his own joke]. I will put a little sail on to get us enough speed for you to manoeuvre us out of the marina.'

Danny quietly asked Screech if he was a keen sailor and got the angry reply of, 'Never done it before.' There were 13 of us on board, the rest of the class would be sailing the yacht tomorrow. Once we got enough sail to move the vessel, Barkley gave the wheel to Screech and rushed off to get the boys stationed around the boat to raise the sails. I could see the panic on Screech's face, so made my way back to help him. I thought of telling him how good I was with tractors but decided against it.

Between us we managed to get in a lane between boats that looked like it would get us through the hole in the sea wall. The problems were that as the sail filled with wind, we began to increase in speed. Also the wheel was on the same level as the rest of the deck so we could only see 30 yards in front of the bow. We both worked up a sweat swinging the wheel back and forth. Finally we just missed the sea wall and were out at sea. Barkley walked back to us and grabbed the wheel and said to Screech, 'Well done LH, you have not lost your touch I see.'

The next four hours were fantastic. We got out of Plymouth harbour, put up all the sails and raced up the coast. We each got a go at steering and hauling the sails up and down, then changing course with the sails swinging from one side to the other. We then headed back to Plymouth and found a spot about half a mile offshore and Barkley said we would anchor for our luncheon.

Once anchored, he declared it a wonderful afternoon and we should all have a dip before luncheon. He gathered us on deck and took a section of the guardrail away and lowered a ladder into the sea. Laughing, he shouted, 'We cannot have any wet clothing spoiling my deck so we will go swimming in our "buffers".'

We all looked to Screech, who was standing next to Barkley, to take charge of the situation. Barkley put his arm round Screech and said, 'Come on LH Yelton, let's show them the way' and proceeded to take his kit off. Screech looked from him to us and back again. He had a decision to make!

He only started to strip off and him and Barkley jumped in starkers. Mick said, 'Well now we have seen his bum and willie.'

'Not much of a talking point for the future,' Danny replied. We had planned to refuse but by this time half the boys had thrown off their robes and jumped in. So, not to be left looking like party poopers, we joined them.

Back on board wearing skimpy towels provided by Barkley, we drank fine wine and ate canapés. The scran, as we called it, was not well received, starting with what's this vinegar? Haven't they got any beer and why have we got babies rusks with cold fish on them? What is wrong with pies?

We set sail for home and the saga continued. Barkley started sending four at a time down for a shower. He was a cunning bugger (no pun intended) as he sent Screech down in the first four. He explained this away by saying he wanted to be the last to shower as he had to put his full uniform on and rush off as soon as we docked for a function. He did not know that we knew, so his plan would seem very clever to his shell-shocked mind!

Sure enough, we had all showered except Danny and Barkley. We passed Plymouth docks and were not far away from the marina. So Barkley slowed us down by lowering all the sails. Only leaving up the one that allowed us to gently leave the marina earlier. He then gave the wheel to Screech and pointed out the direction that would take us to the marina entrance.

Down in the shower Barkley happily jumped into the room with Danny. Danny gave him the space and waited for any approach. It came as a surprise as Barkley wrapped his arms around thinking he would be strong enough to hold him. They were both wet and Danny just dropped to the ground and jumped back up and head butted him. Barkley had not been brought up in the East End and the vicious kick into his groin left him on the ground.

There was a key in the bathroom door so Danny locked him in and put the lights out and nipped back on deck. Walking up to Screech he said, 'The Skipper is feeling unwell and says for you to take us back to the jetty.'

'OK, but how do we slow the thing down?' he asked with panic in his voice, followed by, 'It has no engine.'

One of the guys piped up with, 'He taught the six of us to use these buckets with ropes, we throw them over the side and let them fill with water. Then we pull on them and it slows the boat. As you come into the marina you shout to us and we slow it down.'

'Is he taking the piss?' asked Screech.

'Apart from ramming the jetty what other method have we?' I ask.

We drift slowly along the lanes of boats until finally we see our jetty. The plan we have agreed on is that as we approach, we pull down the sail, the bucket pullers pull like hell and Screech swings us alongside. Two guys with ropes jump onto the jetty and pull the yacht into the jetty – simple!

What happened was – we struggled to lower the sail so we were going too fast. The bucketeers could not slow the boat and all finished up at the stern together eventually having to let go of their buckets. Screech lost sight of the jetty when the yacht got within 20 yards of it. The yacht smashed into the jetty at speed and we all fell down!

The two rope guys got up quickly, ran to the front and jumped onto the jetty and pulled the yacht alongside. Once we had brushed ourselves down, we informed Screech we should get in our transport and leg it quickly.

Screech put his hand up and said I will take it from here. To his credit, he went down and talked to Barkley. When he came back he said Barkley had agreed, he had knocked himself out when he fell in the shower. He was sorry we had to bring the boat in on our own and he would mention us in despatches. He would say we performed an almost impossible task bringing a yacht in under sails and it was a good job the Leading Hand was an experienced yachtsman!

Screech finished by saying he had told Barkley to stop trying it on with sailors in the shower, he was obviously not very good at it.

Over the coming weeks, the subject of Screech died down. We got enough fun retyping his reports. The boys had now got his signature down to a tee. You were issued with three important documents when you joined. Any of which was a punishable offence to lose or damage. The Pay Book that had all your medical, clothing stamps and other information about you. Also your ID card and finally your Leave Card that you put in the main gate when you went out and collected it when you came back. We left the ID card alone but the other cards often went missing for a few days and mysteriously popped up in the most unusual places. We discussed Cotton and King at length and the overall opinion was that they were led by Screech but did not know about his strange brutal fetish. Screech was the good looking one and the main attraction of the three. He needed wingmen to feed off and give him admiration and respect. They hung onto his every word and no doubt enjoyed the fact he was the one that got the girls for them. The documentation we had seen also indicated that Screech would be alone if he had carried out any attacks.

We continued to go on long-range route marches and spent days on the parade ground. Days were also spent firing rifles and machine guns. When we asked the armourer why we did not fire pistols, we were told that only Naval Officers were allowed pistols. 'Was John Wayne a Naval Officer then?' came a question from the back. 'Shut up' was the armourer's reply. 'I supposed Roy Rogers is out of the question then?' was whispered but not heard by the instructor.

Some of the instruction in the classrooms did help us understand how the naval organisation helped mould us into the men they require. One such lecture was by a naval schoolteacher who told us there had been much thought in how to get lads to become their own man.

He started by saying most children spend ten years in school with the same friends and then find work and spend years with the same work mates. Imagine instead every two years you changed schools and joined a new school knowing nobody and in the next two years just as you were finding your way around you started another new school. Then did the same in the workplace. You would be a completely different person than you are today.

In your naval career you will be sent to a new ship or shore station every two years. You will arrive at a new ship, trained to do your job in the rank you have achieved. First day on the ship you will know nobody and will be expected to take over the duties of the person you are relieving. You will see that guy for about one hour and he will be gone, his bed and locker will be yours. The equipment or duties he looked after or performed will be instantly your responsibility. As you enter the mess deck all eyes will turn on you. It is a matter of fact that whoever helps you first and becomes your friend, after three weeks you will be edging away from them. They are lonely people who need you more than you need them. Your equipment will have faults that nobody knew about but you will have to fix it. Blaming the guy who has just left is not acceptable. If you are a Leading Hand in a mess there will be old guys who have never bothered with promotion that will do their best to undermine you. You are on your own on a ship of 250 men, avoid any advice for the first three months. After two years you will be on your own again, only this time you will be better at it.

What the Navy expect to achieve by this method is that every man will be totally in charge of himself. In battle you must have teamwork but in that team all men have to be able to complete their tasks without any help. Teammates do not cover for each other; they expect their mates to be up to their own job.

Christ, we thought, does he really believe all this shit? Anyway, he is a non-combatant school master who does not even go to sea! Over the years I have often thought about that lecture and it is probably correct.

Passing out parade

With a few weeks left we are preparing for our grand march out. We will form the guard and march around the parade ground, accompanied by a Royal Marine band. Even Screech is excited about it, he gets to march behind us with his stick rammed up under his armpit. Shouting and screaming and often getting his lefts and rights completely different to the ones we are trying to keep up with. To get in step, you have to perform an ungainly shuffle and sometimes we shuffle for 50 yards before we are all in step. By that time Screech has surpassed his name and has reached notes men should never be able to achieve. Once he shouts halt, we then shuffle about until we are in a straight line. This is what Screech is waiting for, he now walks between us correcting our arm and hand positions on the gun we are holding. This is usually achieved by him rapping you on your knuckles with his stick. Guess which four get the most attention? After today's performance he will definitely lose his Pay Book and Leave Pass this evening. I am voting for the ID card as well.

It is important to pass this march out, as if we fail, we will be back classed and not be going home for two weeks. After leave, I will be going to HMS Collingwood in Fareham, which is about six miles and a ferry ride away from HMS Excellent in Portsmouth, where my London buddies are going. We plan to meet up in London during our leave. I don't think Wiltshire is ready for them and I am looking forward to seeing London again.

We were in our usual spot in the social club and Patty was collecting our glasses looking rather distressed. We told her to sit down and, looking around, she sat down slowly.

'What's up?' we asked.

'If I tell you will you promise not to tell anyone?' she replied.

Danny took over and said, 'You can trust us Patty.'

'Last night someone tried to grab me as I went along the path above the parade ground,' she quietly said.

We were stunned and began looking from one to another. She continued, 'He was swearing horribly in a very strange voice and had hold of one of my arms pulling me into the bushes. I caught my shoe and fell and my arm wrenched from his hands and he fell back as well. I just got up and ran into the bright lights and reached some guys walking to the main gate and stayed with them until I got to the main gate. Then I crossed the road and my dad was late. When he eventually turned up for some reason he was angry with me.'

Still we just sat there in a stunned silence. Finally, Danny asked, 'Did you recognise him?'

She shook her head.

'Have you told your dad?' he asked.
She shook her head again and said, 'If I tell him he will stop me working and I will be stuck at home.'

'We have to report this,' I said.

'If you do, I will say it did not happen and I was messing about with you all,' she said with some panic in her voice.

'So what do you want us to do?' said Mickey.

'I don't know,' she replied.

Danny held his hand up to stop us all asking her questions and arguing about her answers. 'One or two of us will escort you to the main gate for the rest of the week,' he stated. 'If we are not in the club you have to ask one of the staff to walk you to the main gate saying you thought you saw a man in the bushes. No – wait a minute – we will tell the club manager that we were walking behind you and saw a man in the bushes and he should make sure all his staff are escorted to the gate. We will also inform the Naval Patrol what we saw and get some others to report it as well. In the meantime, we will escort you for the next week on the quiet.'

We went down to the main gate and inside the office was a Regulating Petty Officer (RPO). We told him our story and described the man as over six foot four with dark black wavy hair (Screech). The time was 11 o'clock and all the NAAFI staff were walking past to the main gate. We said we had been talking to other guys in our hut and they had seen a similar guy moping about. Luckily the RPO did not spot that we should have been back at our hut by 10.30.

Back in the hut we asked the lads if Screech was in his cabin. He and his two henchmen left about eight and have not returned, they replied. Sitting on our beds whispering we agreed the only thing we had not told the RPO was about the guy actually grabbing Patty.

With this and Screech's stash under his cabin, we decided that in the next few days we would send an anonymous letter to the RPO.

We checked and the NAAFI staff were leaving together every evening. Patty said she preferred one of us escorting her. Who is your favourite we asked? Patty grinned and we all argued about which one she nodded to. I have only been in the navy for eight weeks but it seems an age since I left boring but safe Wiltshire. Were we making a mountain out of a mole hill? Are we inventing a problem that was not there? Even so, the next afternoon Danny slipped an envelope into the in tray of the main gate addressed to the RPO. The letter within explained where and what could be found under Screech's cabin.

The next day was the last before our marching out parade so we spent a day of practice on the parade ground. Screech accused me of looking like a farmer waddling along with his pitchfork instead of a sailor marching with his rifle. Then all 25 of us were stuck in our hut working long into the night cleaning, ironing and whitening our belt and ankle straps. It took at least three hours getting the shine on our boots up to military standard.

Today's the day, if we pass we all become members of the Royal Navy and are given a badge for our uniforms.

We also all leave HMS Raleigh and travel to our homes across the UK. After two weeks leave, we go to the various training establishments to learn our trade before going to sea. Marching out takes about four hours of inspections and rifle drill.

The marine band plays the national anthem and we, as the guard, hold our rifles in front and stamp to mark the beginning of the end of the parade. We then form into three long lines and march round the parade ground. Finally the line of sailors, with rifles on their shoulders, approach the stand where an Admiral awaits our salute.

To pass, we must get all three lines dead straight and of course stay in step with each other. Marching in front of us was a Naval Officer and behind us was Screech. Both the officer and Screech were shouting 'Left, right left right!'. The problem was they were not in sync and when the officer shouted 'Left', Screech was shouting 'Right!'. Someone within our ranks shouted very loudly, 'Leading Seaman Yelton [Screech], shut the fuck up and listen to the officer!' There was only 20 yards before we reached the dais but we all quickly did a few shuffles and passed all the top brass and grown-ups in three very straight lines. We marched to the end of the parade ground and there was a CPO in charge of the parade. If he shouted 'Right turn' we would have passed. If, however, he said 'Left turn' we would have to march around again and failed. He shouted 'Right turn' and we all cheered. This ten-week nightmare was finished and we could now see what the Navy really had to offer.
We marched up to our huts laughing and singing. Screech brought us to a halt and gave us the command to right

turn. We all stood in line waiting for Screech's speech. Instead, an officer came round from the back of our hut and said, 'Leading Seaman Yelton leave those men and come with me.' Screech went off with the officer and a PO came and stood in front of us and said, 'I am now in charge of this class. Go to your hut and pack up all your belongings and I will issue you with your Leave Passes, travel warrants and draft documents in two hours.'

When we were finally dismissed, we hurried into the dormitory and rushed to the windows to see what was going on. The door to Screech's office and cabin was locked. Outside there were at least six regulators of various ranks. Danny had his ear to the office door and said they are ripping the place apart. We decided to pack and get ready to leave, then go down the NAAFI for a farewell drink and find out what was going on. It was still only midday, so we went over to the PO and told him our plan, which he was happy with. Before leaving we asked what was going on? 'It's above your pay grade,' he snapped.

The social club was full as all the trainees had got the afternoon off after an end-of-course ceremony. No sign of Patty, so we asked one of the other girls where she was. She didn't know so we went and asked the manager, who looked at us suspiciously.

Danny said, 'We arranged to meet her for a farewell drink, we have just passed out and are leaving this afternoon. She has looked after us over the last eight weeks.'

He looked around and led us out the door and said, 'She is

missing. She went out of the gate with the other girls and her dad was not there so she walked with them into town. When she got to her road she walked off on her own and has not been seen since. Apparently, her dad was set upon by someone on the way to meet her and is in hospital.'

We just sat in silence while all round us the boys were celebrating. Finally, Mickey growled and said, 'Where was Screech last night?'

'How would I know, I spent most of the night shining my shoes,' I replied.

We finally got back to the hut and all but one of the regulators had left. He seemed to be guarding the outside door to Screech's room. Inside our dorm was the PO and we went straight over to him.

'Is this,' pointing to the office door, 'anything to do with the missing girl?' we asked.

'What makes you think that?' he replied.

'Well, it's a bit of a coincidence as we have just been told by the NAAFI staff that she is missing.'

'Best ask the Leading Patrolman outside,' he said.

Outside we asked the guy and he said they had a tip off but there was nothing here. 'Your Leading Hand is down the main gate answering questions,' he said. He then demanded our names and said, 'He would have to tell the RPO we were interested.'

'No problem,' said Danny, she was a friend and we are happy to help. The guy then went into Screech's office and phoned the RPO. We followed and could see the hole in the floorboards exactly where the stash was, they had the right spot. The leading regulator put the phone down and said, 'You four are to report to the Regulating Office at 08.00 tomorrow morning for an interview with the police.' No point in arguing. We informed the PO and he said, 'Stay here the night and go on leave after they have finished with you.'

We each told the police exactly what we discussed all evening. Patty was worried that someone was following her and stalking her. She told us and we reported it to Regulating Branch. We thought we had it covered. Every evening either we or the NAAFI workers escorted her to the main gate and watched her meet her father. Before that she said she had escaped several attempts to snatch her. One night we got a glimpse of a large guy about six four with black hair.

They asked if we knew who sent a letter about the cabin at the end of our block. 'The only people who had access to those rooms were the three Leading Hands and the door was always locked,' we said. When asked if I thought she had run away, I said, 'It's a bit of a coincidence that the father who was supposed to pick her up was attacked. If he had been able to be outside the gates then wouldn't she be OK?'

Sitting on the train from Plymouth to London Paddington we agreed to meet in a week's time. They gave me the phone number of the local pub and a time to ring. In the early sixties, only posh people had phones at home.

I got off at Swindon station and on the 30-minute bus drive to my village thought about my ten weeks in the Navy. The advantages were my three new friends and the fact that I had escaped HMS Raleigh in one piece. Here I was approaching my village in my brand-new Navy uniform, ready to walk from the High Street through the village to our council estate. I feel chuffed and proud. I had to somehow try and put the last few days aside and try to enjoy being with my family and friends. There was nothing I could do, and doubt the three musketeers from the East End of London will be any help. All the news we got was on the radio or Dad's *Daily Mail* and there was no story about a missing girl from Torpoint or Plymouth.

After a few walks about the village and evening trips to the pub with my dad, I soon realised I looked a right dick in my uniform. From the first impression and proudly telling everyone how great the Navy was, it became obvious that all my mates and the rest of the village folk did not want to know what they were missing. I decided not to tell them the truth, that they were better off staying where they are. With everyone going about their normal business, all I could do was wander into one of the many pubs at lunchtime and play darts with the village layabouts. I finally hooked up with three of the village ex-gang leaders who were now all in the Army. Apparently, the Wiltshire judiciary had a leaning to the Army rather than sending their guilty felons to borstal. These guys were a lot of fun and took me to places in the village I had previously not known existed. If that opened my eyes, I was then whisked off to Swindon and introduced to an underworld of drinking, gambling and all sorts of dodgy dealings. Managing to turn down a few invitations of night raids on factories and stores was not easy. I did say, however, that when I got back from my six-month electronics course I would be able to help with burglar alarms and listening devices!

A trip to the Big Smoke

Within a week I had phoned Danny and we agreed to meet up at Paddington Station in two days. I told my mum and dad I was off to spend a few days in London with my three pals from the East End. They were then immediately worried. The East End is a place to avoid, I was warned. Why not stay with my sister in Fulham, my dad urged, it will be much safer.

'One of my friends has an Italian restaurant in Brick Lane so I am staying there,' I said.

'Give me the name and I will make some calls,' said Dad. I had no idea of the name. The results of them nagging for the next two days meant me having three phone numbers that I should call if I needed rescuing.

I enjoyed the memories of our family outings whilst travelling to London. The train and underground were breathtaking to a small boy from a Wiltshire village. The steam engine approaching and screeching to a halt had me grabbing for my mum's hand. The lectures from my experienced parents on the safety of travel I remember particularly well, especially if you get lost on the underground always get off at the next station. I remember when messing with my sister, I let Mum, Dad and her get on a train and rushed to the next set of doors planning to jump in and surprise them. The doors closed and left me on the platform! They sped off into the tunnel and I was left on the platform stunned. I had no idea how much trouble I was in or what to do next. I must have switched into training mode as minutes later another train arrived and I got on. Seconds later it whizzed into the next station and as it slowed I saw my parents holding onto my sister. I jumped out and had about 30 yards to run down the station. To this day I swear, they were breaking the plan and getting on that train. Just as they were halfway in the carriage they heard me shouting as I approached at top speed. Their relief only lasted seconds before the anger kicked in and I was threatened with stoppage of Chelsea football. Dad said he was getting on the train to see if I was on it? Yeah right!

I arrived at Paddington and at the end of the platform station stood Mick and Danny. They were dressed in what I supposed was the latest gear. Coloured jackets and rollneck jumpers, I must have looked like I had just come up from the country. Their first words were, 'Dave, we need to get you down the market, we cannot be seen with you on our manor looking like an overgrown schoolboy! Even our mums would laugh at you.' I thought they were joking but no, we jumped on and off a few buses and finished up in or around Spitalfields Market where I was soon suited and booted. Which was what the boys suggested I did with my old clothes. I did decide to keep them as I thought it best if I wore them when I got off the bus back at my village as they would not understand a deep red jacket (bless them).

We went to a pub nearby and chatted around the obvious subject until I had to bring it up. They told me they had asked a family friend who was a detective who might be able to help.

'Yes,' said Danny. 'We are getting together with Alan tomorrow night to see how we can get it moving as its going nowhere at the moment. Tonight we are meeting Robbie a Lieutenant in the Regulating Branch he is just back from Plymouth, We have been talking to him about our future in the mob [Navy] as we are not happy with being seaman. Gino is thinking the same and he will be joining us tonight when he has finished in his father's restaurant. Robbie could come with us to see Alan tomorrow, let's decide that later.

'Alan has been told all the details of everything, and we mean everything. He has taken it all away to study it and make a few phone calls. He agreed not to let on about the source of the information until we agree the way ahead tomorrow. We have also provided the very same to Robbie. He is family and arranged our joining up in the RN to keep us safe. For the last two years he has been with the RN Criminal Investigations Unit in Portsmouth.'

I had to ask them, 'What does keeping you safe mean?'

They looked at each other and Danny said, 'It's very complicated. Both Mick and Gino's families have always lived on the edge of the criminal bosses in the East End. They grew up with their dads working for my dad, they were foot soldiers that delivered and collected but were not on the enforcement side. You could say they were small fry but they were very well paid. The most important skill was to remain loyal to the big players like my dad and keep him informed of any external danger. When my dad died his brother, Albert, took over. There are now foreign groups who are infiltrating London and getting very powerful. So far, they have not had the nerve to threaten the East End. Mick and I were encouraged to get in with some Cypriot lads and run with them. The Cypriots were getting very powerful and our crowd needed information on the opposition. We fell out with them and the daughter of the top Cypriot boss accused me of assaulting her. We were in trouble and Robbie, on hearing of our problem, suggested the RN. So here we are. We visit our families but do not socialise locally. We have a pad paid for in the West End and that's where we entertain when in town. Gino's family's restaurant is in the East End and it's safe for him there. Being Italian, they have their own set-up. So, Alan is police but keeps an ear out within the force and gets brownie points when he captures criminals provided by his snouts.'

'Makes everybody happy except us sons that have to do what we are told,' whispered Mick angrily.

The plan now is I stay at the West End flat with Danny and Mick with Robbie and Gino meeting us there. After a few drinks we will go on to their favourite rock and roll club to meet their mates and grab some girlies. Sounds good to me, having won a jive competition at the Swindon Locarno I was ready to show them some moves.

The flat was massive with three bedrooms, kitchen and a very large lounge. Danny showed me round and said the place was theirs whilst they don't upset any of the family. I was introduced to Robbie who produced what looked like a forced smile.

'I have heard a lot about you,' he said, which seemed more like a question than a statement. He quizzed me on my background and didn't seem to listen to any of the answers. I had the feeling that I would have to be careful around this man. Gino and I hugged and passed pleasantries. It felt great to be greeted by someone who was pleased to see me.

Robbie's news was confusing as he said, 'I have just returned from Plymouth and gone over the case with the Navy regulators. Screech had not been charged with anything and would soon be on a Leading Patrolman's Training Course. His Navy records have not got any information on the incident you lot describe but as it was a police investigation and off the base, perhaps Alan will have more info tomorrow.'

'Let's get this straight, Screech is soon to be LRO (Leading Regulator) a member of the RN Police?' I asked.

'Yep,' Robbie replied.

'Where's the course?' I asked.

'HMS Excellent at Portsmouth,' Robbie replied.
Danny cut in with, 'That's where we are going in two weeks for our gunnery and seaman training, we can check him out.'

'Should be fun,' said Mick.

'I should be able to join you as it's only a ferry ride across the water from Gosport,' I added.

Danny said, 'Spookily Mick and I are planning to do the same as Screech and change to the regulating branch. After a two-year stint at sea we can request to change branches. We would spend all our time chipping decks and painting them if we stay in the seaman branch.'

Gino then said, 'Yes I am planning to change to the catering branch.'

'So in a few years you three could be on a ship with you two controlling the discipline and spotting all the cons and dodgy dealing and Gino will be in charge of ordering all the food from ashore,' I grinned.

'Bought at special prices,' Gino commented.

'Delivered by vans straight into the heart of the ship's storage rooms,' said Danny rubbing his hands.

'Smuggling must be an issue now and being done daily across the fleet,' I said, 'but, I have no doubt you will do it better.'
'Meantime you are fixing the radar,' laughed Mick. 'Once I am at sea give me a year and I will have a plan that you can use.' We all raised our beers and Mick shouted, 'To the big meeting in one year!'

Then we went to a big dance hall in Hammersmith and danced to live music. There was a bit of standing on the edge of the dance floor pint in hand staring at the talent to start with. However, there was a live group that apparently were quite famous and they were outstanding. All four of us were well into jiving and were soon on the dance floor. It took a few violent clashes with a number of girls before I worked out what was the norm in trendy London. Once I had achieved it, I homed in on the lady I had been watching all night. We danced well into the night until we finished up in a sitting area near the bar. Finally we could hear each other speak and we exchanged names. I find I have been dancing with Sophia and I should call her Sofie. We both looked at each other and were obviously shocked by our accents. Sofie sounded like the Queen's daughter and I sounded like I had just got off my combine harvester. We then found our homes in Wiltshire were about 17 miles from each other. She lived in a big posh mansion; I did not mention my council house. She knew my village and said it was only a 30-minute drive away (or four hours on your horse I thought). Mummy and Daddy had a flat in Chelsea and she used that when she was up in town. We were slowly joined by the other three, now turned into six. The boys were all with loud London girls who were whooping and shouting. I looked at Sofie and she was way out of her comfort zone. To her credit she slowly came round, I did not realise that an East End accent was just as hard to understand for her as mine. She whispered to me, 'Nice people, where are they from?'

'Born and bred Londoners,' I said.

Danny suggested we head for the flat and the rest of the evening was a great laugh. Finally, we dispersed into three bedrooms with Gino and his lady left in the lounge.

In the morning, my bedroom door was kicked open and Robbie stepped in with a big mug of tea and shouted in the true naval manner, 'Hands off cocks and hands on fucking socks!' Sofie sat bolt upright and displayed her wares magnificently before grabbing the blankets. Robbie with a big grin on his face saw a way of getting another look by handing her a mug of tea hoping she would drop all to grasp the cup. I leaned over, took the cup and said, 'Piss off Robbie.' He left shouting over his shoulder, 'We have breakfast booked in the Italian over the road in one hour. Should be time to give her one more,' and slammed the door.

'Sorry about that,' I said, 'you have just met Robbie.'

'Who is Robbie?' Sophie enquired.

'I am not sure but he seems to have some sort of control over my three mates.' I then spent some time telling the story of our joining the Navy and subsequent adventures over the last four months leaving out the criminal aspects.

Breakfast was another triumph, lots of banter and exaggerated stories of what we got up to last night. Danny suggested we should all do it again tonight but there were excuses being drifted about. He then asked what's the best band and venue in London tonight. After much discussion amongst everyone, the girls came up with a name and followed it with we will never get in there.

'OK,' said Danny, 'if I get us in, hands up who will come?' They all cheered and even Sophie's hand went straight up in the air. He then named a pub down the road where we all had to gather at seven. Danny added, 'By the way, it is Robbie who will get us in, so if when you get to the pub you see him at the bar, the gig is on.'

Robbie pulled me aside and said, 'I have got you a present,' and waved Chelsea tickets in my face. 'Change of plan, we are all going to the match and we will meet Alan at your dad's old pub on the Fulham Road, the ground is nearby.' I told Sofie about my dad playing the piano there many years ago. We said goodbye and I hoped I would see her tonight. In the early sixties, we were many tiers below the likes of Sofie's family and she was probably not used to mixing with the likes of us.

As Robbie swanned back over to the others, I was left wondering why he was going to all this trouble to make my weekend so special. I could just about see the Chelsea tickets but my dad's pub as well? I was left thinking how he knew but realised I had probably mentioned it to the boys on an annoying amount of occasions. Still, something did not quite ring true. I decided to enjoy it while it lasted.

Robbie and us four boys travelled out to the Fulham Road to Durell's. As we sat in the taxi we discussed our girls we were with last night. I got a lot of stick because Sofie seemed to come from the landed gentry. Robbie kept saying I was punching above my weight and I replied she was just a simple country girl. After a while they left me alone and turned on Danny who was with a stunning little blonde girl. Typical Danny conquest they all agreed, five foot midget and would look great in a school uniform.

They all poured into the pub, looked round the room and asked where my dad played. This was very embarrassing as I had never been in the bloody pub! You are talking between 1951 till 1953, I was about seven I explained. My dad's house was just up Munster Road. We sat down with

Alan the detective who was smaller than the rest of us. At about five foot nine he was wiry, fair haired, slim and once again a very smart looking fella. He dished out a printed report to the five of us.

Leading Hand Adam Yelton had an alibi with Leading Hand Terrance Cotton from the next hut. He said he spent the five hours from when Patty left the NAAFI until two or three in the morning with his friend. They said Terrance Cotton has signed a statement to the fact that he was with him all evening. First they were servicing their motorbikes and then they went down the NAAFI for a few beers. We cannot confirm this as the staff do not remember them. The problem is that it was the night before everyone was going on leave and it was packed. He said they were going ashore but he had lost his Leave Card and they could not talk the guard at the gate into giving him a temporary one. He added that he had a run-in with the duty PO a few weeks earlier so was told to piss off. The duty PO confirmed he refused to let Screech leave the camp. They then said they went back to Cotton's cabin and had a few beers.

Adam Yelton had a few run-ins with the police as a young teenager. He came from a rough estate and both parents were heavy drinkers. The Navy took him on after he was threatened with a light sentence to borstal. He had anger issues and all the arrests were for fighting. He was also accused of assault on a girl but the charges were dropped. Since joining the Navy he has had very good reports, constantly being recommended for promotion. He was made up early to Leading Hand with exemplary reports since. Only the best get selected to become instructors.

As an instructor he is well thought of, the only criticism was his determination to make men of the recruits; this sometimes meant he needed to be reined in.

Patty had run away from home twice whilst at school. Police were called when the social services suspected child abuse. Mother and father were interviewed and angrily denied any harm to their child. Patty refused to confirm or deny it. Patty was on a concern list. The school and social services had to file regular reports. She did not seem to have any close friends or a boyfriend. This seems strange as she was a beautiful looking girl and the NAAFI manager said she was great with the customers.

The father had a good naval record and had been promoted to CPO early. He was assaulted on the night and left unconscious in bushes near the normal location he met Patty. He said he was asked for a light by a hooded bloke and was hit immediately and remembers nothing else. He said he met her every night as he did not like her walking home alone late at night.

There was no mention of the documentation we informed them of. There was a hole dug under the hut floorboards but it was filled back in and nothing was found. The refill work seemed to have been done recently.

Alan summed up by adding the girl had either ran off or been abducted or killed.

As she has a history of trying to leave home this should be our main focus. However, if she ran off then it has to be assumed she went with whoever attacked the father.

We have not been able to find any boyfriend or anyone close to the girl. If she was abducted then the guy knew about the father and dealt with him first. Then he followed the NAAFI workers until Patty left them. It would make sense that the abductor either lived on the camp or worked there. The police cannot treat Yelton as a suspect unless they can collapse the alibi. At this time, they cannot even prove he left the camp.

Putting my hands up I said, 'It's amazing how much influence you guys have to get us all this information. The facts are we are nowhere near solving this puzzle. If you can do a number on Screech when you join him in HMS Excellent that might help. If Robbie can find where Cotton is so we can have a drunken chat with him in a bar somewhere, that could also work. I may have read too many whodunnits but the mother might be the key. If she knew about her husband's abuse and the reason Patty kept running away she might have arranged the escape. All we can do is get on with our lives and wait for something to break.'

Danny nodded and said, 'We will keep trying and see if we can wrinkle something out.' Then he raised his glass up and said, 'Alan and Robbie!'

Robbie said, 'You guys go on to the stadium, Alan and I will catch you up.'

As we walked down the Fulham Road to Stanford Bridge I carefully enquired about Robbie and Alan. Danny sighed and said, 'They both work for the firm, god knows what they are planning.' Mick added the Navy has more than one hundred ships spread all over the world.

'What's that got to do with it?' I asked.

'Do not quote me but there is not a safer way to get stuff from A to B than in a warship.'

I looked ahead and could see the ground so I just shook my head and let the comment pass.

The match was against Cardiff and Chelsea were not playing well this season. They had only won once so far. The crowd were disgruntled and in the famous Shed Stand you would be a brave man to sing the Welsh national anthem. In the end we lost 2–3 and there were fights and scuffles all the way to the tube.

We gathered in the pub in the evening and Robbie was there waving tickets. The London boys and girls were all gathered in a crowd at the bar throwing back drinks. I checked out Danny's little blonde girl and she looked even younger under my sober scrutiny. Sofie turned up at the last minute and we sat down and seemed to find it difficult to find things to talk about in the quiet corner I had selected. After a few difficult silences I suggested we join the rowdy crowd at the bar. The night repeated itself and Sofie and I had a great time on the dance floor and had no difficulties talking, shouting and laughing whilst pouring drinks down our heads. The night repeated itself and in the morning we were soon back in the Italian having breakfast and preparing our individual goodbyes. Sophie and I swapped addresses and I had her telephone number and quietly mumbled I did not have one. I did think of staying on but it was pretty obvious I did not have money, clothes or the knowledge to escort Sofie to her normal

London haunts. She did suggest the theatre but when she looked up and saw my mouth wide open in horror we both knew it was not a good idea.

On the last night, Robbie invited us to a posh fish restaurant. I had never ever been in a restaurant of any kind, so was completely out of my comfort zone. The four of us were led to a table and a man pulled the chairs out for us, then gave us a small book and told us the specials for the evening. I opened the book and found we were in a place called Bentley's and they had been serving Londoners for over 60 years. Looking around the place it was very busy and I felt underdressed.

The list of food was confusing until I came upon 'Fish and chips'. Thank god! I thought, I will have that. Robbie took charge and ordered a bottle of white wine and beers all round. Danny leant over and whispered, 'Robbie likes to play the big shot, we will just have to put up with it as he is paying.' Just as well, I thought, my fish and chips were two weeks' wages. I was playing it cool and pretending that I did this sort of thing every week. So I thanked Robbie when he ordered me half a dozen oysters to start followed by a lobster bisque (which meant nothing to me).

My plan was to copy everything they did, so when shells arrived (with what I can only describe as a large snot in the middle) I became worried. Robbie then took a little bottle of sauce and shook some drops on the oyster. He then lifted it to his mouth and let the slime fall in! The other boys were doing the same, but Danny whispered watch that Tabasco sauce, it's hot. Well my mother has never mentioned or used a chilli so consequently when I picked up the bottle I thought it's not hot, so it must have cooled down. I copied their actions to perfection but put more sauce on to cover the thing in the shell.

When the oyster hit my mouth it exploded and I had no idea what to do. With my hand round my mouth I stood up, sat down, stood up and sat down again, but refused to scream out. Robbie grinned and said, 'Hey Dave, you had that oyster swimming in Tabasco, very impressive.' I ate the rest of the oysters without the Tabasco and with my mouth still burning. The soup and fish and chips were amazing.

Robbie ordered a pudding I had never heard of, but was delicious. We then sat back and were served with very large brandies. I was pleasantly well fed and watered. I leaned back and surveyed the room and thought what a great way to spend an evening. Robbie, Danny and Mick were in an intense discussion about a guy in the East End who was taking liberties. I was not included in this discussion so continued to look around the room. A very beautiful girl walked up and stopped by the elderly couple sitting to the side of me. The girl asked if they were enjoying the evening and the food. They continued with small talk and the old guy asked her what country she came from? She told them Denmark. The old guy said, 'I was in Denmark just after the war ended.' 'Where?' the girl asked. 'Aarhus,' he replied. With a yelp of delight the girl said, 'That's where I am from!' and introduced herself as Freja. Losing interest, I continued my people-watching around the restaurant.

An hour later and another brandy, the lovely Freja arrived at our table to enquire if everything was OK. Robbie was immediately captivated. Slightly drunk he chatted her up. Finally she left and watching her rear end disappear, Robbie growled and said, 'I love Swedish girls.'

Danny replied, 'There is no way she is Swedish, she is Dutch.'

Robbie said, 'A fiver says she is Swedish,' and stuck his hand out. Danny shook the hand. Mick looked up and said, 'Here we go, by our rules Dave and I can come into the bet. I bet Norwegian,' he said.

'Well Dave?' said Robbie, 'Can a country boy afford to lose a fiver?'

Gambling is something I have yet to add to my sins and Robbie was right, I did not have a week's wages to risk. I grinned and said, 'The only reason I am hesitating is I know where she comes from and it would not be fair to take your money.'

They all laughed and said, 'That one won't work, put up or shut up.'

Robbie was deliberately being disrespectful and treating me like the country bumpkin he had decided I was. So rather than feel guilty, I shrugged and said, 'Danish.'

Sitting in this place with all these rich people made me very uneasy, normally I would not rob my friends but these people at this moment did not seem like my friends. There was some sort of rivalry or even hatred between Robbie and Danny. Mick was accepting it and I, it seemed, was being dragged along.

Danny was anxious to win the bet and was looking about for Freja. When she next walked past, Danny leant back and asked, 'Is that accent Swedish?'

She kept walking and looked over her shoulder laughed and said, 'No Danish.'
Mick grinned and Danny and Robbie stared angrily. 'How did you know that?' demanded Robbie.

Thinking as I spoke, I lied, 'I have an uncle who has a Danish wife and they have stayed with us quite a lot.' Followed by, 'I did tell you I knew and you refused to believe me.'

Robbie full of brandy would not stop and was trying to find a way to have another bet. Finally he came up with, 'We bet you cannot tell us where she comes from in Denmark.' Danny chirruped up with, 'Over half the Danes come from Copenhagen.'

I was getting angry now; they were still treating me like the village idiot. 'I could have a bloody good guess,' I said, 'and it would not be Copenhagen.'

'Where then?' demanded Robbie.

'Is this a bet?' I counter-demanded.

'Yes,' said Robbie and turned to the other two and said,

'Are you both in?'

With Robbie looking at them, they look at me, I shake my head and mouth, 'No.' They opt out and I say, 'Aarhus.'

Freja passed by and I asked, is that an accent from Aarhus I can hear? 'Yes' was her reply, 'How did you know?' 'I have an uncle married to a lady from Aarhus,' I said.

They threw what they owed at me, it was nearly a month's pay but I tossed the money back and said, 'Put it towards the bill.' I wondered why it all got so intense. The devil in me almost said, I bet I can tell you her name, but even drunken London yobs would become suspicious if I got her name right as well. I also thank god the old couple had left their table long before the betting began.

I agreed to get together with the boys when we both got settled in Portsmouth.

Back to the village

On the train back, I changed into my Wiltshire clothes. I did not come out of the train toilets in a country smock, milking coat and floppy hat, just my normal clothes that would stop me being stoned as I stepped off the bus into the village. I risked my new London look with the army boys on trips to Swindon and it went down a storm. Dancing the night away and mixing with girls that spoke my language was initially great but every now and again I thought of sophisticated Sofie.

Time to leave the village and, to be truthful, I had outgrown it. Which seems stupid as it's been less than a year. My future is the Royal Navy and I resolve to study hard to understand how it works and how to enjoy it.

HMS Collingwood

I joined HMS Collingwood and began my technical training and I loved every minute of it. We had weekly sports afternoons and we had to name two sports we enjoyed. Getting asked to volunteer was a pleasant surprise from the last establishment where the aim was to find out what you hated and then make you do it. I named tennis and football. I eventually made the Collingwood first team reserve at football and travelled to other Navy establishments to play (sometimes). The after-game drinking sessions were great. Finished off with a coach ride and a sing-song made a fun day out.

The tennis took a very different turn and it was a while before I could work out the problem. It started by me being sent in to see the CPO PTI (Physical Training Instructor) in his office. He had my records and looked up at me and said, 'It says here that you like tennis?'

'Yes Chief,' I replied.

'You come from Wiltshire, I cannot think of any places in that county that have tennis facilities.'

'There are hundreds of country estates and mansions that will all have tennis courts but my council house was not so lucky,' I grinned. Then I went on to explain our new school.

'Well you are the only tennis player here who is not a Naval Officer,' he said. 'It is hard to understand but I have to ask permission to use the tennis courts as they are for Naval Officers only. This I have arranged; do you have a racket and tennis clothes?'

I shook my head and also pointed to my black, Navy-issue plimsoles. He found a white shirt, shorts and socks but failed on the shoes. We walked across the parade ground to where the officers lived. We did cause a few long stares as we entered our court; I think it could have been my black daps. I was using the Chief's spare racket but I soon got used to it. Playing nearly everyday for four years at my village school with four of my close friends meant I was pretty good at the game. Derek, my best mate from the village, was even better than me and he was in the Navy somewhere.

I beat the Chief very easily and when we got back to the gym he said I should play for Collingwood. The PO who shared the office shook his head and asked the Chief how he would make that work. On our own later, the PO said that there are only officers in the team and I would be so out of my comfort zone before and after the game I should ask not to play. I just shrugged my shoulders, what could I do? Later in the week, the Chief arranged a game with the team captain who I found out later was a Lieutenant Commander. I made my way over to the courts and was met by a very tall thin guy who looked like he was in his late twenties. He smiled, shook my hand and said, 'Chief says you're very good so let's find out shall we?' We played for five long sets and I just had the edge on him. I felt the only reason we played for so long was each time I won a set he was determined to get even. Eventually I won three sets to two and to his credit he shook hands and said, 'Well done, you deserved to win.' I returned to the gym where the Chief was waiting and immediately demanded to know the score and if I had beaten him easily. When I said, without boasting, that I always had the beating of him and kept him running around, the Chief gave a fist pump and whispered a loud 'Yes!'.

It was now obvious that the Chief was on a mission and he had found a vehicle to complete it. As I left the gym, the PO caught me up and discussed the situation. He said the CPO PTI has been arguing with the Station Commander that rank should not have anything to do with sport. His first achievement in the 1960s was to have a Leading Hand captaining the rugby team with officers in the scrum. Then the cricket team being 90% lower deck was pushing it. However, his final plan was to crack the tennis team. 'You, my son, are an accident about to happen!' shouted the PO as he walked away.

The day happened the following week when I was picked up in a minivan. I was in my best uniform as under training I was not allowed off the camp in civvies. With me I had a new racket the gym had purchased and whitened plimsoles, white rugby shirt and shorts. I made my way to the back of the van. When it arrived at the wardroom (officers' quarters) there were five men all in white slacks and white pullovers. An Officer's Steward loaded some stuff in the back. They jumped on and waved a hello to me. The skipper got on last and shouted, 'This is REM Dave Samson who you have all heard about.' The two guys who shuffled up to the seat in front of me turned and made some small talk as we made our way. I asked who we were playing, and where, and they replied HMS Dolphin the submarine base, didn't you know? 'I was just told when to be ready,' I replied. Then I asked the format we were playing. They said I was seeded second behind the captain and after all the singles we would play three doubles matches. Richard, one of the guys talking to me, was my partner in the doubles.

Luckily the courts had a changing room. With some guys playing in white flannel trousers and some in pristine shorts, I came a long way last on the fashion front. They had three courts prepared and the three highest seeds played first. We won all three and then lost all the rest of the singles. So, we were drawing with Dolphin at the beginning of the doubles. We won two of the doubles to win the match five four. I enjoyed the games and having won both my games I was feeling pleased with myself as I got changed back into my uniform. The rest of my team were now in jacket and flannels.

Once I was showered and changed, we walked outside following the Dolphin team. Their team captain pulled me aside, everyone else carried on down the road. He began with, 'I am afraid there has been an awful blunder, we had not been informed that a junior rate was a part of the team. I only noticed just now as you came out of the changing rooms. We have arranged an early supper in the wardroom which would be impossible for you to attend.' He held his hand up and waved an Officer's Steward over. He was told to take me to the junior ratings NAAFI. He shook my hand and thanked me for the game and finished with, 'You should be able to get suitable refreshments there.'

The NAAFI was closed but a night-time automat just outside was open. It had four tall tables each with four tall stools. The machines did hot pies (sold out), sausage rolls (I got the last one), lots of chocolate bars and fizzy drinks. The guy told me that if I wanted anything else I had to go out down the road to the nearest pub. I stupidly had not brought enough money so assuming they were only going to be two hours tops I thought I would balance on a stool and wait. After two hours I thought I would give it another hour. Then I grabbed my holdall and racket and wandered about finally asking the security patrol where the main gate was. As they walked me to the gate, they asked what an HMS Collingwood rating was doing loitering around at night in HMS Dolphin. When I explained, the Leading Hand went ballistic. He strode into the main gate house with me and banged on the door marked Duty PO. The story was told again and it was discovered a minibus full of drunken officers singing their heads off had left ten minutes ago. The Duty Officer was called and he came in and rang the Dolphin tennis team captain and shouted down the phone. He then rang Collingwood and shouted, 'I don't care what fucking time it is, you get a vehicle here within 30 minutes!' The van driver arrived and he said, 'I asked them where you were and they said you had gone back on your own.' I did not reply. I was fed up with the lot of them.

Next morning a runner knocked on my classroom door and told the instructor I had to report to the Camp Commander followed by a 'Now Sir!'. I wished I had put a clean working uniform on and had not grabbed the wrong hat as I rushed out the door. I was taken to a posh building and shown upstairs where the CPO was waiting.

As I stood before him, he asked why I thought I was summoned. After a bit of thought I replied, 'Probably because I missed the bus last night.'

'Where from?' he asked.

'HMS Dolphin,' I replied.

'What were you doing there?'

'I was a member of the camp tennis team.'

'Tell me the whole story,' he said.

At the end of my tale he nodded and said, 'It is important I know all the facts so we can have some fun.' He then knocked on the door next to him and went in.

I stood there for about 15 minutes and the door suddenly opened and the CPO shouted 'Atten-shun!'. I leapt to attention and that's when someone else's oversize hat dropped over my eyes. I lifted it up and stuck it back on as he shouted 'Quick march!' and then halted me in front of the Commander's desk, who looked up and said, 'Stand easy.' I have heard last night's saga, apparently you are quite the tennis star. Your team say they thought you had left the camp and made your own way?' he questioned.

I knew I had to be careful but I felt he was a man who preferred his men to stand up for themselves. So finally I said, 'Sir my team left me outside the courts and walked down the road chatting to our opponents. I was taken to a small NAAFI automat and left to fend for myself. Apart from a football bus I have not left the camp. I had never heard of HMS Dolphin and had no idea where it was. I assumed having put me in that building I would be picked up when the rest of my team had finished their supper. Sir, I doubt I had enough money for a taxi and did not know the bus routes.'

The Commander smiled and looked at the CPO and said, 'What should we do?'

'I would suggest we make Samson tennis captain, Sir.'

'So REM Samson what do you think of being the tennis captain?' the Commander asked.

I cleared my throat and said, 'Sir, after my experience over the last three weeks I do not believe the landed gentry of England at this time would allow any tennis captain in the country to have a deep Wiltshire accent.' I followed with, 'And 19 might be a bit too young.'

'Thank you, Samson, you may go. Oh and get that hat changed.'

The CPO marched me out and sent me back to the classroom. I saw the CPO PTI next time I was in the gym and he said, 'Sorry I made you part of my little experiment, it did not fail. They now know how stupid the Navy sport rules are.' He then added, 'If you like you can play in the home games.' I agreed as it wasn't the tennis players' fault and I enjoyed showing how us council house boys beat them at their own game.

I had finished all my courses and got high marks which could allow me to be promoted to Leading Hand quicker. I also received my REM (Radio Electrical Mechanic) badge so I was now ready and willing to go to sea and fix all the radios and radars on any ship.

However, knowing the Navy, I should have realised it would not be that simple. I was hanging around HMS Collingwood as part of the external painting party. I had been chosen as a specialist in chain fencing and after three weeks on my knees in rain and mud I justified my selection. I was finally relieved of my paintbrush when a guy arrived on a bike and said I had to double (run) at once to the drafting office. On arrival, the PO said, 'Pack all your kit and be outside this office in one hour. You are joining HMS Folkestone, it is in Portsmouth harbour and sails this afternoon.'

'Where to?' I asked.

'No idea,' was the reply. Then a shout of 'Get going! You are joining a ship so will only be allowed Pussers (Royal Navy) bags and suitcases.'

The Navy give you a round kitbag that stands five-foot high, a large green suitcase and a small suitcase. I seriously doubt if anyone has tried to fit all their kit into these bags.

I rammed the most expensive items in the bags and left 30% behind, knowing I would have to buy them again at the next kit muster (if they had them on ships?)

Without any clear orders and with no idea what the norm was, I put on my best suit, hat and shoes. The PO treated me with a 'Where the hell do you think you are going? To a fucking wedding? The ship is in the dockyard so you should be in working clothes.' Then he added, 'Too late to change, get on the truck.'

I am not sure if I should have felt important but there I was leaving Collingwood sat in the back of a very large truck on my own.

The truck screeched to a halt and the driver got out and came round the back, dropped the back boards and said, 'It's chaos out there, I cannot get within 100 yards of the ship. There are stores wagons everywhere you will have to take your kit and walk.'

Once on the road, with the lorry disappearing, I took stock. I should have asked the driver to point out my ship. I could foresee many problems, the first being I could not possibly carry my kitbag and my two cases. The second, I had no idea what my ship looked like or where it was. Portsmouth dockyard is massive and I could see ships alongside walls in all directions. I had yet to meet a naval dockyard person (dockyard matey) but there were plenty of workers in the same coloured overalls. I assumed these guys would know where my ship was. I stopped a gang of three and asked if they knew where the Folkestone was moored and they just asked was it a frigate or destroyer?

My reply of 'I have no idea' was met with mirth, a shake of heads and a 'can't help you mate'.

Having staggered around for over an hour pleading, begging and accosting these strange creatures in brown overalls, I had got nowhere. I was now imagining having to explain how the ship sailed without me because I couldn't find it! An angel appeared in the shape of small fat sailor with HMS *Folkestone* on his hat. I refrained from hugging and kissing him and explained my dilemma. He just picked up my two suitcases and said, 'Follow me.'

There she was, a nice little ship with decks crawling with guys carrying boxes and food up four gangways and one gangway that was empty. Joey my saviour ran up the gangway with my two cases. I was struggling at the bottom with my overweight large kitbag. Just as I was about to step up there was a loud shout of 'Get out of the way, officer descending!'. I looked up to see a red-faced rotund officer waving his hands at me dashing down the steps. He reached the bottom, stared at me struggling with my kitbag and bellowed, 'Salute a Naval Officer and report!' I dropped the bag and said, 'REM Samson, joining the ship Sir.' He then looked up the gangway and shouted, 'Cook, get this box to my cabin asap.' Joey headed back down the gangway to a very large box. Joey was an officer's steward and spent his day running around after officers. I manhandled my kitbag up onto the deck and then ran back down to help Joey. 'That bastard is the Gunnery Officer, he is one thick ignorant twat and is the bane of my life,' said Joey. Whispering over his side of the box he said, 'Stay away from him.'

Once Joey had disappeared I approached the PO standing guard and said I was joining the ship's company. Just then a CPO came and said to the PO, 'We are sailing in 4 hours and are not anyway near getting all the stores aboard. Call all hands on deck to muster at the gangway.' He turned and looked at me and said, 'Who are you?' I told him and he said, 'Leave your gear over there and join the team on the third gangway.'

My next three hours were bizarre and confusing. I joined a gang passing boxes of messy vegetables hand over hand. The guy I was passing to commented on the fact that I was wearing my No 1s (best suit). The produce changed every now and again but did not get any cleaner.

At last we were finished and all the gangways were removed except one. We were huddled at the bottom of it when an Admiral appeared at the top. The Captain of Folkestone saluted and the PO and two seamen piped him off the ship. We were told to get on board as the gangway was about to be removed. Once on deck I looked around for my luggage and it had disappeared. I tried to explain to the PO. He told me to worry about it later and as I was wearing No 1s to go and join the ratings standing along the railings as we sailed out of Portsmouth.

As I stood to attention, we were spaced evenly along the railings watching all the families waving with some wiping away tears from their eyes. There were hundreds of them scattered on the battlements of Old Portsmouth. I could not help wondering where the hell we were going and why. We then sailed along Southsea beachfront before turning right and out to sea. The tannoy shouted for us to fallout and dismiss. Everyone then went about their business and left me with the task of finding my kit and someone who actually cared if they had a new shipmate.

Eventually someone told me (wrongly) to go and see the Coxswain. I found out later he was the most senior CPO and reported directly to the Captain. He was also in charge of all disciplinary matters on the ship. I found his office and the door had its top half open. The office was full of people but I knocked anyway and they all turned. I explained that I was told to report to the Coxswain. A Lieutenant Commander looked me up and down and said my uniform was disgusting and to go and change it and report back. It was not the right time to lose my temper, especially in front of the Second in Command and the Coxswain. However, without so much as a touch of my forelock I explained my situation without stopping for breath.

They looked at me and after a few minutes the officer asked me if I had made my phone call. My face obviously looked puzzled and he continued, every member of the ship's company was supposed to contact their family and tell them we were going to be out of touch for the foreseeable future. I replied I had an hour to pack and was dropped at the wrong end of the dockyard and I did not even know the ship was a frigate. They told me to report to the Chief Electrician who I would be working for.

The Chief Electrician was a kindly man that did not seem phased by anything. He was sat at his desk which was part of a large workshop. He sent two guys to find my luggage and said the Coxswain had told him what happened.

'The Navy likes to think it looks after its men. It doesn't. We all have to take the crap and fly by the seat of our pants.' He laughed and said, 'If you think the last five hours have been bad, wait until you see your mess deck and what it's like to share a little ship with 225 men.'

The Chief asked a guy to get me a mug of tea and said he would come back later and settle me into my mess deck.

I began talking to Taff (David Jenkins) and asked where we were going. 'The rumour is that a ship has had to drop out of a big exercise off Scotland and we were on standby so we are to go up to replace it. We were supposed to have five weeks alongside in Portsmouth so we are all pissed off. Then we were due to go to the Mediterranean so now we will leave the exercise and go straight to the Med. The next land we will see is Gibraltar in six weeks.'

With that statement Taff had nothing more to say on the subject. 'What's it like on this ship?' I asked.

'Unbelievably bad,' said Taff in a thick Welsh accent.

I had already decided to refrain from my natural gift of the gab and ask hundreds of questions. My plan was to get amongst the men on this ship and just listen. Not something that came naturally, but I would also be studying everything and everybody to see how the ship functioned.

This was easy to achieve when I was led along the main passage of the ship (Burma Way) and down a steep hatch into my mess deck. The space had three tables on one side (starboard) and two tables on the other side (port). There was a bench that sat five on either side of each table. There were also two areas where 29 hammocks were stowed then rows of metal cupboards for uniforms and further metal units with two small cupboards on top of each other. The room was full of men – and I mean really full – everyone had a cigarette in his hand or mouth. Most of them were sat on the benches because there was not much room to move. The CPO and I got as far as the foot of the ladder and with my kitbag and two cases we were stuck.

The Chief pointed to the large beer-bellied man standing next to us and introduced Punchy Gutteridge. His actual name was Anthony but he was a character known and loved by everyone on board the ship. I just stared and turned round and round studying my new home, mouth open, saying nothing.

The Chief left and Punchy shouted for quiet and said, 'This is Dave and he is going to tell us where he is from and something about himself.' So I said, 'This is my first ship so it's no good asking me anything technical as I don't know nothing. Nobody told me when I joined that none of you could speak English so if I don't answer you it's because I cannot understand a word you are saying. Before you ask, I won't be shagging any sheep because they wouldn't let me bring my wellies and you cannot do it properly if you haven't got somewhere to stick their back legs.' They answered with lots of shouts of 'Oh arrr Oh arrr'. I finished with, 'I cannot see any beds, do we have separate sleeping quarters?'

So 29 men had to eat, sleep and live in a room the size of a Hooray Henry's boot room. I will not go on and on about the disgusting conditions we lived in but just this paragraph describing a day down our hatch. After receiving my hammock training I was not looking forward to my first night in a very rough English Channel. The rule for hammocks was that they could not be put up until 21.00 (9 o'clock). Everyone was allocated a pair of hooks to tie the ropes on. The head end had a stretcher (stick of wood with a V in each end) to keep the head end apart. Inside was a sheet, pillow and blankets. There was a bar to pull yourself up, you would then use your feet to separate the hammock sides and jump in. When all the hammocks were up there was no deck head space left. The whole room was filled and to get around the room you had to stoop down and shuffle about to your locker or to go up the ladder. To get out of the hammock you pulled yourself up and lowered your body past your own hammock.

The separation between each sleeper was about 12 inches. The hammocks were over all the tables and it took practice to lower yourself out and not step on the table that we all had to eat on. All hammocks had to be taken down and put in the stowage by 8 o'clock in the morning. A different five guys would each day get the food from the galley at breakfast, lunch, tea and evening meal. A Leading Hand was supposed to watch the food on the table to make sure we only took our fair share. If the lunch was a pie, it was served up in a large tray and the last slices would have nothing under the pastry. There were heaters to put in any food left for the men on duty. The only seats were the benches round the tables.

We each had a small locker which would only take a third of your clothes. Punchy showed me round and there was always a 'but' with every description. 'These are shoe lockers but don't put anything in them. They will go missing, sometimes they only pinch one shoe which is really annoying,' he said. There was a long coat storage the length of the bulkhead (wall), Punchy said, 'It's safe to leave your best suits and raincoats here at sea. But when we approach the shore take them away to your part of ship [workplace] or someone will go ashore in your suit if it's in better nick than theirs.' He then said, 'Take all the rest of your kit and suitcases and find somewhere on the ship to hide them as there is no room here in the mess.'

After a night swinging with all the other sleepers and holding the sides of the hammock as the ship crashed down onto the waves. I am sat eating my breakfast of toast and tea. An old guy sat next to me and said, 'Are you having fun yet?'

I said, 'It's hard to believe they expect this many people to live in this little space.'

'Have you been on HMS Victory?' he asked.

'Nelson's ship?' I replied.

'On that ship in Nelson's time they had a bench like this behind every gun. Ten men would sit at their bench and eat and drink, that would be their only space. Above it they hung their hammocks and slept. They had been kidnapped and forced on board and would be flogged if they complained, but we volunteered for this. How stupid is that?' he said. 'They did however have a wooden door in front of the gun so they could see or get some fresh air in, unlike us enclosed in steel. Things haven't improved much, have they?'

My decision to just listen and learn did not last long as I added, 'In our village in Wiltshire if there were 29 pigs enclosed in this space it would be illegal and cruel. The farmer would be stoned, beaten and banned from the pub!'

Things brightened up when I went up into the ship and was introduced to the Chief in charge of all the electronic maintenance teams. I was assigned to the ship's two long-range radars. The radars had their individual rooms and I joined a PO who was in charge and two other guys. As both of the radars just hummed away 24 hours a day at sea there didn't seem much to do. Petty Officer Jim Rowe then took me into the darkened operations room which was full of radar displays, each with an operator studying the screens. He whispered his explanations of the various units. When there was nothing to fix, he took me through all the manuals and circuit diagrams of the radars and displays. Jim told me the reason for his generous help was because when there was a call-out in the middle of the night, I would be expected to fix the simple problems and leave him in bed. I did not care. He took me on the bridge to explain the workings of the radar unit up there.

During a military exercise, the bridge was a busy place but after a few visits I got the feeling most of the guys up there were just standing around hanging on the Captain's every word. Up there they were pretending there was a war going on but down below none of us had a clue and we were just going about our business. I would regularly go up and pretend to be checking the radar just to look out and see all the other ships on the horizon in our war game and listen how seriously it was being taken.

As the days and weeks went by, I got used to my daily routines. I had found a good stowage room for my stuff and place to escape the mess deck. It was down below the radar room which just had power units supplying the radars above. I volunteered to keep the place clean and managed to get the shipwright's workshop to make me a spare key. I was told the officers had a furniture store where they kept spare furniture. So I asked Joey, my officer's steward friend who worked in the wardroom, to help me furnish my new space. He took me to the store and he agreed I could have an old broken armchair and camp bed in similar condition. The guy in the shipwright's workshop let me fix them both up. I still slept most of the time in the mess but I had an escape hole if required.

The food was bad and usually cold. As an 18-year-old junior we had to go to the back of the queue. The NAAFI shop was our saviour, selling soup, snacks and drinks. The main problem with the mess was that being a young junior we were not involved in the day-to-day mess business of rum and beer.

Rum

The rum ration, or 'tot', from 1850 to 1970 consisted of one-eighth of an imperial pint (71 ml) of rum at 95.5 proof (54.6% abc), given out to every sailor at midday. Senior ratings (petty officers and above) received their rum neat, whilst for junior ratings it was diluted with two parts of water to make three-eighths of an imperial pint (213 ml) of grog. The rum ration was served from one particular barrel, also known as the 'Rum Tub', which was ornately decorated and was made of oak and reinforced with brass bands with brass letters saying 'The Queen, God Bless Her'.

The time when the rum ration was distributed was called 'Up Spirits', which was at 12 noon. Each mess had a 'Rum Bosun' who would collect the rum from the officer responsible for measuring the right number of tots for each mess. The officers did not get a rum ration. Tot glasses were kept separate from any other glasses. They were washed on the outside, but never inside, in the belief that residue of past tots would stick to the side of the glass and make the tot even stronger. Sailors under 20 were not permitted a rum ration and were marked on the ship's books as 'UA' (Underage).

Punchy was our Rum Bosun and took his appointment very seriously. All the ratings of 20 and over would be ten to a table around two tables. Each position on the bench was allocated and set in stone, and woe betide anyone who sat out of place. Rank took precedence, then age. Punchy would arrive with his Rum Fanny (bucket) at the first table and he would put his thumb in the measure and fill it and then tip it in a glass and hand it to the next senior mess member. The thumb was his tip as the Rum Bosun. After moving tables and measuring out all entitled men's rum the remaining liquid in the Fanny would be Punchy's own tot and 21 thumbs worth of everyone else's tots! He would return to the first table and sit and hold court.

Guests would arrive from other messes invited for a 'wet', of sippers or gulpers (you could not make it up!). Sippers was a sip for a small favour and a gulper was a large gulp for a seriously good favour. If a guest was invited for a sippers and he was a fairly popular shipmate, Punchy would offer another sipper from his large pint glass. Some other mess members would also hand their glass to the guest. That's the reason it was worth being invited as a guest, he would leave our mess well-oiled and then go back to his tot in his own mess!

Gulpers was about an eighth of your tot and was the main currency in the ship. It would not be exaggerating to say that you could almost get anything done in the ship for a whole tot or three days' gulpers. A gulper's guest would sit next to the guy who invited him and be given a glass and this guy would pour an amount of rum into the glass. Punchy would watch on and growl if he thought the amount was not generous enough. Once again, other mess members would tip in an amount of their choosing if they so desired. Once Punchy had been told of the service that had been provided by the guest he would not offer any of his but could order you to tip even more in the glass.

We got an hour and a half for lunch and this ritual would last an hour. Towards the end, beer would be introduced, guests would be asked to leave and the rum drinkers would eat their lunch. By 13.30 every day 80 per cent of the below decks ship's company were drunk. The man who acted the most sober was Punchy, who had probably drunk well over a pint of rum and four cans of beer. As an 18-year-old what do I know, but thinking back the best way to keep 200 men rammed into that bucket was to create alcoholics.

All of us who were underage had to keep well out of the way during lunchtime. We either stuffed some food into a container and went on the upper deck to eat or did not even bother. We had a small window of opportunity when all the men were staring at Punchy making sure he did not put more than a thumb in their measure. I have heard heated arguments about a thumb should not be allowed but the little finger. To be fair, it's much easier to hold a measure with a thumb stuck in it than a finger. Anyway, until a Leading Hand joins who is much bigger and nastier than Punchy and could win a takeover battle, they should think themselves lucky it's only a thumb.

We UAs, while eating a hastily grabbed handful of chips during lunch hour, always say 'When I am old enough there is no way I will be joining that drunken rabble.' It makes no sense to get off your face every day and find somewhere to hide and sleep all afternoon. When one of our ranks became 20 we would watch him slide into his hallowed place on the farthest bench and begin his apprenticeship. Punchy would perform a form of baptism and his road to alcohol dependence through to full-on alcoholic would begin. Bless him! I wish I could say I did not fall for it as well.

The ship was dead every afternoon, you could walk through empty corridors which in the morning were jammed with people. Even the CPOs and POs would be nowhere to be seen. I suppose as they had their rum neat they were suffering from the same illness as my fellow mess members. At the time I wondered if the officers upstairs knew where everyone was, but it happened everyday so over the last fifty odd years it must have dawned on them.

I used to enjoy afternoons as I would take my toolkit and visit the darkened operations room and talk to the radar operators and play with spare radar displays. Then up to the bridge and check out the display up there. I would talk to the midshipmen who were near my age. They were shat upon as well, but it is hard to feel sorry for them as they got into a little jacket every evening and had dinner in a dining room with servants pouring them wine. I soon became a known face in these two important places on the ship. I was totally ignored because I was a minion but they accepted that I was allowed access. I told my CPO and PO and they agreed my job was to look after all the radar displays as I had proved I could fix the normal problems; anything else I would call out the PO. I watched and listened to the gossip between officers on the bridge. Studied the admiralty charts to see where we were and listened to the radio chats between the ships. I got to know the comms guys and the bunting tossers (flag wavers and light signallers).

I had nothing to do with any of the full-grown officers on the ship except the Gunnery Officer. He was South African and treated all ratings as he probably treated the black people in his home country. I did not know anything about South Africa but they did have a thing called apartheid, which if what they said was true sounded disgusting. It did not start well on the gangway as I was trying to join and from what my mate Joey Cook said the man was evil.

One day standing on the upper deck watching the shite hawks (sea gulls) diving to feast on our gash (food waste) from the galley, Joey came along. I asked him how he was getting on with the mad Gunnery Officer? He explained it was now beyond a joke, the guy was on his case from dawn to dusk and he did not know how much more he could take. He said he had a plan to get even and I should watch this space. Joey drifted off and I was about to leave as well when a gang of drunken chefs arrived on the ship's stern. I was on the mortar deck above and just watched the frivolities. The shite hawks were swooping down to the chefs to catch the bread they were throwing. Once they caught the bread they soared up into the air squealing and throwing themselves left and right, then when reaching a certain height they plummeted into the sea. More shite hawks joined the throng and soon the waves beyond the ship's stern were filled with diving birds. The game continued until the chefs ran out of bread. I went down the steps to the stern and asked the chefs what the hell was that all about? They said we soaked the bread in Tabasco sauce! (been there!). 'Everyday we have to come down on the stern and tip all the galley waste food into the sea and those bastards don't wait. As soon as we lift the bin and before we can tip it over, they attack us and shit all over us. This is payback time!' I walked off shaking my head trying to decide whose side I was on. Working on the principle of you do not argue with a gaggle of drunken chefs I laughed and said, 'Nice one.'

My second run-in with the Gunnery Officer began at 9 o'clock on a very stormy evening off the coast of Scotland. Lt Victor Schuab was an ape of a man as wide as he was high, looking like the typical South African rugby hooker he was. Joey says he was very well connected in the South African Navy and was almost untouchable.

I was looking forward to this particular night as I had heard in the ops room that this evening's exercise was us and three other anti-submarine frigates protecting our fleet of ten ships from an attack from three of our submarines. I had listened to the brief earlier and the sonar and ops rooms would be directing all three frigates' defence and hoped to sink at least one of the subs. When a ship had locked onto a sub with its sonar it then closed onto it quickly until it got within range of its mortars. It dropped a couple of grenades over the side to indicate to the sub it had registered a kill. If the sub got into a position undetected where it could torpedo a ship it would send up a flare.

All the fun would be in the ops room with minute-by-minute updates from the sonar room. The captain and Radar Ops Officer and the Anti-Submarine Officer would all be controlling the ship's actions. They would tell the Officer of the Watch on the Bridge what speed and direction to steer. What was required was an Officer of the Watch that had the ability to quickly think on his feet and make sure the ship stayed safe as the ops room sent all three frigates hurtling around. At the briefing, the captain's last words were, 'Remember the ship's safety is more important than a successful submarine kill. It is, after all, only an exercise. Victor, I rely on you to keep a good lookout up top!'

I went into the ops room and kept out of the way in amongst the blackout curtains. The exercise got underway and within the hour a contact had been detected by the sonar room and the info sent up to the ops room. Just then Victor shouted on his mike from the bridge – 'My radar display is down, I am blind up here, send for the maintainer.' I went over to the Radar Controller and said, 'On the way Sir' and ran up the ladder through the officers' corridor and up onto the bridge. Victor was at the display shouting, 'Fucking piece of shit!' Assuming he was not speaking to me I said 'Excuse me' to the Navigating Officer, who was trying to assist Victor, and gently moved Victor aside.

'What's the problem Sir,' I asked.

'What the fuck are you doing here? Get me the PO or CPO in charge of this crap.'

I noticed when I pushed Victor aside he had his hands on the signal knob and the sea clutter knob. I turned the sea clutter down and the gain up and the radar picture instantly came back into view.

After adjusting all the other knobs the idiot had twirled in blind panic, I stepped aside and said, 'I think Sir you will find the display is now working correctly.'

'Well done lad,' said the Navigator and went back into his chart room.

Victor informed the ops room that all was now well and he had a radar picture on the bridge. When the Captain asked what the problem was Victor said, 'It just came back on Sir.' I then asked Victor if I should hang around in case it happened again. At that moment the Navigator popped his head out of the chart room and winked at me. I was ignored and I stepped back into the shadows.

On both bridge wings two anti-submarine seaman who normally fired the mortars (depth charges) were stationed to lookout for submarine signals. I popped out to have a chat with one of them but did not stay long. They had thick watch coats on with binoculars round their necks but they were still freezing and soaking wet. The gale force winds did not make talking easy but we stood behind a windbreak and the guy said, 'Once the shit hits the fan we will be doing about 28 knots and hard over turns to port and starboard. One minute you will be climbing up the bridge wall and the next minute thrown to the ship's railings hanging on for dear life. Oh yes, and they darken the ship and we are not allowed to use a torch.'

'Shouldn't you rope yourselves onto something?' I asked.

'No, we have to run to the bridge door and tell them if we see a flare and we may have to drop grenades over the side if they throw the door open and shout.'

I asked to see the grenades and he took me along to a

small red box, lifted it up and there were six grenades just like I had seen in the children' comics.

'Jesus, what happens if you drop it?' I asked.

'I would not be here to tell you,' he said. 'You just hold the lever, pull out the pin and chuck it.'

Soon I would be grateful for this five-minute chat.

Over the last hour, we had darkened the ship and chased the submarines at high speeds. Every time Victor was ordered to perform hard turns his voice got more and more excited. He strode across the bridge throwing open the doors and shouting out to the lookouts to look out for periscopes. In those seas you would have to be superman with his supersonic eyes to see a bloody periscope in the dark. A couple of times we had a strong contact and we should have caught the sub, even Victor shouting, 'Let's kill the bastards' had not helped.

I was getting bored and deciding whether to bed down in my little room or swing in my hammock with a thousand farts when a 'full speed ahead' came from the ops room. This was followed by a 'hard a starboard' order. At the same time, the starboard bridge door swung open and the lookout fell in. He was clutching his arm and had a bad cut on his head. The signalman and I gently pulled him into a corner out of the way of the action. The sickbay attendant was called and in the meantime, we carefully eased him out of his coat. Victor shouted down to the ops room, 'We need another lookout up here now.' He then looked at me and said, 'We are going

97

in for the kill, you there, go out and report any sightings to me.' Followed with, 'I will relieve you as soon as his replacement gets up here.' The coat was thrown at me, followed by the binoculars; the door was slammed as soon as I had made it out.

Taking stock, I could see nothing and just hung on to something, waiting for my eyes to become accustomed to the light. When they did, I could still see nothing. The next 20 minutes were just as the lookout had described to me earlier. I hung on fixed to a spot, willing the relief to turn up. Then I saw a flare pop up in the distance. I thought, sod the rules and shone my torch on the ground, found the gyro and worked out it was about starboard twenty.

Then staggered back to the bridge opened the door and shouted, 'Light at starboard twenty.'

Victor strode across, pushed me aside and looked out. 'Where?' he demanded.

I pointed and he roared, 'That's the starboard bow, idiot!'

'The ship is turning,' I replied. The door then slammed and I was back in the dark. I did shout to the slammed door, 'Where is my fucking relief?'

Thirty minutes later the door flew open again, it was Victor. 'Drop two,' he shouted.
'Two what?' I shouted back.

'Grenades!' he roared.
'I am a Radar Mechanic and not qualified!' I pleaded.

'We have to inform the submarine now, drop two that is a direct order,' and the door slammed.

I went to the red box, opened the door and there they were. I got my torch out and clipped it on a cable nearby and gently took out the grenade. Sure enough there was a ring pull and a lever. I remembered reading about how they worked in a war comic and also took into account the lookout's words. Part of me was for going into the bridge and saying, 'Fuck your sodding order, go and drop the things yourself.' The ridiculous thing that was also spinning through my head was that everyone would think I was chicken and I would become a laughing stock. I was a member of the armed forces.

Those thoughts must have lasted a couple of seconds, then I told myself sod it. I pulled the pin out, holding the lever tightly against the grenade, leant over the guard rail and dropped the grenade over the side instantly ducking down. After an age, there was a 'thrump' from under the water. I then quickly repeated my actions and let the second grenade drop into the sea. After the second 'thrump', I opened the bridge door, shouted, 'Two dropped!' and shut the door.

I have not been in many scrapes in my life but hanging over a guard rail on a ship rising high in the air and crashing down in the waves whilst listing 30 degrees one way and 30 degrees the other in complete darkness in a 40-mile-an-hour gale (I will stop now!) with a live grenade in my hand still wakes me up at night.

I was relieved two hours later and strode onto the bridge seething.

'Where's the Gunnery Officer?' I asked.

'He is off watch, the Navigator has the ship,' was the reply.

So I went to my little machinery room and laid on my camp bed and spent the night planning my next move. I decided to play the innocent (which I was). So next morning I spoke to my Radar Chief and said, 'I think I have a complaint but do not know what to do about it.' He said we should speak to the Chief Electrician as he was in charge of regulating the electricians' branch (all other branches call us Greenies).

I explained exactly what had happened. They both quickly asked what the hell I was doing on the bridge? I told them the cock-up Victor had made of the display and his telling the captain that it just went off. Followed with my opinion that he did not have a clue how to operate the display and, when I suggested I stick around, he did not argue. Also whenever he used the display, I would discreetly slip over and reset the controls. They laughed.

I was surprised how angry they were that I had been exposed to dropping live grenades. They were absolutely astonished. I innocently asked if I should make a complaint. They said that it might work against you, best let them be the ones to complain as they cannot be fobbed off. If I complained it would go via the Electrical Officer to the First Lieutenant and then the Captain. As an 18-year-old kid I would not stand a chance and they could easily get rid of you! The Chief explained that I work for him, and the officer had no right to give one of his men an illegal order. 'Leave it to me to complain, I will say I heard it from the mess deck and then demand that you tell me the truth. Go and tell Punchy and then tell him to say nothing before he reports it to me.'

Well, once Punchy had been informed and seen the Chief Elec., the whole ship knew by lunchtime. So much for keeping my head down, it was now difficult. Every time I lifted my arm someone would shout, 'Grenade, everybody down!'

I was summoned to see the Coxswain and questioned at length. When I got my chance, I said, 'I did not ask for this investigation, I was in the wrong place at the wrong time and did as I was ordered. After the first order I said I was a radar mechanic and was not qualified. The order was repeated. Should I have refused the order?'
'How did you know how to throw a grenade?'

'I didn't,' I replied. 'I used to read children's war comics that's all the knowledge I had.' I laughed.

'It is not funny,' he said sternly.

'It certainly was not last night, I was petrified,' I answered. 'Also the signaller who sat by the bridge door must have seen and heard everything that happened.'

The Coxswain had heard enough. I was dismissed!

A few days later I was called to the Electrical Officer's

cabin with the Chief Elec. We three sat around his desk and it was obvious the officer did not have a clue how to say what he had to say. He kept trying to bring the Chief into the conversation hoping he would help him out. The Chief was not forthcoming. After lots of umming and erring, the officer said, 'We have looked into your unfortunate incident and dealt with it, so we can now put it behind us. We are most impressed with your work and are recommending you for promotion. As a Leading Hand in the near future, if you keep this up you should make PO quickly. Well done, have you any questions?'

I said, 'It has been explained to me how important and well connected the Gunnery Officer is so I, of course, can see that I was in the wrong. I have one question. As I should have obviously refused the order, to make sure it does not happen again, is there a book that lists the orders we should refuse?'

My Division Officer is not a fool, a smile came on his face as he failed to answer the question. I looked at the Chief and thought, good job they cannot fob you off.

I am still not clever enough to find out how the buzz (word) of my reply got round the ship, especially as Punchy was word perfect when he told the mess.

The lower deck's nickname for Lt Victor Schuab was now officially Scab! It was mooted before the following happened. At sea, if you want to get anything sent out over the tannoy, you have to ring the wheelhouse and request a message to be relayed. Unfortunately, the rating taking a call from the Captain to ask the duty officer to go to the bridge did not know the Gunnery Officer. So he looked on the duty roster and read Victor's name and passed the following message: 'Lieutenant Scab is requested to go to the bridge!' Minutes later, the door to the wheelhouse flew open and Scab shouted, 'My name is Lieutenant Schuab [pronounced swab in English]!' 'Is that like swab the decks Sir?' the rating enquired. The wheelhouse door slammed.

Every evening the Ships Daily Orders were distributed. Also an information sheet giving everyone an idea of the happenings for the next day was thrown down the hatch to each mess. What may have not been known by all, was that shortly after, another sheet called the Lower Deck Times was thrown down to the messes. The Scab story made the headline that evening.

The Navy has a nice way of keeping you out of your comfort zone. The following week, my navigation radar stint was finished and I was assigned to the Gunnery Radar section. When introduced to the Chief Electrical Artificer, who ran all the technical parts of the 4.5 inch gun, he told me that Scabby, as he called him, very rarely came down to the Gunnery Control Room. Technology is not his forte as he has no idea how the system works. He sticks to the bridge for firing and loves it inside the gun bay and down in the ammunition stores. The radar was looked after by Leading Hand Bill Young from our mess deck. I hadn't had much to do with Bill as he had recently left Rum Table number two and has risen to table number one. As earlier explained, a UA like me does not tend to chat in the mess with the grown-ups. At least I had every afternoon to myself as Bill had a little grotto next to the Control Room where he slept.

With exercises finished, we were heading to Gibraltar with a week to go. All us Greenies were performing maintenance and tests now that our equipment was not being used in the pretend war. As I no longer had access to the bridge or ops room, I was no longer in the know. So I spent my time learning the gun and its computer.

During our passage to Gibraltar, I had another incident with my friend the Gunnery Officer. This time only as a spectator. The Chief got me to help him with a recorded trial that tested the system and gun. The idea was that the equipment controlled the gun and recorded it swinging on a bearing and the barrels would raise to a certain elevation. The gun would fire and the recoil time and lots of other stuff would be recorded. The system could then be analysed and be passed as fit for purpose.

The equipment was installed in the Gun Control and ops rooms. Scab would be in the Gun Control room and the Ops Officer would be ensuring that no ships were on the horizon. The Captain would be on the bridge. The Chief would be in the gun bay watching over the test equipment. Bill Young's task would be in the Gun Control room to assist Scab.

The Chief said the problem was explaining it all to the Gunnery Officer, who disliked relying on the Chief to achieve a successful trial. So at a meeting, standing over the equipment, the Chief described the events and suggested a meeting should be had with the Captain to explain the importance and itinerary. The gun would fire seven minutes after the start of the trial and would fire of its own accord. We needed permission to fire before we started the trial. Scab said there was no need, he would inform the Captain and explain the exercise.

'This is an accident waiting to happen,' said the Chief after Scab had left. 'I will write an official memo explaining the trial and highlight the timeline and each person's actions.'

The ops officer and the Captain met with the Chief and went over his memo. He also explained that all actions and audio commands would be recorded and sent as part of the trial. The Captain waving the memo said he would discuss the trial with the Gunnery Officer.

Next day I am in the ops room keeping out of the way but ready to assist if there are any questions. The ops officer and Captain have agreed a ship's course and a bearing on which the gun will fire.

In the Gun Control room, Scab is hovering over the trial computer asking L/H Bill Young to explain the coming events. At his shoulder, Bill explains that when he wants to start the trial all he has to do is press the enter button and the trial will start automatically.

At this point, with Bill looking on, Scab, whilst studying the computer accidentally pressed the button. Chief from the gun shouts 'Trial underway'. The ops officer says, 'Roger, clear to fire.' The Captain says, 'Permission to fire.'

Scab steps back and asks Bill, 'What's happening?'

'You just entered the start the trial command.'

'How do I stop it?' he shouts.

'Hit that emergency button,' says Bill pointing at a big red knob on the gun control consul. 'You better be quick because we will fire soon,' he added.

Once again the Gunnery Officer has to make a quick decision. There are two obvious choices, one hit the red button and the gun will swing back to standby and not fire. Two, the trial has started and the Captain, ops officer and the Chief have all given the go ahead so let the trial continue and the gun will fire safely. He chose number three and grabbed the microphone and said, 'Captain Sir I would like your permission to – boom!! – stop the trial.'

'Why?' asked the Captain angrily.

At that moment, the Chief said, 'Captain, gun bay. Go ahead gun bay.'

Chief EA Sir, the trial is completed and the results look fantastic.'

'Well done Chief,' says the Captain.

'Gunnery Officer Bridge,' commands the captain.

Scab turned to Bill and said, 'The computer started the trial on its own, didn't it Leading Hand?'

'Sir,' replied Bill. 'The pushing of the button was recorded and all our voices were recorded. It will all come out when the fleet gunnery team analyse the results.'

So Scab headed up to the bridge to tell the captain that he accidentally started the trial without knowing it.

Punchy was quickly into the control room and asked Bill, 'Did you have that recorded?' Bill nodded. 'Let's hear it,' he said and roared with laughter and said, 'Give me the tape, I will copy it and bring it back soonest.' Sure enough, he was back within the hour.

For the next few days, Punchy would leave the mess with Bill 30 minutes after he had dished out the rum. Halfway up the ladder on the first day of his missions he stopped, sought me out and laughingly said, 'Dave this is going to get me some rum,' and waved a tape at me. I had arrived! Punchy had called me Dave for the first time! Punchy and Bill were the star guests in all the other messes. The fact the Gunnery Officer had started the trial by uneducated prodding was hilarious to all naval ratings. It was the headline in the Lower Deck Times thrown down the hatches that evening.

Unfortunately the Victor Schuab saga ran on and on. Unknown to me and most of the crew, two days before we were due to arrive in Gibraltar the officers' mess laid on a 40th birthday dinner for Lt Schuab. I heard later from Joey that the Captain was invited as a special guest and the good Victor had supplied a collection of fine South African wines. The party went on well into the night and a final few staggered to bed at first light. Joey and another steward had to stay up and serve them and then clean up the wardroom and lay it out for breakfast,

A still very drunk Victor staggered into breakfast mid-morning and apparently demanded food. He was politely told by the Chief Steward that the galley was closed. He stormed out of the wardroom and rammed on his hat and it was filled with poo! Aghast, he ran into the ops room still covered in shit and in the darkness strode over to the main broadcast tannoy and shouted to the whole ship's company, 'Some bastard has shit in my hat, when I find him he will be castrated – trust me!'

Coxswain and his Leading Patrolman were seen moments later running up the Burma Way (main ship's corridor) and up the steps to wardroom as was the 1st Lieutenant (second in command of the ship).

Unfortunately my main source of information was now at Punchy's rum gathering. I sat quietly out of the way but within easy earshot as they were all shouting. Punchy invited a Leading Steward to the mess to provide us with all the happenings in the wardroom. Day two, we had Leading Patrolman Pete Faulks who refused to talk. This all changed when Punchy applied depth charges (vodka sunk in beer). Thus, after much rum the regulator changed from nothing to say, to revealing all. Note: Punchy and his chums had an illicit still hidden in the depths of the ship and his neat alcohol was laughingly described as vodka.

From Pete we got that the 'powers that be' expected it to happen again. Punchy's comment of everybody hates him so much there could be 'copycat hat shits' had us all falling off our benches. Then Pete said all the officers have their hats on their own pegs outside the wardroom. They also have a hat peg outside their cabin, which means if the hat is there he is in his cabin. If an officer goes ashore he leaves it on the wardroom hangers. At a gathering of all officers and the regulating branch in the wardroom it was suggested that the hats could be swapped to see if 'guns' was being targeted. Pete said the other officers were not happy to get their hats involved. The meeting ended with the Coxswain tasked with gathering a list of suspects and interviewing them.

I was wandering on the upper deck and Joey was leaning over the rail gazing at the goffers (waves).

'So, my friend, was it you?' I whispered.

'Couldn't possibly say,' he replied, 'but after the way we were treated on his birthday I would not be surprised if it happened again.'

Careful,' I said. 'They will be watching the hat rack outside the wardroom but not sure about the one outside his cabin door,' and continued my wander.

Next day I met Joey again and I said I had a plan. They will send the next poo away to see if they can find out whose shit it is, so you have to be clever. I then told him how I would play it.

We enter Gibraltar with lots of other ships. I have never been to a foreign country. The ship is buzzing with excitement and I remembered Punchy's warning and removed my best suit from the mess locker. Punchy gathered the whole mess and said he had been ordered to take us all ashore, especially the new boys 'He's lying,' whispered one of the other Leading Hands. He moved us away and carried on talking. 'He will collect a kitty off you all and get you pissed out of your brains and leave you where you drop. The kitty will carry on with him. Remember Punchy can drink 15 or more pints and you will collapse after 7.' 'Are you not going with him then?' we asked. 'Of course I will,' was the reply, 'He knows all the places, all the people and is fearless. You should at least experience one of his runs ashore before he kills himself.'

Punchy's tour of Main Street

There were about 16 of us as 25% of the crew were on duty on board ship everyday. We gathered on the gangway but once on shore Punchy made us fall in three abreast. He then walked up and down inspecting, adjusting lanyards and collars. Stepped back and said, 'I am very proud, stay close watch and learn.' The Officer of the Watch was stood up on the gangway shaking his head. He knew that a gang of Greenies were about to be educated and it would all end in tears. Punchy shouted, 'Left turn. By the left quick march!' We glided towards the Dockyard exit, Punchy taking the salute as we went through the gate and entered Gibraltar town. As we marched into town, we passed a rabble of our officers including Guns. They were dressed in posh civilian suits and highly polished shoes (Joey had done a good job). As a joke, Punchy shouted the order, 'Eyes right.' As we all sharply turned and looked at them Punchy shouted out, 'I hope you gentlemen have all hidden your hats!' His next order was, 'Eyes front and stop fucking laughing!'

After a few left and right turns he called us to a halt and said, 'This is the first one of my 20 favourite pubs.' He shouted 'Dismiss!' and headed to the bar where he bought 16 pints.

The old hands formed a chain behind him and passed the pints back. We were never asked what we wanted and never knew what we were drinking. We worked our way down through the Main Street, out towards the airport and by now we had visited about eight pubs and us lightweights were tipping some of our beer into the glasses of the seasoned campaigners. Worryingly, we crossed the border into Spain and here Punchy suggested a short with our pints. This bar had food called tapas which Punchy ordered enough for us all. We attacked the plates with a frenzy and the food was gorgeous. Luckily the shorts were left on the table with the food so they could be avoided. We were having the time of our lives, the humour and one-liners of 16 drunk matelots was a joy. Punchy gathered us together and said, 'Now we go to the cabaret and then we have to get back over the border. Make sure we all get over together, after that you can do your own thing in Gib.'

The cabaret was a stage with girls dancing and taking their clothes off. Three ladies in Spanish dresses came on stamping and clicking their castanets. One of the guys said that this dance was the famous flamenco! A few minutes later he said, 'Dear me, I have never seen it when the girls just finish up in their boots!' 'It is also dangerous with those castanets clacking so close to their nipples,' I cried. The place was rammed, packed with mainly Navy but with a smattering of Army and RAF. Our gathering was 15 feet from the stage and instead of the chat and jokes we all just goggled at the girls in silence. We got bored after a while and Punchy shouted, 'This is the last act in this session, after this we go back to Gib.' we all nodded. A large woman of a certain age (probably 40) came on the stage circling around waving her arms. The audience went ballistic they were still cheering as she started removing her clothes. Unfortunately, what happened next has never really left me!

She slowly removed her clothes to the sound of Rule Britannia echoing off the walls. Finally, she was down to just her panties (large baggy ones). The music changed to the Scottish national anthem and she pulled out a Scottish flag from her fanny! The Scots in the room roared their approval. Tied to this flag was an English flag, the music had changed and all the English cheered. The small flags depicting the Welsh, Irish, Army and RAF and others carried on being gently pulled out and each one had a different musical accompaniment. Last but one to 'those in peril on the sea' was the Navy Ensign. Finally, the Union Jack was slowly drawn out. We all stood as one to attention, saluted and proudly sang the National Anthem. We sung with great gusto and nearly took the roof off. In other circumstances, I am sure Her Majesty would have been very proud that her uniformed armed forces were so patriotic. I was even so proud that there were tears in my eyes! The dear lady bless her, probably also shed a tear as the Union Jack was much bigger than the rest of the flags and had toggles!

Punchy herded us out and across the border and into Gib, got us safely onto Main Street and promptly disappeared with what was left of our kitty. I last saw him going down an alleyway with his arm round Pete the Patrolman. We scrambled about in our pockets for enough money for some fish and chips and joined a long queue. The whole Med fleet was in Gibraltar and most of the crews were shuffling in close order up Main Street. The Naval Patrol with their big sticks were on every corner waiting to wade in as soon as a fight developed. The street was so crowded that they had to bash lots of innocent souls before they got to the centre of any problem. A large fight began in our queue which I think was about whose ship was better. We left quickly as for some god forsaken reason I had come on a Punchy run ashore with my best hat, which would not survive a patrolman's night stick.

As we climbed the gangway, we were escorted to our mess. I had to wait awhile until I could get up to my little hideaway. With the radars off in harbour, the machines in the room were silent. My mother's little drunken sailor slept the night away. (What would you do with him?)

Next morning I was lying on my camp bed thinking of the night before. How on earth did the Spaniards in that nightclub interpret the British Forces standing to attention, saluting and singing passionately as a fat old lady pulled flags out of her whatnot? Also, what about the Gibraltar people leaving their flat this morning to trot to the shops to get a paper and stick of bread. Wading through a mass of bottles, half eaten fish and chips. Also torn uniforms covered in blood and vomit. I suppose if you open over 150 pubs and invite 20 or 30 warships for a little drinky-poo, you are asking for it. Finally, Punchy's private tour of the delightful drinking houses and night clubs of the area – brilliant! I learnt during our pub crawl that Punchy was famous for these tours. In fact, this evening he will be escorting the stokers' mess and the next day the seamen's mess would be providing the kitty. I stowed all these opportunities into my brain for future use.

I am sat in the UA corner meekly sipping a cup of soup feeling unwell when Punchy comes bounding down the ladder, Rum Fanny in hand, singing some disgusting song. 'Come on boys, let us get pissed again like we did last night.'

Following him down was Pete the Patrolman. I understood the reason. Pete worked for the Coxswain and so Punchy would know all of the ship's business, even the stuff between the Captain and Coxswain which other officers would not have access to. Watch and learn, Dave, watch and learn.

The rum distribution had not even been completed before Punchy said, 'I hear there has been another shit in a hat Pete?'

'Yeh the bastard got Guns outside his cabin. Quite a load as well, he must have been ashore, he wouldn't eat that much of our food! I have just been to the meeting, they have sent the evidence ashore to the hospital to see if they can extract any clues. They did discuss sending a memo out to all the ship's company but the Coxswain said it would be copied and stuck on the window of every bar in town.'

'Too right,' Punchy said nodding.

'They did say you and your guys had mentioned hats as you marched past.'

We were all laughing away as our leader replied, 'We were checking that they were taking adequate precautions. If they had removed all their hats, there would be nothing to shit in would there?'

'That was discussed as well and it was considered unbecoming of an officer to cow down to the lower deck antics. So instead of locking their hats in their cabins they are leaving them out and saying shit in them if you dare. Madness – let's change the subject,' said he-who-should-probably-be-obeyed.

The new subject was how Big Fat Nellie managed to remove so many flags from her whatnot. Many explanations were shouted down. One guy was suggesting she had them in the back (before he finished someone shouted 'passage!') of her knickers. Finally, after the thoughts were getting even more ridiculous, Punchy lifted his hands for silence and said, 'As soon as Nellie came on I recognised her from a night club in Mombasa (Kenya). This night club had a boxing ring where sailors could fight Africans and get a wad if they beat them. Between fights they had cabaret acts, jugglers, contortionists and tumblers. The star act was Nellie, who came on every night to loud cheers and applause. My tour was watching one night when an African weirdo, dressed in a lion skin and carrying a stick with skulls on, leapt over the ropes and ran at Nellie who was halfway through her act. Nellie, who was sat on her stool, jumped up and ran across the ring pulling her stool behind her. The stool, whilst being dragged, was leaking flags that were increasing in size as they came out.

'What Nellie does is put three or four small flags inside her, and when they are out, the last has a string with a loop on it. The special stool has a string with a toggle on it. She puts the toggle through the loop and the first small flags are now connected to all the bigger ones that are carefully stowed in the stool. These are then dragged out between her legs!'

There was a stunned silence as we all tried to work out if he had just made it up or was telling the truth. Punchy, grinning, said, 'I went back to the club last night and told Nellie her secret was safe with me as long as she bought the drinks.' She then told me the guy who tried to attack her was the local witch doctor, and he had decided that her act could affect the birth rate of the village.

Two days later Pete was back at the rum table with the results of the 'poo tests'. He had a big grin on his face and took an age to tell us. Finally he got up from the bench and said, '52% large dog, 48% barbary ape!' There was a stunned silence. 'Let's get this straight,' said some smart arse from the back. 'A large dog and an ape from the rock joined hands and ran up the gangway up the stairs to Gun's Cabin, grabbed his hat and each had a shit in it and then legged it back off the ship?'

'Type that up,' said Punchy. 'We will have this tale stuck on the wall of every bar in Main Street.'

Joey, being a Steward, was off duty and entitled to go ashore as soon as the ship had docked. To find cool air he walked up the rock road towards the peak and took in the stunning views. As he looked down on the dockyard below, he could see his ship. It felt great to be so far away from that nasty evil man who treated him like shit. He smiled sweetly as he watched the apes waving angrily at him. To annoy him, one came close, sat in front of him and stared then popped his bum up and produced a large pile, then turned sharply with a 'Cop that lot if you will' and left. Thank you, thought Joey, just what I need! Later, on the way down, Joey stopped and sat on the lower slopes and watched the stray dogs at play. Eventually they moved on and left Joey with some fantastic steaming creations. Although Joey was no expert, he reckoned Dave would be impressed with his final selections. As he ran up the gangway the guard said, 'Get some good rabbits (pressies)

Joey?' 'You would not believe,' he replied.

The officer hats were now safe (as long as they treat us nicely).

Over the last few months, I have got to know and like two Scottish lads. They are the same age as me and we have shared the UA's table in the mess. At first I thought they were speaking a foreign language but slowly, whilst sharing most parts of the days together, I began to understand them.

They both come from Glasgow, are very close friends and between them there is a lot of banter and laughs. When Punchy shouts one of his Scottish one-liners they shout back angrily in unison and are not amused. Results of Scottish football and rugby cause much argument, despair and delight depending on the results. Rory Gallagher is short and wiry with thick straight black hair. Davie Hamilton is the same build with fair hair. Slowly I found the reason for the heated arguments – one was Protestant and one was Catholic. Having led a sheltered life in a small village, if we had a Catholic church it was news to me (I later found out we had a small little building that I thought was a house). I learnt in Glasgow the two religions had separate streets, schools and even football teams. You could not marry out of your religion and when the two go back to Glasgow they cannot mix together.

The first night we went ashore together, as soon as they got drunk they got into a brawl, were thrown out of the pub and proceeded to batter each other rolling about in the gutter. Neither would give in and the hatred that oozed out of their faces was frightening. It took the other six of us to split them up. We then went our separate ways, each group holding onto a very angry Scotsman. I got back on board with Rory. All the time Rory was ranting about Davie as we put our hammocks up and went to sleep. Rory's hammock is next to mine and sometime later Davie's head rose up between the hammocks and he grabbed Rory's and swung it upside down. Rory fell straight down hitting a table and then the floor. Davie was instantly on him. In the dark, stuck in my hammock, I could hear the punches hitting home. Eventually all the lights came on and Punchy separated them. Davie had two black eyes and Rory's arm had taken on a strange shape. Punchy switched the lights out and said go to sleep and say nothing. In the morning I came down the ladder from the washroom and there were Rory and Davie sat together drinking tea. Rory's arm was in a sling and Davie's head was bandaged up. I looked at them with a puzzling question on my face.

'It's your fault,' said Davie. 'All the mess knows we are not allowed to go ashore together. All our life we get pissed at the pub in Glasgow and at closing time we go looking for some Fenian (Catholic) twats to beat up. A red light goes off in our heeds and we canny stop it.' As they have both been on board for over a year I ask around about their problems. The answer is a shrug, the Irish are bad but the Scottish are even worse. These two are no different from the rest of them. If Rory goes ashore without Davie he will stagger back and tip Davie out of his hammock and this after Davie has taken the trouble to put Rory's hammock up before turning in as it's not easy doing it drunk. Next night the reverse would happen.

We have eight days in Gib. I walk round and up the rock. Keep well out of the 'up and down the rock race' designed to strengthen Royal Marines and kill and maim matelots. With ten ships in the harbour there is lots of inter-ship football and cricket. One of the CPOs asked me to play tennis. I agreed, and then he came back with the only courts are for officers. Been there before.

Danny sent me a letter and said he and Mick were on HMS Benbow in the Mediterranean Fleet and our ships would be together in Malta. We did not manage to meet in Portsmouth so it will be good to see them.

Before we set sail to join up with the UK's large Mediterranean Fleet we had to receive and stow stores and provisions. I, being a lowly junior rating, would be called to the dockside many times over the next four days to join gangs of my fellow workers to get the gear on board. Remembering the conversations I had with Mick and Danny about the Navy being a good way of smuggling dodgy stuff, I watch the goings on with interest. Once at sea I discuss what I saw with Joey whilst we are looking at the waves. We are often joined by Jimmy a chef working the officers' galley and the conversation extends from just provisions and stores to the day-to-day working of the ship.

They tell me how the CPO Steward and CPO Chef get together with the Catering and Store CPOs. From this power base, everything that goes on and off the ship is controlled. Only they know what is in all the stores spread about the ship. The Coxswain and the Bosun run the rest of the ship. Joey says his CPO supplies the CPO mess with wine and spirits from the wardroom stores. He said the officer in charge of their wine is a young lieutenant and does not have a clue and relies on the CPO Steward. Also all the fancy food cooked in the wardroom ends up in the CPOs' mess. Jimmy says the caterer gets kickbacks from all the suppliers and there is always a bar chosen ashore where all the chefs get to drink for free. The stores CPO is always available to supply anything if the price is right. When I mention smuggling goods to and from foreign countries they shrugged. Very easy to do, all they would have to do is put the goods into boxes marked the same as the other produce and deliver it with all the other stores. The stores party would just hand over hand into the ship. The best way to check would be to watch what left the ship and was taken away with the delivery van as that would be suspicious. I plan to study what happens when we get to Malta.

Arrived at Malta

I was part of manning the upper deck for our entrance into Malta. There were 12 ships sailing in line and as we were only a frigate our squadron came in last. We were also the Bum Boat of the Frigate Squadron so we came in twelfth. So we stood on deck for over two hours. Malta looked magnificent with the limestone churches and palaces. Finally, we anchored in Selma Creek as there was no room for us on a shore berth.

Rory was an electrician and had the job of sorting the phone line from the anchor buoy to the gangway. I asked him if I could help so I could see all the goings on in the harbour. Also, Rory said I could test the phones by ringing Danny's ship and asking to speak to him. It took a couple of hours as the Captain had to have his installed first.

I eventually got to speak to Danny and he agreed we should all meet up asap saying Gino was also in Malta. As I was locked into Punchy's mess run ashore – called 'The Delights of the Gut' – I suggested I get the tickets. Danny took some convincing, but agreed. I then had to find Punchy and convince him as well. We agreed to meet at the jetty where all the ship's boats delivered their sailors to begin their adventures in Malta. The ship's tannoy was warning that up to 5,000 matelots would be going ashore and for us to behave ourselves. This was followed by a warning that gonorrhoea was rife and we were to collect protection from the sickbay.

It had been my birthday two months ago and my mother had sent me a food parcel. Pete the Regulator said that she had forgotten to pay for an airmail sticker so it came by sea. The only godsend was there in amongst the rotting pate, mouldy cheese and melted chocolate was a 15-shilling postal order. Everyone in the mess stopped opening their mail, which they had been desperately waiting for, to stare at my parcel. Next came two tins of cow's tongue followed by a tin of spam. 'Who eats cow's tongue?' was shouted.

'Who puts it in a tin?' was the next question. The bananas had gone black and the apples (from our garden) were full of maggots. Oh and she had made my favourite quiche and cheesecake. Unfortunately these two items had now become one and had mould on as well. Punchy said he knew just the place where we can change the postal order ashore. He had a sly grin on his face as he said it, which I should have clocked onto.

Punchy's tour of the Gut

We all crowded onto the ship's motor boat to take us to the jetty. Before getting on the boat we were told the last trip back would leave at 23.30. Punchy said if you miss it just get a Dyso (Maltese call it a Derse) boat, the harbour was full of them. As I looked across the creek there were boatman standing up and pushing on both oars together facing forward. It looked awkward but they seemed to be buzzing around quite successfully. Once ashore, I found Danny, Mick and Gino and roughly explained that I had no idea what would happen but this run ashore seemed to be famous. I added that for them it was a free night to go some way towards repaying them for my London weekend.

Punchy fell us all into threes, walked up and down the lines adjusting collars and lanyards. When he got to me he said, 'That hat's disgusting!'

'I was told never to wear your best hat on a Punchy run ashore,' I said.

'Correct answer, quick march!' he shouted.

We stopped at our first bar and once again he went to the bar and beers were passed back. When we had gathered, Punchy said, 'We are now at the beginning of Strait Street, this is only the start of the Gut. It is dangerous down there [pointing up the street]. Put your money in your socks and stay together. The Malts and their women will pick off the back markers and strip you. The place will be rammed with our Navy guys, do not help them unless I tell you. They should be able to look after themselves. At the other end of the street I will leave you so get a garry (horse and cart) back to the jetty. Do not walk back into the Gut on your own. At that time of night if you pay them you can race each other back to the boat. Finally, only drink what I give you, Micky Fins will knock you out. Here endeth the lesson.'

So off we marched into the Gut and into the first selected bar. The bar was full of girls/women. We all sat down at tables with a girl between each of us. Punchy bought us all beers and the ladies a red drink which we all asked to taste. Our leader roared, 'Leave their drinks alone!' The girls spoke in Navy slang, it was a shock to have a lovely face look into your eyes and say, 'I fucking love you, no shit.' Mine then downed her red stuff in one and waggled the glass at me. When I refused to pay, she rammed her hand between my legs and squeezed hard. My yelp was in unison with my mates and as I looked up they all had a girl's hand holding their crown jewels. Punchy was doubled up laughing and he said, 'If you want them to stay, buy them a drink, if not they will leave.' After a repeat performance in three more bars we were all feeling very sore down there. Next we went into a bar without women and we were served with plates of oily pasties filled with white cheese, followed by rabbit stew and chips. Punchy said the pasties and stew were traditional but I think the chips were added by him at the last moment.

We were now in the middle of the Gut. On both sides of the road there were bars with women outside beckoning us in. The street was full of drunken matelots staggering past and stopping to barter, all surveyed by the ominous Naval Patrols slapping their sticks in the palms of their hands. Our leader then turned into a bar only to be greeted by a large oily Maltese who wrapped his arms round him. Punchy was obviously expected and no doubt made a deal with the guy for a visit for all the other delights of the Gut tours he had planned for the next two weeks. He had already given Danny and Gino his flyer with an offer of 20% for them on any kitty takings.

We were supplied beer and introduced to the owner Isaac and his wife Daniela. Punchy pulled me aside and asked for my postal order. 'Issac will give you the best exchange rate,' he lied. Now very drunk, I gave it him with a shrug. The bar had a mini stage which had girls in bra and panties gyrating to Arab music.

Suddenly Punchy jumped on the stage and lifted the arm of the girl dancing and began waving my postal order. He demanded silence and shouted, 'Samson's mother has bought him a birthday shag!' The guys grabbed me and pulled me onto the stage. The girl grabbed me and the postal order and pulled me through a door and up the stairs. All I could think of was gonorrhoea. I had read that you could have all sorts of complications and die from it (I was confusing it with syphilis). Beautiful though she was, I was too drunk and scared to comply to the task. I have always thought quickly on my feet and I just blurted out that I had gonorrhoea. The girl stepped back and luckily spoke in perfect English with a 'What the fuck!'. I held my hand up and said, 'I know, I know. What say I give you my postal order and some more money and you help me play a trick on my friend? It will help me keep face with my shipmates.' She nodded and the plan rolled out of my mouth and it surprised me as much as her. So she replied, 'You want me to lead you out holding your hand up shouting champion? Then when we get on the stage, I say this a challenge between champion and you and grab Punchy's hand and take him up for a fuck?'

I pointed out that the postal order needed a signature and gave her another five shillings. We agreed I would sign when she had finished with Punchy. 'Who will you choose as the winner?' I asked. 'Depends how he treats me,' she replied.

So it played out as described. I was cheered as I skipped onto the stage. Punchy did not know whether to hit me or play to the crowd when Angel and I called him out. He stared at her, growled and led her to the door. The bar went silent and everyone listened and watched the ceiling. Sure enough there were loud bangs and thumps to be heard. I asked about my noises and they said they hadn't bothered to listen! When they came back down, Angel grabbed me and led us both onto the dais and, with a short delay, lifted my hand up shouting 'Champion!'.

Later my opponent pulled me aside and said, 'Clever little sod, aren't you?'

I grinned and said, 'After all you have done for me, sharing my birthday fuck with you is the least I could do.'

'I will write to your mother and thank her,' he replied. Four days later Punchy went down with gonorrhoea. When asked if I had any symptoms, I got out my ID card wallet and waved a french letter.

With only about 20 yards of the Gut to go, Punchy has released us and has turned and headed back in. I expect he will now drink free for the rest of the night and sort out new venues for his next day tour. I believe he is taking the CPOs' mess tomorrow so perhaps he has to find some more upmarket bars. I doubt he will get a free fuck on their tour. We safely leave the Gut behind and after a few drinks walked over to the queue of horse and carts.

It is four to a cart and I finish up with Davie and two of the other lads. I arrange to meet Danny, Mick and Gino later in the week. We set off in a slow trot and soon after we are overtaken by Danny and crew so I stick some coins in our driver's hands and he gives chase. We pull alongside shouting expletives at each other. Danny's cart swings off left to where his ship is and we have now reached an impressive speed. We hear cries and singing from behind which makes Davie leap up and around. 'Fenians,' cries Davie. Sure enough, a cart with Rory standing up next to the driver comes up beside us. Whatever they are chanting is driving Davie insane.

He jumps down besides the driver and shouts, 'Faster, faster.' Davie's anti-Fenian or pro-Protestant ravings are frightening our driver who is now showing his age. He hands the driver a ten-shilling note. Christ, that's two shags I think, I am not sure the driver's up to that. Our horse speeds up, probably more scared of Davie's screams than the whip on his bum. As he gets more manic, he tries to steal the driver's whip and in doing so falls between the cart and the horse. The driver pulls the reins as hard as he can and we look back to see Davie lying in the road. We turn round and get to him as he lies there moaning, which might be a good thing. Before we reach him, someone rushes past and it is Rory. He gently sits Davie up and, with his arm around him, asks him quietly in what must be Scottish for 'are you OK mate?' Remarkably, although he is still to speak, he seems alright. The moans have stopped and he is rubbing his arm. As we are all very drunk, neither he nor we can say how he is or whether something is sprained, fractured or dislodged. The rest of the lads go off in the other cart and Rory and I bundle Davie into our cart. The driver, although looking very shocked at the happenings, has no doubt stayed around hoping for another one or two shags.

We are at the jetty and are all alone. It's a moonlit night and I can see the Frigate Squadron tied up in a line across the water. I shout Dyso (or something similar) and a boat light comes on with the sound of oars and 'OK' was heard. Davie is slumped on the floor and has still not said a word. He did however manage to walk, aided by Rory, from the cart to here. After much discussion, we finished up paying the driver another half a shag for his troubles.

We get Davie into the boat and he immediately falls asleep on Rory's lap. I tell the boatman the name of our ship and he points to the one furthest away – typical. We have just passed the second ship and Davie wakes up and he sees Rory and 'Fenian bastard' is roared before the expletives turn into unrecognisable Scottish. He stands up and swings an almighty punch, misses completely, and falls towards the water pulling me and the boatmen with him. If he had been sober I am sure Rory would have remained in the boat but – not to be. He dives in to save us all. This leaves the boat to drift swiftly out of our reach. The boatman would now disappear off chasing his boat, no doubt wishing the Maltese boatmen did not have to wear fancy dress to go to work. His buckle shoes weren't the best for swimming in. We did not see him or the boat again (no shags for him).

Even Davie was now treading water but not for long as he suddenly made a grab for Rory who then introduced an impressive front crawl and sprinted away from us. I surveyed the scene with Davie back to treading water and, I think, beginning to sober up. Before we set off doing a slow breaststroke to the ship, I spotted our hats bobbing about together, well out of our reach, so decide to leave them. Rory was swimming strongly, so I did not have to worry about him. Then I realised he was heading for the wrong ship so would wait a moment to see him get safely on-board HMS whatever. Rory got to the pontoon and went up the steps running up the ship's side, up he went onto the ship and saluted. The ship's guards walked towards him and pointed to our ship. Then one went to grab him, Rory squatted down, turned and ran onto the steps and down onto the pontoon and dived back in!

He was now swimming slowly to our ship and would get there before us. He swam past our hats and ignored them, they were worth at least three shags. He once again climbed the steps, very slowly this time, saluted, then walked towards the guards and collapsed. We arrived ten minutes later and crept up the steps. Looking over to the ship's deck we saw the medic, duty PO and the guards attending to Rory. We sneaked past and went down into the mess. I could not get Davie into his hammock so I left him in his wet clothes in a blanket under the table. When I awoke in the morning Davie was still under the table and there was no sign of Rory or his hammock.

As usual I lay in my pit going through another wash-up of a mess organised tour in my head. There were no flags pulled out of ladies' whatnots this time but I did spend my mother's birthday treat on a shag for Punchy. I'd been for a swim with two weird Scotsmen, not to mention a wild horse race in the night. I cannot wait to sign up for the next one!

I pop into the sickbay to check on Rory and there sat next to his bed was Davie! To be fair, they were not holding hands but he sat close and they were both laughing. I wondered if I was the source of the amusement? One day I will find myself an intelligent Scotchman to explain to me what makes this nation behave like this. It's obviously not sexual, their women seem contented. Davie in his drunken shouting did mention something about an Orangeman beating Rory in the year 17 something. You would think Rory would have forgotten that by now but no, he tipped Davie out of his hammock in rage at just the mere thought of it.

Malta tennis competition

With the Med fleet ashore getting blinding drunk everyday, it suddenly became important to get everyone representing their ship or Squadron at sport. First the four frigates had to play each other at all the sports to enable the Squadron PTI to pick teams to represent the Frigate Squadron against the other ships. I played for the ship's football and cricket teams but failed to be selected for the Squadron. Right, that's sport out of the way, I thought, now you can begin to explore the island. Navigating round the Gut even in daylight, I found the rest of the island very interesting. The fact they managed to keep the Germans out even though they were completely surrounded was impressive. I visited the rooms where the RAF controlled the aircraft and went to the submarine bunkers. I arrived back at the ship one afternoon only to be met by our PTI who wanted to talk about tennis.

The Navigation Officer, Timothy West, had volunteered to play for the ship and had asked the PTI to find another player on the ship. Having spotted that I had played for my previous establishment I had been volunteered. He listened to my moan about previous experiences and said, if we won the frigate knockout in singles and doubles, he would use the ship's fund to buy me a racket and tennis clothing to represent the Squadron. So my new friend Tim called me up to his cabin and told me he had arranged a few practice matches. He had three rackets and lent me one. I was very short of practice but by day two I was beating him. Tim was a nice guy and we chatted as equals. His wife and children were coming over to Malta for a holiday. They were going to stay with a Navy friend and his wife in a house near the tennis courts.

We went on to win the Frigate Squadron Tennis doubles trophy and I won the singles beating Tim in the finals. I met Tim's wife Fiona and their children Petra and Jeffery. Fiona was a classic blonde beauty, tall and slim with a smile that made it impossible not to smile back. Petra aged 15 and Jeffery aged 13 were almost smaller versions of her. With Tim cutting a dash as well, they could easily be in a fashion magazine as the perfect family. They were very posh and excited that their dad had collected a cup.

They invited me to supper at the house they were staying in. I tried to make an excuse, but they insisted. Pulling Tim aside I explained how impossible it would be. I had to wear uniform in Malta, can you just imagine jolly jack tar being stared at by officers and their ladies all in their finery. The amazing thing is that Tim did not even know I had no civilian clothes, and at that time rules did not allow us to carry them.

So instead we had afternoon tea at the tennis club. Fiona and the children pumped me with questions which I answered truthfully. My answers had Tim grimacing with embarrassment as after each one they looked at Tim with questions he would have to answer later.

'We have been on your ship and looked at Daddy's lovely little cabin, where do you sleep?'

'I share a room smaller than this [waving around the room] with 27 other men and we have to sleep in hammocks as there is not enough room for bunks.'

'Do you have a nice lounge like Daddy's?'

'No we have to eat in the same room on benches and tables under the hammocks.'

I think Tim now realises why going to his cocktail party would not have been a good idea. It would have been as excruciating as me taking him and Fiona for a quiet drink in the Gut.

We progress to the semi-finals in Fleet Championships for both the singles and the doubles. Next day when we play the semi-finals, Danny, Mick and Gino come along and join us at the tennis club. We win the doubles and in the singles I win through to the final. Unfortunately, Tim loses his game. We all gather in the Tennis Club for drinks after and enjoy each other's company as the sun goes down. The boys are in great form and have the kids in stitches. Tim and Fiona come from London as well and were impressed with where Danny's flat was in the West End. I hear during the discussions Tim's dad is a famous criminal lawyer. Fiona is also a lawyer and works for her father-in-law in his practise. Danny says if ever we get into trouble we will be sure to call.

Next day is the big final. I am told by Tim that the Captain will be coming and hosted by Fiona at the club. An Admiral will also be attending to present the prizes. I had already invited Danny, Mick and Gino. When I told Tim, he was pleased and said perhaps they could help with the teenagers whilst Fiona was chatting to all the other VIPs.

Punchy, who was the main ship's sport supporter, was well known for gathering the ship's company in large numbers to attend our football and rugby matches. They were very loud and had learnt and written some great songs. The PTI always encouraged Punchy and often laid on transport for the ship's company fans. At breakfast, my Mess President slid up to me and asked, 'When is your match?' It was at 5 o'clock which meant about 3.30 the tot parties would be going ashore. I had no choice but to tell him, as if I evaded the question he would definitely find out and attend. This was a bit worrying so I got hold of the PTI and told him of my concerns. He said, 'No problem, I will have a word with him.' Now I was definitely worried so I said, 'I will tell Lt West that you have it all under control and you will help seat the ship's supporters and keep them quiet. Well you will be there as tennis team coach,' I said and left.

The final with Tim went well, he was a master at doubles. He had explained that he had been playing most summer weekends since he was six. His father came from a well-to-do family so many days they stayed in large houses and the kids would be sent to the tennis courts straight after breakfast. Our master plan was for me to try to smash winning shots and win my service game with my big serves. Tim would be at the net and intercept our opponent's shots. It worked, they were better tennis players than us, but we played as a team and won in the last set. Tim was delighted and we hugged for what seemed like an age. Over my shoulder I could see the Admiral and our Captain stood up clapping. My first thought was, put me down Tim, this is not going to help your career path hugging a junior rating. A vigorous handshake and me saluting him would probably have been more appropriate.

After the Admiral presented the Cup to us, we each had to tell him what and who we were. He then said it was absolutely super that an officer and rating had won as a team. We moved over to our little crowd and Fiona filled the cup with champagne (another first for me). I moved away from the crowd to chat to Danny, Mick and Gino and was surprised to see Robbie in the group. He was wearing a very smart suit that was obviously made for the Malta temperatures.

'Careful,' said Danny, 'he is dressed as an officer now.'

'Lieutenant Robert Appleton no less,' I say.

'Thank you Dave, impressive stuff. Tasty moves, you made them look like right fucking plonkers.'

Just then, Tim came up with the Coxswain and a cup filled with champers. I introduced them to Robert and to my amazement they then had a long conversation about what he was doing in Malta with Robbie talking in his version of posh. I saw the boys, all in different groups, stop and drop their mouths open and stare. It was hard to actually understand him, Tim bless him was nodding intelligently. Later, Tim pulled me aside and said, 'Who is that chap and why is he here and is he foreign?' Not in the mood to help Robbie become a posh git.

I laughed and replied, 'Ten minutes ago he was Robbie, a guy I met in London speaking to me in very broad Cockney swearing in every sentence. As soon as you and the other officers turned up, he started speaking his version of what we call posh.'

'He says he is an Assistant Provost Marshal and working with the fleet on security issues,' Tim replied. I explain that apart from meeting him when staying in Danny's flat for the weekend, I knew nothing about him.

I leave everyone to prepare for the singles final. The guy I am playing beat Tim in his semi-final. He is six foot four and Tim says he hits the ball so hard that he had difficulty hanging on to his racket. Apparently, he was well known in the Navy tennis circles and the son of a Duke. I did not ask if I should call him 'Sir' as he was also a Lieutenant Commander. As long as he did not call me boy, Sir it would be.

Myles Cooper Bland nearly broke my fingers with his handshake. He smiled sweetly as he did so, holding on as long as possible. Being right handed I wished I had offered up my left for execution. With a 'best of jolly good luck old chap' he strode with purpose up to his end and prepared to serve. The first serve was called out by the umpire. I did not gain any information on it as I did not even see it, all I heard was the whoosh and thump as it hit the wall behind me. In order to make sure the second serve is in, it is usual to slow it down. Not his lordship, he hammered that one as well. I saw it, got my racket to it, but did not hit it! As my game was a hard serve and a lethal forehand my chances were reduced to nil when he treated both with utter contempt.

Sitting on my seat resting between changing ends and losing two games to love, I surveyed the scene. In the stands, our Captain was sitting with Tim and all the other ship's officers (even Guns). Just below was Fiona, Jeffery, Mick and Gino. Danny was sitting across the aisle talking intently with Petra, a few seats along was Robbie (what was he doing here?). No sign of Punchy (thank god).

Sitting there I realised it would not be possible to win this match. So how could I stop this man making a fool of me in front of these guys (and dolls)? My answer was, instead of me being the power guy, I would be one of the guys that annoyed and sometimes beat me. The plan was to just dink the ball over the net and make him run to get it. He was very big and strong but ran like a carthorse.

It was nearly working and I only just lost the first set. I had my supporters cheering whenever I had Myles getting to the net too late and falling into it. During the second set, with the score four games each, I was about to get up from my seat to begin the next game when I heard 'Hi Hoooooo! Hi Hooooooo!'. There marching along the seats was Punchy and his Ship's Supporters Club fresh from their four-hour rum session. I had to walk to the end where they were supposed to be sitting. The closer I got, the louder my name was chanted. Unlike professional tournaments, the umpire did not have a microphone. So you will not be surprised if his standing up in his high-chair waving a pen and shouting, 'Quiet please ladies and gentlemen' had no effect. I looked up to our Captain and officers group who were probably deciding whether to pretend they did not own this unruly mob or file out quickly to the bar. The problem was, all of the chanters had HMS Folkestone in fine gold lettering round their hats.

The Captain sent the Gunnery Officer over to solve the situation, followed by the PTI hanging onto his coat tails. A Gunnery Officer is supposed to be known for his ferocious voice that roared across a parade ground. Ours stood on the court looking up to the seats with his hands held aloft screaming. As he walked towards them they burst into the song that they had written for him months ago. The song described how much they hated him and it questioned his parentage and was not kind about South Africa. The chorus of 'We shat, we shat, we shat in his hat. What do you think of that? We shat in his hat!' rang around the court.

Next, striding across the court came our Coxswain. As he approached the supporters, their volume slowly lowered until there was silence. Except for Punchy, who was facing the supporters, oblivious to the Coxswain's approach, waving his arms and conducting whilst loudly singing 'We shat, we shat...' etc. The Coxswain tapped him on the shoulder and smiled. Then he whispered in his ear and Punchy slunk over the wall and found a seat and, with that, all his men sat down abruptly as one, and fell silent. Every single Navy man from the Admiral down to me knew there would be no more noise in the stadium from my supporters. The main man, as far as the lower deck is concerned, is the Coxswain. The Captain and officers are to be saluted and avoided, the Coxswain is to be listened to and obeyed.

My plan of making Myles run miles and miles worked well enough to win the second set. Even my supporters clapped enthusiastically and there were a few muffled whoops.

My opponent got wise to my trickery after the score was five all in the last set and I began to think I might have a chance of winning. Sitting looking at my very large opponent slumped knackered on his chair gasping for breath, I decided to dink the ball just over the net on every shot. I remember at school the PT teacher saying if your opponent is better and stronger this was the way to beat him. He then made us practise everyday sometimes the court was dark before we finished. To most players it's a risky shot but not if you practised as much as we did.

His first serve thundered down and I just angled my racket and the ball dropped just over the net. Myles had only got halfway to the net and roared, 'lucky bastard!' The next serve I repeated my dink, this time he just stared at me. He got so angry that he served two uncontrolled thrash's into the net. To win the game I then dinked another one over the net and I shouted, ' I am a third time lucky bastard.'
The final game consisted of me serving accurately within myself. Myles lost three points trying to power balls past me. One I dinked as he rushed the net and the other two went over my head. So match point. He returned my serve carefully, I dinked one over the net Myles flew to the net and lobbed it back to me, I then ran back played the ball into his court with my back to the net. At the same time Myles fell into the net shouting expletives. Once back on his feet he congratulated me, Putting his arm round me we walked towards the umpire. 'You crafty little bastard,' he whispered.

After the match at the presentations, we were all back in uniform. All the officers had changed into civvies and the reception was just not made for us. In the future Officers

140

and men might be able to mingle in these circumstances but not in the early sixties. The fact that there was no way the winner of the doubles and singles champion would be able to wander around and chat with his opponents at such an evening is sad but true. So with my London buddies I headed off and joined Punchy in the Gut (where our dear officers would think we belong). I was however welcomed like a hero and it was many a long time before I had to put my hand in my pocket. We got very, very drunk and arranged to meet the following night. My ship would sail the morning after so it would be the last time we would see each other for a while. We headed back on to our different ships this time without my Scottish friends, which meant me and my hat got safely back on board without getting wet.

Next morning, I was killing time on the upper deck and looking down over the guardrails. I saw Robbie and our 'can man' (NAAFI Canteen Manager) on a boat tied alongside us. They were arguing and Robbie was prodding his chest hard to get his point over. I ducked down below our sea boat and got in a position where they could not see me, but I could just about see them through a small gap. The argument stopped and the can man shrugged and accepted a large envelope. They shook hands and Robbie gestured with his arms and a Dyso rowed up and took him back to shore. The vessel was loaded with boxes of all sizes, I was very intrigued as to what was going down. The tannoy then piped 'Stores party gangway'. Never one to volunteer, but this was too good to miss as there was no way anyone was ever questioned about turning up to hump stores. I joined the can man at the gangway and volunteered to take the last leg by the store.

He tossed the keys to me and said, 'Stow all the boxes at the back of the store.'

The store is down a vertical ladder, I stand at the bottom and the guy above throws the boxes down to me. I get to inspect each box before I walk into the room and stow it against the far wall. I have my seaman's knife with me to slit any box that irks my ire! A box arrives badly dented and with a small slit. I use my knife to increase the cut and manage to get a cardboard box ten inches square and an inch deep. It has some foreign language on it and a picture of a man and woman doing something naughty. I open it and there is a cinema reel of film. It's obviously a dodgy movie so I hide it near the door and decide it's too risky to mess with any other box so the rest go into the store unopened.

I look around at the bottom of the ladder and there is a metal unit along the wall. I repack the film and hide the box behind the unit. The can man comes down and counts all the boxes and checks them against his list. 'Any problems,' he asks. I say a few boxes have dents in them and one was split but not enough for any of the contents to fall out. I got the box out and he checked it and said it was OK. I gave him the keys and left. That evening I got the box and hid it in my little hideaway, deciding what to do about it later. I was confused and puzzled why a man with a great career in the Navy would stoop to shipping dodgy films into the UK. I also wondered what other goodies were in the NAAFI store. As this was the first reel of film I had seen in my life I had no idea what to do with it or how to check what was on the film.

Only Gino turned up that evening, so we decided to go up market and keep clear of the Gut and, after a few beers, find a restaurant. I would be back to cold soggy slush, so a meal was my idea. The restaurant we choose had the Maltese speciality of rabbit. The waiter almost convinced Gino to order the delicacy. I then explained that my youth was spent sat at the edge of many a field with a gun shooting rabbits with myxomatosis. This was to stop them jamming up the combine harvester as they ran blind around the field. Their faces covered in sores that shut their eyes and drove them mad. The waiter said their rabbits did not have this disease. Gino nodded and ordered steak.

We spent some time discussing the difference between our ships. As we were from different trades the common denominator was our living conditions. Gino's had bunks to sleep on and a dining room to eat in. The food was served from a hatch that you queued up and was served onto trays. Then all you had to do was turn around and find a place to sit! 'Holey moley, what bliss!' I cried. Then quickly told him about our daily nightmare.

'So,' I asked, 'what do you do at tot time?

'Stay in the dining room and drink tea or coffee,' he replied. Half of me was glad that it was not the norm in the Navy to have to put up with our conditions, the other half was why me?

As is always the case when two of the mates were missing, the obvious topic of conversation would be about those who were not with us. I started with, 'Robbie and who is he

143

and how come he keeps popping up when least expected?' Gino shook his head and said, 'I know little about him and he is still a mystery to me. He is well known and respected in the organisation. Danny, when asked says he was close to his dad and now looks after him. He was chosen to keep him on the straight and narrow when his dad was killed. Danny had mental problems after their deaths, when they were shot down in what was thought to be a gangland killing. George, Danny's dad, was the top man in the organisation, and the official report on the deaths was that a rival gang was responsible. Albert Smith, George's brother is now the top man. The real reason we are all here in the Navy is that, when he was not right in the head, Danny attacked a girl who was part of the Cypriot gang we were spying on. It was Robbie who got us all in the Navy. Robbie says he is here to check on smuggling in the fleet, how that is connected with his pals in London we have no idea. Danny just brushes it off when we ask about Robbie. He once went as far as to warn me that it was best not to make enquires about him,' said Gino. 'We are also suspicious about Robbie's relationship with Danny's mum. If we are right, Albert would not be amused.'

Anyway, Robbie has flown back to UK today so maybe he will leave us alone now.

'Danny seems alright now?' I question.

'He has dark moods but is brilliant at keeping it to himself. He is a fanatic on cleanliness and personal hygiene. You can see how he dresses, always immaculate, and never passes a mirror without checking himself out. You cannot help but like him, he is generous, and helps his friends when they are in trouble,' says Gino. Then Gino laughs and says, 'His taste in girls is young and blonde only. Spookily just like his sister.'

'What about Mick?' I ask.

'He always seems a straight guy,' Gino replies. 'A hard man who does not suffer fools and always hangs on every word Danny says. I think deep down he is jealous of him. Quite often he goes on walks without us. If you ask where he has been you never get a clear answer. His dad worked for Danny's for years, so he was always walking on eggshells.'

I decide to leave it and chat about Navy routine. We have a great night and we say our goodbyes at the jetty.

Depart Malta – back to sea

We sail from Malta to begin a big exercise with the Italian and Spanish ships. Life on board soon got back to normal. My latest workplace was in the electronics workshop where I fixed equipment brought in by the other sections. I spent most evenings designing circuit boards in the workshop. The Chief REM would also be in there working; he often came over to see what I was doing and helped me when I got stuck. He did say he wanted a percentage if we succeeded designing anything worthwhile.

For three weeks the officers played with their toys and pretended to sink submarines and shoot down aircraft. I keep away from the bridge as, after my session as submarine lookout, I am probably thought of as a troublemaker. Then I heard that Tim the Navigation Officer did not sail with us when we left Malta. Surprised, I went up to the bridge and into the Navigator's Chartroom. The Leading Hand who spent his day updating the charts was working away. I apologised for the interruption and asked about Tim. He looked at me with a 'what's it got to do with you?' look. I explained that I was the guy who he played the tennis finals with and the last I had seen him was at the finals.

He put down his pencil and said very quietly that it was not to be repeated but that Tim had stayed behind to look for his daughter. He followed up with, 'She went missing the night before we sailed and that's all I know.' I nearly

146

collapsed but nodded a thank you and headed for the upper deck where I held onto the guard rails and tried to stop myself from being sick. My head was spinning as I tried to comprehend the absolute mind-blowing disastrous news. What is going on, I thought, first Patty and now Petra. This cannot be a coincidence, was Screech on one of those ships in Malta? Here I am 18 years old and instead of learning my trade and enjoying myself, part of me has spent the last 12 months fretting and worrying about a girl that I hardly knew. The other part is telling me it has nothing to do with me, it's a police matter. Similarly I have only spoken a few words to this girl. Now there is another girl missing, once again why am I feeling responsible?

It is just not possible in my position on the ship to contact anyone. I cannot believe how this could have anything to do with Danny, Mick, Gino or Robbie but it would have helped to talk to them. After three days I was going stir crazy and had to discuss it with someone. Punchy was best approached in the morning before the rum changed him into Punchy No 2.

We sat down in one of the radar rooms and I explained everything, finishing with if there is a connection with the two kidnappings then the team looking for Petra should be informed. Punchy said, 'I understand how you are feeling but just because you knew both these girls, tying the two things together does not make any sense at this stage. Anyway, this guy Robbie is an Assistant Provost Marshal and he knows everything you guys did. Being in Malta they would have already got him on the case. He has investigated this Yelton guy for the first crime and he will soon find him again. You are a young kid, do not get involved. Trust me, they will not listen to you. My advice is to keep your nose out and let the experts fuck it up.'

He was right I was being stupid. I marvelled how that man could switch between the many characters he played. After that advice, within an hour he was being a buffoon at the rum table. Throwing one-liners out to amuse his audience, followed by scathing putdowns that raised even louder laughs. And then two weeks later this happened!

Punchy bows out

Punchy died today and I am devastated and in deep shock. It all started four or five days ago when Punchy began his campaign to advertise his birthday. Apparently, last year he had the time of his life and this year, he boasted, would be even better. The officers' galley had promised T bone steaks, chips and beans for the rum table at lunchtime. Followed by depth charges with beer chasers. For the evening party, the main galley would bring to our mess fish and chips with mushy peas, followed by his favourite figgy duff with syrup and custard. He had purloined wine and beer. The ship's skiffle group would provide the music and the mess would put on a Sods Opera (we all have to dress up and perform comedy sketches). All this would take place as our little warship sails quietly through the Mediterranean Sea on station and escorting a large battle cruiser and aircraft carrier. I did question how this great event would act out without anyone knowing. Punchy is legend and he has probably invited all the senior CPOs to pop in on the evening do, I was told. Also Pete his mate will have got the nod from the Coxswain who will have told the First Lieutenant and cleared it. The biggest problem is getting all his guests into this mess.

With the prospect of steak and chips, I, with my fellow UAs, were keeping out of the way over in the corner of the mess, as far away from the rum table as possible. As it was Punchy's birthday, a 'stand in' Rum Bosun stood over the Rum Fanny dolling out the tots to the two rum tables, it was a full attendance. In the centre of the main table was a large pint pot. As each person received his rum, he tipped some into the pint pot then lifted his glass saying 'Punchy!'. At the end of the ceremony there was nearly two pints of rum (junior ratings drank two parts water to one part rum, the rum however was 95%) waiting for him. The food arrived along with a big surprise birthday cake. The four chefs who delivered the goodies were asked to stay and soon had glasses of rum in front of them. A runner was sent to find Punchy and he soon came back saying he will be with us soon but has had a few invitations to other messes. I caught him just as he was going into the Chiefs' mess. He said to start without him. As the rum tables were still performing their rituals, we slid quietly over and sneaked some steak and chips. Once finished we did not have the nerve to cut the cake!

Our mess party had now cleared the rum stage eaten food and reached the cans of beer stage. With still no sign of Punchy, the main table with his two pints of rum, a birthday card and the uncut cake awaited him. The vodka for the depth charges was hidden under the table. Finally, there was a tremendous roar and what sounded like a spine shattering yippee! Followed by Punchy sliding down the ladder at great speed. His feet hit the floor with a loud thud. He was lying back on the ladder and then he pushed himself up and fell forward staggering towards the rum table. His main henchmen sitting either side of the table stood in unison and being very large men, grabbed Punchy before he could flatten the table. They sat him down on the end. He was not making much sense but, between giggles, was telling what a great time he had in the other messes. Someone had brought a big bag of his presents that he had received on his rounds. He was dipping into the bag waving a pressie with delight saying how kind everyone had been.

He then looked around slowly almost at each individual face and finally said, 'Now I am back home with my friends.' We stood up and someone started lighting the candles and gave him his card. We all raised our glasses and sang happy birthday. As we did, Punchy stood up unaided and grabbed one of the full pint glasses of rum and sank it in one!

I just stood in utter amazement. I knew it was bad but did not know how bad. A sigh of relief all round as he sat down again and started chatting. Someone made him a chip butty and he took a massive bite and seemed OK. He picked up the other glass of rum and the guys sitting next to him grappled his arm. He just stared at them and said, 'I'm OK,' shook off the hands and took a couple of very large gulps and said 'Get some glasses'. He then tipped most of the remaining rum in the glasses and handed them round. Punchy's head eventually slumped forward and he began to snore. He was then lifted up to be taken to his normal afternoon sleeping arrangement in amongst the hammock stowage. They lifted him and half threw him into the middle of the hammocks and left him. The lights were dimmed as usual and us UAs went back to work and everyone else not on watch went to sleep off their daily lunchtime session.

We came back down into the mess when the ship piped stop work. As usual, the mess lighting was still dimmed.

Someone switched the lights up to the usual swearing. Two or three of us together looked in horror at Punchy. He was lying half on his side, his face was grey and there was blood dribbling from his half-open mouth. Someone rushed to the sickbay to get the attendant. I rushed to the Chiefs' mess to get the Chief Electrician, he thought the world of Punchy and had pulled him out of lots of scrapes. He came to the door and I told him Punchy was either very ill or dead. What followed next was utter chaos. We were eventually thrown out of the mess and congregated on the upper deck asking each other what was going on.

Derek, the next senior in our mess, joined us and told us Punchy had died. He said they had tried to revive him but he was already gone. He had overheard the conversations of the Captain, First Lieutenant and the Coxswain. Apparently Punchy had visited the forward and after seamans' messes then the stokers followed by the chefs and stewards. What about the PO and CPO messes? 'Not mentioned,' said Derek. This meant that he had probably been given at least a pint of two parts water and one of rum in each mess which meant he would have had at least six pints before he fell down our ladder. We all did these calculations in our heads and imagined the damage that had been done with that much alcohol inside him.

The problem was every morning he went up the mess ladder with his little electrician's tool bag and his test meter. He was in charge of all the lights and sockets throughout the ship. He could wander into any mess or the officers' wardroom/cabin, open a fuse board sometimes to fix a fuse, but most times to listen to whoever was in the room. It would not be long before they were getting Punchy's opinion. His main aim was to be rewarded for fixing their equipment. The result was an invitation to join their rum table at lunchtime for sippers. Thus he was known and liked by everyone on board. This popularity killed him.

Punchy was put in one of the ship's freezers and we returned to the mess all sitting around in silence thinking of the man.

In order to survive on a ship like ours with old-fashioned ways of mixing eating and sleeping in the same space, no dining rooms or bunk beds, no decent washing facilities and very cramped conditions, we needed protection and Punchy provided that. He looked after us. Mess decks were full of old sea dogs usually recruited from the national service or the courts. He would scan the mess and go over to any of us sitting quietly or even quicker if he spotted any bullying. He always knew all the scandal and cock-ups made by officers. He would play the room and go barging in on each of the benches to relay the latest news. It was strange we all thought of him as a good friend, but if he had survived and you met him in the future, I'm sure he would not even have recognised you.

Derek and the other seniors in the mess started describing him and they said he had CDF (common dog fuck!), which in Navy slang meant he was a player with the gift of the gab and instant witty answers. They then mentioned he was fearless in many ways. He could get away with walking up to the Captain or any senior officer and begin a conversation. Then how he would take out anyone who threatens his men when ashore. We were told he had a lovely big blonde wife and two matching daughters, eight and ten, which would bring tears to his eyes during the last couple of hours of his drinking sessions. They lived in a little village in the Yorkshire Dales. I tried to imagine Punchy with his massive barrel chest and large beer belly strolling down a cobbled street, arm round his wife and holding the kids' hands. Mind you, he would need to have them in the pub garden by 12 o'clock.

Punchy always said he was not an alcoholic because he did not drink at breakfast. After that he strolled round the ship until the magic hour of tot time. Then his day consisted of drinking until he collapsed and waking up to do it all again. So bless him, he was in control of everything and everybody on the ship, but not his life.

There was an internal investigation on the ship that got very heated. They (senior officers) were trying to find someone to charge. It was easy to see that the best way to make this disaster go away was to blame someone and to get them off the ship into jail. The question was who? It is against the law to give any of your rum to anyone else, also to invite someone from another mess to drink your rum. The messes had met quietly on the upper deck and sort of agreed that if anyone is charged then every man who tipped some rum in a glass in all seven messes would admit to the charge. At a rough count, that would be somewhere between 80 and 110 charged with Punchy's demise. The Coxswain was quietly informed of the plan.

The lower deck lawyers are also compiling a book of Naval known traditions. The rules of Sippers and Gulpers are set in stone in today's life in the RN they believed.

The first thing they did before the external officers arrived to investigate was to arrange a secret ship's search for booze. Even though the whole ship's company were warned that a search was to be made in the dead of night, a large amount of illegal booze was found. All the players complained it was impossible to find enough spaces to move it to. I found it quite amusing that the whole ship's company (and I mean everyone) was running around all night with bottles. They took the booze from its hiding place before the search party got to it. Then they carried it along the upper deck and put it back in the original space after the search party had left, hilarious! In the end, only the booze that had not finished fermenting or stilling was allowed to be found. The Navy has not changed since Nelson's day. The whole lower deck, including all the CPOs will always stick together. Even the Coxswain who will appear to lean towards the officers will decide which fights are worth fighting and advise accordingly. The important thing was that an amount of half-made booze was captured for the First Lieutenant to report the search as a triumph to the Captain.

Having removed all illicit booze from the ship, the long and tedious rounds of interviewing of all the potential culprits began. It was a complete waste of time, everyone said they gave Punchy a card and a present and sang happy birthday as he drank his favourite tomato soup! Listening from my far table as the plans were being discussed, I felt like holding my hand up and suggesting they should vary the soup from mess to mess. Whatever, if the messes are to be believed Punchy died from drowning in tomato soup.

On the science front, the body was taken to the aircraft carrier and flown ashore for forensic tests and a post-mortem.

Eventually, the Mediterranean fleet became involved and a team arrived on the ship. The latest stage of the enquiry was announced by Pete, a guest at our rum table with rum in hand. New mess rules were imposed and a UA (sometimes me) was sat on the top rung of the ladder stopping anyone rushing down to witness guests drinking our rum. If you walked down the Burma Way, a junior would be sat at the top of each mess ladder from 12 o'clock each day. Life goes on. Derek gave Pete the floor and he said a doctor had been flown in from the UK, who was already heading a team studying the drinking habits of the fleet at sea. On his insistence, they planned to ask every mess to do an internal account of exactly what Punchy drank in each mess. The President of each mess would only have to give an amount, no names would have to be provided. Also no charges will be made. They will then do a study using the post-mortem to measure the actual alcohol consumed. It is important that the amounts are very accurate and that no one holds back because the amounts look bad on their mess. Someone enquired whether the CPO's mess was included, to which he answered not to his knowledge. Much discussion followed and all agreed Punchy was seen entering their mess. So it was agreed a tot of neeters should be added to the count.

A few weeks later we had a rough idea of the findings. Punchy had drank just under six pints of 2&1. He died of alcoholic poisoning. When he came down our ladder he already had enough alcohol in him that, even changing all his blood at that time, could not have saved him. The mess agreed we did not kill him, he was already dead when he came down the ladder!

A few days after the death I began having very frightening

nightmares. The dream consisted of me lying in my hammock looking down on the mess. The problem was I could not move or speak. I was trying to get up and shouting for help but life went on down below and I could not move or communicate. In the dream it seemed to go on forever. Eventually I would wake covered in sweat, panting for breath. This went on for weeks and I began to be afraid of falling asleep. There was no cure even if I went to our very strange Sickbay Attendant. He would tell me the same as he did to everyone. 'Fuck off, come back when you have broken something' was the usual response from our compassionate and caring nurse.

It is the naval tradition for the whole ship's company to attend the sale of Punchy's effects. We all mustered on the upper deck and all Punchy's belongings were laid out before us. We would bid on each item paying silly money. All the money raised would be sent to his widow and the children. I felt a bit guilty because I had always admired Punchy's brown cowboy leather belt. He got it in America. How he got it, changed every time I asked him. Whether I bought it because I have always wanted it or because it would be a keepsake to remind me of our times together did not matter. The bidding went on and on and I finished up paying more than two months' pay for it. It has taken pride of place in my locker for many a year. Try as I might, I have never got fat enough to wear it.

A fast battle cruiser attacks!

Finally, something happened to amuse the lower deck. It was late afternoon and on the tannoy came an excited Gunnery Officer. 'You hear there,' he roared. 'A fast battle cruiser is going to fire her six-inch guns at a splash target pulled by us,' he said proudly. 'If you go on the upper deck you should be able to witness what our battle cruisers can do.'

The Chief said, 'Come on Samson, you should see this even if they cock it up and miss the target as usual.'

We stood by the guardrail as the ship's winches belayed a large metal type anchor with wings out off the stern. The ship picked up speed and it was soon producing a large waterspout which I assumed was to be the target. When it was a good distance away, Scab shouted 'the cruiser is about to open fire'. We all stared at the target, the Chief had given me a set of binoculars but I decided I would have more of a chance of a better view without them if they missed the target. Just as well I did as suddenly there were two very loud whooshes, a double splash and two objects entered the water about forty yards from me. Almost immediately, two more hit the water and another two seemed to go over our heads. I say our heads but when I looked round there was no sign of the Chief, he had scarpered. The ship then put on maximum of starboard wheel making all of us hang on desperately. Those on the upper deck had no choice but to stagger to the nearest object and hang on. We then increased speed to flat out and the ship vibrated violently. The action stations alarm started ringing permanently and over the tannoy came 'Action Stations Action Stations'. My station was in the radar room just inside the hatch from where I had been standing. I was not too happy as I was now thinking I had witnessed six-inch shells missing me by 20 feet or so.

Finally, after all the damage control teams have searched the ship and found no damage, they stand us down. I rush down to the mess to see what the buzz is. The word is that the cruiser's gunnery radar locked on to our ship instead of the splash target. The next message is the cruiser will steam past us to apologise. As she approaches us we all put our hands up to surrender, a few smart alecks are waving white flags. The two Captains are shouting posh abuse at each other over the large loudspeakers on the bridge wings. It's very hard to sound angry if you start the rant with, 'I say old chap.' Suddenly there is frantic waving, they are yelling there is a hole in our ship's side near the waterline. The ship immediately stops in case water was forced into the hole as we steam into the waves.

Everyone is now on the upper deck peering over the side as the Shipwright is lowered over the side from the forecastle (ship's bow). From his cradle, he disappears through the hole into the ship. The damage control party are waiting by the door with all its levers clamped shut. Then they hear someone banging on the door and out comes the Shipwright. The shell in the paint shop had no explosive in it. A normal shell would have wiped our paint shop out and gone through the other side of the ship. The problem was it was not safe for us to steam forwards as the temporary patch on the hole would not last. So our dear Captain had the embarrassment of entering Gibraltar harbour backwards (astern). I will leave you to guess the disgusting signals being sent between ships.

Punchy's Memorial Run ashore

On arrival in Gibraltar on the first night, it was decided that we would have a mess memorial run ashore dedicated to the memory of Punchy. At the lunchtime rum table, the itinerary for the run ashore was discussed in great detail. One of the guests from another ship suggested that we should all try the new chicken and chip shop. Seeing the glares of 'who asked you to put your oar in', he held up his hand and said you don't understand.

This takeaway shop has a giant rotisserie (a new invention!) with about 30 odd small chickens rotating round and round whilst being roasted. The normal portion is a half a chicken and chips. The story has it that one evening a drunken big bad stoker ordered a whole chicken. He ripped the chicken's arse open, got a cloth up it and stuck it on his hand. When everyone saw him walking back to the ship with a beer in one hand and a chicken on the other hand, they all wanted one. The rest of the queue changed their order, only wimps order a half was the cry.

Fez the Moroccan who owned the place stood back in amazement as racks of his chickens were disappearing. He watched as very drunk men tried to stick their bare hands up his very hot chickens. In the kitchen he cut up cloths and presented them with each order. That evening all the rest of the Navy lads looked on with envy as they watched men walking back to the ships biting

161

large lumps of chicken with a free hand to wash it down with their beer.

The next day he had bought gloves and then re-engineered them to fit his chickens. As a man who was brought up in the souks of Tangier, he knew he had stumbled onto a winner. A sign was soon outside the shop which said, 'A bird on your hand is worth two in your bush.' He was laughingly told by a joker that 'bush' was rude so he crossed it out and put 'tree'!

The whole mess was laughing, a few said he was taking the piss. It's straight up, he insisted. In our mess you wake up to giggles with a crowd staring down at a guy fast asleep in his bunk with a half-eaten chicken on the pillow and his hand stuck up it. We shout, he opens his eyes and screams as he stares into a chicken carcass. It's even funnier when he realises it's stuck on his hand.

The Navy Patrols are thinking of banning the sailors from using the place as Main Street is full of carcasses in the morning. People are getting their shoes stuck in them and babies' pram wheels are getting jammed on them. I think they are trying to get the Gib government to not let him sell whole chickens. The stray dogs are not complaining, even the apes are popping down from the top of the rock for a change from their vegetable diet.

Fez charges four times the price for a whole chicken on a glove over a half chicken portion. There is always a drunken discussion of how come a glove is the same price as a whole chicken. Fez's argument in pidgin English is that 'putting your bare hand up one of my red-hot chicken's arse is not healthy for you or the chicken. My chickens are velly fussy about what glove they likes.'

Our visitor finishes with, 'It is about time Gib had an identity. If you wake up and there is a pasty under your pillow you are in Plymouth. If it's a curry pie, it's Portsmouth. Now if you wake up with a chicken on your hand, you're in Gib.' There was a shout of Bahrain a Kebab and Hong Kong... 'A woman' the whole mess shouted. He said, 'I was going to say Chow Fan.'

A vote is taken and one of the blokes who has the afternoon off is sent with the money for 23 gloved chickens to be collected at Fez's at about 11.30 tonight.

Between the Shipwright and the ship's photographer, a nearly life-size picture of Punchy has been mounted on a board. They had sawn round his fine body shape. It has a handle at the back, so it can be carried, and a stand that can be pulled out thus enabling him to be stood up with us in the pubs. This object has just been brought down the ladder and the guys who made it are paid with rum and Punchy's vodka depth charges.

It also agreed we would get the sail maker to knock up a small flag with Punchy's name on and get it delivered to 'Nellie with the Big Fat Belly'. Apparently her extra charge for pulling out guest flags from her 'whatnot' is very reasonable. She has a few apt tunes she can add to her ensemble for special occasions. It's getting to the end of the rum session as some idiot suggests we take a picture of the flags' extraction as a souvenir for our noticeboard. Bedtime for rum drinkers. They have a long night ahead.

We muster on the jetty, Bill our mess member, who spends every spare moment lifting weights, is tasked with looking after Punchy. Derek our leader called us to attention and held up collection bags. If anyone we meet wants to donate to Punchy's wife and kids, grab a bag and stick it under their noses.

Bill's bulging muscles pick up Punchy and we marched proudly out of the gate and into all the same pubs. Lots of Navy lads knew Punchy and came over and stood next to him and described the outrageous scrapes they had been in together. It was weird as they stood there looking at him, talking to his picture expecting him to answer. These were the guys who had been in the bar all afternoon. Bill stopped them putting their arms round Punchy. Owners and managers of the bars all knew him and put notes into his collection bags. Finally we crossed into Spain and to the bar near the Bullring. As before, shorts and beers came along with the tapas. Someone remembered that we had chips last time so they were duly ordered.

We stagger into the nightclub, Big Fat Nellie comes over and grabs Derek to finalise her act. Money and flag are handed over. There seems to be a discussion as Nellie seems to be measuring the size of the cloth. I think she is used to better cloth than our sea boat sail, someone whispers. We know her secret so in the end she will do it was whispered. Derek returns and gives the thumbs up and says she is going to do it accompanied by Frank Sinatra singing 'My way'. All my mess members are nodding in agreement. 'Nice one,' Derek muttered. I shake my head and think, this night is getting more weird by the minute. Would you all listen to yourselves, I want to shout.

Bill positions Punchy so he can see the acts. There are angry mutterings when the two flamenco ladies are joined by two men with tight black trousers and short little jackets. All four stamp noisily around the floor clicking their castanets behind their backs and up in the air. Finally, the men skip off and our education in Spanish classical dancing is complete. I actually thoroughly enjoyed them, it looked very professional. However there is a right time and place and this was neither of those. The ladies now take their clothes off and a state of normality is returned.

Nellie arrives and runs round and tries to tease us as she removes each layer. 'Is she having a laugh?' shouts someone cruelly. Once she is down to her gigantic knickers she comes over and picks Punchy up with ease and places him in the middle of the stage. Out comes his flag and we all join Mr Sinatra and sing and shout as drunken sailors do. The rest of the act was as before, so after the last line of 'God Save The Queen' we get up to leave. Bill goes and collects Punchy. Before he could escape, Nellie grabs our dead leader and gives him a large wet one on the lips. I know Bill is a weightlifter but I still think it was very brave to use his sleeve to wipe the spittle off from Punchy's face whilst Nellie looked on.

We safely returned to Gib and we are all looking forward to our chickens. Fez was a little wiry Arab with a big smile on his face. The place was packed and had a long queue outside. I was told to hold Punchy whilst Bill went inside pushing past people. Fez's smile slipped when he began the discussions about where our 23 chickens were. Luckily, Bill out-muscled Fez's doormen so we were told to go down a side lane and into the kitchen at the back. There, we were all fitted with a chicken on a glove. In the top, where its head usually is, were a few chips rammed in, which I thought was a nice touch.

165

We stop at the next pub and two of the lads have to take off their chickens to go in and get 23 plastic glasses of beer. Bill was moaning about carrying Punchy with a chicken on his hand. We all agree that it is time for Punchy to leave as he always did. So as this particular pub was one of his favourites, Bill quietly places him at the end of the bar and we all wave goodbye from the door and leave him. The idiot who thought we should leave him with the kitty as that's what would have happened normally was shouted down. Not to be shut up, he then moaned and said the very least we could have done is got him a chicken! It is moments like this I realise how drunk we are.

We, proud as punch, parade and wander aimlessly down Main Street munching our chicken and swigging our beer feeling, how can I say 'on trend'. A guy walks past us and says the Navy Patrol is coming round the corner. We all hurtle down a side street and down the steps only to find HMS Rooke (Naval Base) across the road complete with policemen. A quick about turn and lots of crashing of chickens and spilling of beer and we are back down another side street. A long sit on a wall is required to plan a safe route back to the ship.

I awake on my camp bed in my little grotto. Yes, I have a chicken on my hand but no, I am not frightened. I was one of those sad ones that woke up worried about where it could be and was pleased to see it on my hand.

As usual, I reflect on the night. I remember little of the trip back to the ship. I vaguely remember holding onto two more chickens so the owners can crowd round the quarter master. Then I creep past and on board with all our birds.

Whilst watching drunken fools trying to get in their hammocks still wearing their chickens, I hear the cry of, 'Fenian bastard.' I am on the first rung of the ladder to escape from the turmoil. Looking back to see Davey smash a right-handed chicken into Rory's face. Rory, being left-handed, embeds a chicken in Davey's midrib. I continue to climb the ladder as my Scottish friends re-enact an ancient battle. It took days for the stink of rotten chicken to leave the mess. Fun as it is, I cannot see chicken on a glove lasting much longer.

We were supposed to arrive in Portsmouth in two weeks, but it would take that long to get into dry dock and weld a new plate on our hole. Next day I see that Gino's ship has followed us in so I wander over and see him. He did not mention Petra being missing, so as we had agreed to go ashore that night, I thought it best to talk about it then.

We walk past the bar where our mess had left Punchy's placard last night. Leaning in, I see that much to my dismay it is still by the bar. I never really got the memorial and found it a bit spooky. So I slip in and grab the placard then take it down a side street, break it up and fill a nearby dustbin.

In the first bar, I told Gino about Petra being missing. With his beer glass about to be put in his mouth he just froze. Gently putting the glass down he said, 'No way, not again.' The problem is that I still had no facts. She could have been found and alive for all I knew. Gino had sailed from Malta the same time as my ship and he had not heard from Danny or Mick. I explained all my thoughts and fears and Gino agreed he was thinking the same thing. We agreed to put any actions on hold until we heard whether she had been found.

Robbie investigates

Two days later the Coxswain called for me and said I was wanted for an interview at the Naval Police Office in HMS Rooke. He asked me if I knew what it could be about. I replied that it could only be about Lieutenant West's daughter being missing. I then told him everything about Patty, including Lieutenant Robert Appleton and his association with the London boys. The Coxswain went over it with me two or three times, getting more out of me each time. He then looked up and said, 'I know Appleton and have heard a lot of rumours. He has been fast tracked to an officer and that is not normal in our branch. So I will be representing you at this interview and if I say you are not to answer a question you just say "yes Coxswain".' I nod my agreement.

We arrive at Rooke and the Coxswain headed straight to the Police Headquarters. We were asked to wait outside but Coxswain went off to find some old mates. After about 30 minutes the door opened and Gino came out and shut the door. He held his finger to his mouth and whispered, 'The Nelson at 7.30.' I nodded, it was the bar we had been in last night. The door was soon flung open and there was Robbie. 'Samson,' he said, 'come in and sit down, we have much to discuss. I take it you know that your old Navigating Officer's daughter is missing in Malta?' he asked.

'I was hoping you would be telling me she had been found.

I only heard she was missing two weeks after we had sailed,' I replied.

'How did you hear?' he asked.

'I was on the bridge working and I asked to speak to Lieutenant West and his writer said he had not sailed as his daughter was missing.'

The door was knocked and Robbie shouted, 'Wait!' The door opened and as it did Robbie screamed, 'I said wait!' The Coxswain walked in and sat down next to me and said, 'Coxswain Henshaw representing one of my juniors Sir.' He then got out a notebook and pen and said, 'Have you started without me?'

Robbie obviously knew the Coxswain and even though he outranked him seemed to throttle back his aggression and take a more conciliatory approach. 'I wish to question Samson on the missing daughter of Lt West.'

'As a witness or suspect?' asked the Coxswain.

'As a witness of course, we have no suspects at this time.'

I then answered all the normal questions about when and where I had met her and what conversations I had with her. I summed up by saying I had only spoken to her once over the table at the club with her parents. The rest of the time I was playing tennis and Petra was with her mother, brother, Danny, Mick, Gino and you. The Coxswain asked for the boys' full names. Robbie then asked if I thought the abduction was similar to the one in Plymouth.

'One hundred per cent,' I said. 'It doesn't make any sense but I was very shocked when I heard, I still think about the last one. Was Yelton in Malta this time?' I ask.

'I ask the questions,' Robbie stated. He then asked if I have ever been to Gosport and if so when. At first I say no and then I remember my tennis match. I tell them all about my visit to HMS Dolphin, including being left behind by the other players. He wanted the date of the game. I said 'it was in my diary'. It was agreed I would give the dates to the Coxswain and he would pass them on. After walking me through my every waking movement of my three weeks' stay in Malta, I was dismissed. The Coxswain remained behind and I waited outside. He came out and signalled me to join him and we walked back to the ship.

'I have just told Lt Appleton that Lt West's daughter is alive! She was found the day after she went missing in a disused hut near the house they were staying in. Lt West took her back to the UK after hospital check-ups. The story was put out that she had stayed overnight and was in trouble with her parents. She was in fact attacked and abused but will not speak about what happened. They could find no clues or evidence and it was thought that Petra was more likely to be able to remember what happened in the comfort of her own home. It was agreed that the whole incident would be kept secret.'

I stop walking and look at him in amazement. 'How come Lt Appleton didn't know that?' I ask.

'Leave that to me,' he said. 'He is very anxious to get one of you three boys for the crime,' he said.

Then he said, 'Appleton says that another girl was attacked in Gosport.'

'Why if he is investigating the attack on Petra, did he not know she was alive?' I ask.

Thinking aloud he said, 'On who's authority is he investing all these incidents?' He then added, 'There are many coincidences in these cases and it's not just you boys or this Yelton guy it is also Appleton. He knows this Danny guy and he is running this investigation and the UK one. You all should be suspects including him. I have asked my friends in the force and trust me they all say he is untouchable and he has some very high-up supporters. I have also not been able to find out what the incident in Gosport has to do with the RN, it's a police matter. Very strange,' he whispered shaking his head.

We then walked silently back to the ship. I get my diary and report back to the Coxswain with the date I played tennis at HMS Dolphin in Gosport.

Later I meet Gino in the Nelson and we swap stories. He had a much harder time than me as he was on his own. 'Robbie as much as accused me of the kidnap in Raleigh and also suggested Mick and I did it together,' moaned Gino. 'I told him that you said that your Navigation Officer's girl went missing from Malta after the tennis. Jesus, he said you lot are at it again. I think the Malta girl was news to him but he didn't admit it.

'After that he began discussing you, asking how come we know each other. Then he said, isn't it a strange coincidence that these disappearances started happening after Dave came along. Suddenly the subject changed to Gosport. How often I went over on the ferry and what was my attraction with Gosport. I kept repeating I have never been to Gosport. Then suggested why don't you ask Danny as he had a girl over there for weeks. He never took me with him, maybe Mick went over there with him.'

I stopped Gino in his tracks and told him Robbie had told my Coxswain that girl was attacked in Gosport. He also told him that the only one with an alibi for the dates she was attacked was Danny. The girl Danny was seeing in Gosport is alive and well and has given a signed statement.

'This is all mad,' says Gino. 'There are three possible girls missing or attacked from three different parts of the world. As far as I can see, the only person investigating all three is Robbie. Why aren't the police involved?'

'My Coxswain indirectly asked the same question,' I reply. We then spend a sad evening going over and over all the same stuff and get nowhere. Both our ships sail to the UK in two days so we agree to meet in Pompey. Gino will write to Danny and Mick to see if they can make any sense of the latest news.

Something fishy in the ship's stores

The following morning I am assigned to the store party. We gather on the jetty in a line and throw the vegetables, fruit, bread and boxes to each other from the lorries up the gangway into the ship. The can man arrives just as the last lorry pulls up. I am shocked to see Robbie talking to the ship's caterer. Once again there seems to be a heated discussion. I stay out of sight and decide not to get involved in any dodgy deals Robbie has with the ship's food supply. Being still too frightened to do anything with the film that has been hidden in my grotto since Malta, there's not much point in finding any more evidence. We get moved to the NAAFI lorry which is full of similar boxes as before. Christ, I think, what has Spain and Gibraltar got that needs to be smuggled into the UK? Robbie comes round from the back of the lorry with the can man in tow. He looks into the back of the lorry and then down the line of men throwing the boxes. He spies me and walks confidently along the line and stops. Beckoning me over he shouts, 'Samson! Over here!' Stepping out of the line, the guy swinging a large box to where I was, swears as he nearly does himself a mischief by not letting it go. I march towards Robbie salute and 'Shout, Sir!'. 'Follow me,' orders Robbie and takes me round to the back of the lorry.

Once alone, Robbie says, 'You need to understand a few home truths. Getting Henshaw [the Coxswain] involved was a big mistake.'

I stare at him and say, 'You sent him the order for me to report to your office. It was because I said I did not know why you wanted to see me that he decided to ring his friends in the Gib Naval Police.'

After putting the phone down he put on his hat and said, 'Come with me.'

'Why didn't you tell me the girl in Malta was alive?' he growled.

'Easy,' I angrily reply, 'because I did not know until I was told by the Coxswain when I left you.'

He then asked, 'What does Henshaw know?'

'Only what he heard from you at our interview. When we left the meeting, he asked me my opinion. I told him that there was no way the four of us had anything to do with it. We were all in our mess with 15 other people for the first incident. The Coxswain seemed to agree and said it was a matter for three different police forces.'

'Good,' he replied. Robbie finished our conversation with, 'I will be watching out for you!'

Would you believe, as I watched him walk away the PO in charge of the Stores Party shouted, 'Samson, stop loafing and get back in line!' Next minute I had a crate of cokes thrown at me.

That night, lying in my camp bed up in the grotto, I go through everything that has happened. The main question in my mind is, does this mean that Danny has been messing with these girls? If so, Robbie must be protecting him. Screech must have a good alibi, he would have been put in the frame. Lots of questions no answers.

Ever since Robbie walked away it has slowly dawned on me that I have no choice but to go with the flow. The problem was the real me couldn't just take it without having a little dig back. So my thoughts now went on how do I get the film to the Coxswain without anyone knowing it was me? To get the store searched and the Coxswain onto Robbie's smuggling antics would be very satisfying. However, if it got linked back to me it would be very dangerous.

Drafted to Hong Kong

As we prepare to sail from Gibraltar a big announcement is made. The ship when it arrives in Portsmouth will go into an emergency six months refit. All juniors under training (me) will be drafted to new ships to continue their training. Also all personnel not required during the refit will be sent to temporary postings and will rejoin the ship in six months. We will be in Pompey in two weeks so all departments are in a spin. Most of the married guys families are in Portsmouth so they are really chuffed and trying to convince their officer they are needed in the refit. All of us juniors are just hoping we get a better ship than this one.

After a few days the Coxswain calls me into his office. He was looking at a document and shaking his head. 'I have a draft chit (order) for you to go to a small island just off Hong Kong.'

'Wasn't I supposed to have been sent to another ship?' I asked.

'Apparently they have a desperate need for a novice Greenie in Hong Kong. I wonder why that is?' he questioned.

'When do I go?'

'Three weeks after we get back. You should get your three

weeks leave in and then you report to the RAF base at Brize Norton,' he replied giving me the documentation.

'You need to go to the sickbay in Portsmouth Barracks to get all your jabs for the Far East. Then go to the stores and get your tropical clothing. Whilst you are in Portsmouth Barracks, I would steer clear of the Naval Provost Marshal's Office. They may or may not know you are disappearing for a year.'

I have thought of a cunning plan of how to inform the Coxswain of the smuggling scam. In the mess, Punchy's personal locker is full of all his effects that the mess will deliver to his wife when we get home. The likes of all his photos, jewellery and presents for his children he had been buying in all the countries we have visited. One of the guys who lives in Yorkshire will take the gifts to her personally when he goes home. My plan is to sneak the film and a letter into his locker. It will say this package should be handed to the Coxswain should anything happen to him. This is the letter I will put with the film in the package.

Dear Coxswain,

In Malta whilst walking round the upper deck I heard shouting and looked over the ship's side and on the store's boat was the can man arguing with a Lieutenant. I then witnessed him give the can man a large envelope and leave. The store's party then began tossing the boxes out of the boat. I went down to the NAAFI store and pretended to be fixing a light and managed to get a look in a broken box. This dirty video is only one of many in the store. The boxes are stowed at the back of the room.

177

Knowing the can man well I pulled him aside and asked what
was he filling his store with. He became very frightened and
said that his wife and kids would be at risk if he said anything
and grassed them up. This Lt Robert Appleton was serious
trouble and all the NAAFI managers were scared of him. He
warned me to keep quiet as the same could happen to me.

Sort them out Coxswain
Punchy

Derek, the mess's new boss, had Punchy's keys on a massive
key ring tied to his belt. I had watched which key was
used last time he added something to the locker. After a
particularly long tot session, I extracted the key ring from
the drunken Derek's belt. As Punchy's locker was well out
of the way it was easy to put my large envelope under all
the goodies in the bottom drawer. On the evening before
we enter Portsmouth, we are informed that Punchy's wife
and children will meet the ship and come on board as
guests of honour. We all began to rush around cleaning
the mess and making plans to make what will be a very
difficult day as easy as possible for all concerned. I even
tear up just thinking about how to say hello to a little
family who have lost their dad.

I suggest to Derek we empty his locker and sort out his
goodies and discuss whether we pack them up or present
them tomorrow. Derek removed each item for everyone to
see. Eventually he pulls out the package and says this is for
the Coxswain, after much discussion the consensus was to
open it. I shout, 'Punchy always had our backs, if he wants
whatever that is to go to the Coxswain then that's what
should happen.' It worked, Derek gave it to me and said,

'Take it to the Coxswain.'

'I reckon he planned for his replacement to take it Derek,' I said. He nodded and headed up the ladder.

Later that night, as I wandered up to my bolt hole, I passed the hatch leading down to the NAAFI store. There was much activity and discussion from the many bodies down below. Passing me was the Ship's Stores Officer, I turned to see him working out how to get down the hatch. He was wearing pristine white overalls that had obviously never seen the light of day.

Next day I steer clear of the Coxswain and the NAAFI store. Tomorrow I leave the ship for the last time so I will have to get all my papers from his office. Today I await the arrival of Punchy's family. I half understand why she would want to come and get a feel of how he spent his life, but we all know it will not help. Even though we would do anything to make it better.

As the junior, I have been tasked to look after the children. I am to show them around the ship then return back down the mess for sandwiches, cakes and ice cream. I go down to the galley to collect the goodies from our Maltese PO Chef, Tony. He is there putting the final finishing touches to the tea. 'I will give them my very special ginger log,' he cried. He took two packets of ginger nut biscuits and put them in a bowl. Then he poured half a bottle of brandy all over the biscuits and moulded the pulp into a log and put fresh cream in a piping bag and squirted it over the top.

'It's for F£@ing kids!' I nearly cried, then I thought of

all my mess mates' surprise when they got drunk eating a log. So I ask the chef for five of the brandy logs and one without alcohol.

'It's on the Captain's entertaining budget Tony,' I explain.

'No probs,' he replied in Maltese.

We are all on the upper deck clapping as Punchy's family come up the ladder. His wife is indeed a lovely big blonde lady. His two girls are very like their mother with a hint of Punchy in their smiles. Dorothy has brought her brother Sam who could probably give Punchy a run for his money. I bet everyone was thinking Punchy would have had to behave himself whenever he went home. The Captain welcomed them and gave Dorothy a big bunch of flowers followed by a large cheque from the ship's company. He then took them into the wardroom for drinks. It did seem ironic as the only time Punchy had been in there was to change the light bulbs.

Davie and Rory were assigned with me to entertain the kids. This proved extremely difficult as the cute little girls spoke a type of Yorkshire I had yet to experience. Rory took over telling me that Glasgow might be nearer to Yorkshire than Wiltshire. We were a bit concerned when he started talking as they both looked very frightened and tears began to appear. We gave up in the end and got the guy who lives up there to take over and we went back to the mess to devour a few brandy logs. Dorothy came down into the mess. She was walked around and met each group that Derek arranged. We were introduced as Anthony's juniors. 'Yes he taught us everything,' I said nicely.

'Christ god help you,' she said smiling. I offered her a piece of log.

'Thanks I am starving,' she said taking a large bite. Followed b,y 'Jesus that's strong.' Then she looked over and saw her daughters tucking into a large bowl of log. 'That one's Anthony's favourite,' we said. 'It has no alcohol in it.'

'My Punchy bless him, would be eating this brandy one with a beer in his hand.'

'True,' we nod.

'It is such a shame he died of a heart attack after he had been losing weight and was beginning to get into shape,' she said with a serious look on her face. Then she continued, ignoring the stupid look on all our faces, 'Did you young ones join him every evening at sea doing circuit training?' My two Scottish chums were nodding enthusiastically and I replied, 'Sometimes.'

Her very large brother, Sam, had been listening and came and joined us. We could tell he was not convinced that Punchy's letters home about his being a changed man and a fitness fanatic were true. Straight away he asked, 'Did you accompany him on his long runs ashore when you were in port.'

I decided to act as spokeperson and provide the lies his wife seemed to need. 'Yes,' I replied. 'When he organised runs for the mess we always joined him. Sometimes he would go for runs with the other messes. He was very popular and had lots of friends.'

He mentioned a long run in Gibraltar and run up the rock and asked if we went with him on those. I replied, 'He must have done the rock run with his mates but we did the road one in Gibraltar with him.' I went on to explain that we went all the way across to Spain and round the bull ring and back again. It took a long time but as it's so hot in Gib we had to make quite a few stops and take on board lots of liquid. They nodded and moved off to chat and grill the grown-ups.

We got in a huddle over the other side of the room, all amazed that they had told them he died of a heart attack. 'At least he did not lie to her about the runs ashore,' I said. Typical Punchy, he believed he could add the rock race and still make Sam swallow it.

During the night I have been tossing and turning on whether to tell the Coxswain everything. In the morning, I knock on the Coxswain's office door and he calls me in, asks me if I am OK.

'Fine,' I reply.

He hands me all my papers and explains that he has listed the instructions required for me to safely arrive in Hong Kong. He shakes my hand and asks if I have anything to tell him. This is my chance, but I bottle it and I just shake my head. He opens the door and gives me a card with a name and phone number.

'When you feel safe, ring this number and they will tell you where I am.'

As I go to leave, I turn round and ask, 'Coxswain, why did they have to say Punchy had a heart attack?'

After a few seconds, he asks, 'Who was responsible for his death?' Then he answers, 'Not him, nor his shipmates. Me? What about the Captain, he is responsible for everyone in his command? The Navy? From the Admiral down, we all know what goes on in the ships and Navy establishments at 12.00 everyday. For hundreds of years the naval personnel over twenty are pissed by 14.00. Sippers and gulpers are now part of life in the Navy. I believe at least one naval rating dies weekly of alcoholic poisoning somewhere in the world. How do the Admiralty stop it? Only by stopping the rum issue altogether. To do that they would have to improve the disgusting living conditions you have to put up with. You young technicians are the way forward, as ships get more sophisticated electrical equipment. How can drunks be controlling and repairing it?'

Finally, he said if the Navy issued a statement that Punchy had died of alcoholic poisoning, a lawyer could sue them. It would be impossible to defend it.

Looking back at the ship as I struggle with my suitcase and kitbag, there are tears in my eyes. No idea why, I should be jumping up and down with joy!

I arrive at RAF Brize Norton in fine style. Arthur from my village still runs the milk round that I helped him with many years ago. He came to my rescue as my only other means of transport was a tractor! Bouncing down the country lanes with empty milk crates in the same van brought back many memories. As we pull into the passenger terminal the RAF guard looked at me with disdain and was not impressed with my form of transport. I think he expected two pints and half a dozen eggs to come out of the van instead of a suitcase.

I board a Britannia only to be told by a young crab-fat (Navy's name for the RAF – apparently, when the Royal Airforce was formed the colour of their uniform was the same colour as the fat the navy guys had to put on their bits to get rid of crabs) that the flight is at least two days if all goes well. He saw the question on my face and shrugged, we've had a problem with one of the engines but it should be OK for the next 10,000 miles. I told this to a seasoned matelot I sat next to and he laughed and said that's a crab-fats way of frightening you. He's jealous because he is stuck in Oxfordshire and you are off to Hong Kong.

We flew to Libya and then Aden and on to the Maldive islands and finally Gan. The Britannia had four propellers moaning through the whole journey. As propeller aircraft use more fuel the higher they fly, we spent most of the journey being buffered around in the middle of the clouds.

The plane was full of all different members of HM armed forces. In the early sixties, everyone smoked. I will never forget walking back along the aisle looking left to right and seeing all the passengers flicking their cigarettes into the nearly full ashtrays. The lower the rank, the further back you sat in the aircraft so I could not see up through the smoke to the front rows. Every time we stopped for fuel we all had to disembark. Usually, we were led into a hut with water or tea and stale sandwiches. Pete the able seaman who shared our row at the back would moan at every stop. Look at those bastards going off for pink gin and a spot of supper and fine wine. It was true that an RAF officer escorted the front of the plane, presumably officers, gentry and their ladies, to another building. We were always herded back on at least 30 minutes before the other lot who staggered back on board laughing and joking.

As I sat on board amongst the smoke and farts of 290 men and women my thoughts came to the first two years of life in the RN. After barely surviving Mr Nasty and all the other happenings in Raleigh. Then enjoying the electronics training at HMS Collingwood. Especially as I found keen and friendly experts who were able to turn a farmer's boy from a council estate into a radio electronics engineer. Then my first thoughts of seeing for the first time that old frigate with just one 4.5 inch gun, a couple of machine guns and six anti-submarine mortars. As the missing girls come into my thoughts, I quickly change the subject, deciding to give it a rest and look forward to being happy and safe.

Pete was drinking something from a large pop bottle and decided I needed educating. Out of nowhere, obviously having stared at the females getting off and on the plane, he stated loudly, 'Isn't it strange officers' wives are ladies and ratings' wives are women? Also officers' wives have bottoms and ratings' wives have arses.' From as far as ten rows up the aisle, people were turning round staring at us. Why do they think I am agreeing with him just because I am sat next to him? I give him a nudge and whispered for him to shush. 'Hey why is it that if a ship goes down or an Army lose a lot of men they say that the ship or regiment lost 20 officers and 200 men. Are they a different animal? They must be or they would just be 220 men.' The back half of the plane are now all laughing and clapping. 'If officers are not men, what are they?' (a few whoops were added).

One of those 'not men' was now on his way from the front to the back. Pete's bottle was empty. I whisper, 'The pig in charge is coming at a rush, pretend to be in a deep sleep.' I grab the bottle and shove it through to the seat in front. Leaning over, I ask the guys to pass it on. Pete is now lolling against the window with his tongue out. The officer arrives, complete with bow tie and states.

'I am Major Bradley and I am in charge of this aircraft, what were you shouting?'

I explain it was not me and point to Pete, 'He is having a bad dream and keeps shouting out strange statements.'

'What is he saying?' asks the Major.

'He is complaining that after an incident they announce the number of officers and then the number of men who have died.'

'What's wrong with that?' demands the Major.

'Sir,' I reply. 'If you wish me to interpret a man's dreams, I would say we are all human and why should you be announced dead different to us ratings?' (loud cheers from the troops). Strange snores were now coming from Pete.

The Major turned to stride back up to the front. We then hit a cloud or something and the plane drops suddenly and leans over about 30 degrees. The Major disappears from the aisle, ramming his hand into a big guy's face sitting by the window. Unfortunately, the chap had a lighted cigarette in his mouth at the time and nearly swallowed it. As the Major got back into the aisle there was a shout of 'If you are in charge of this flight, piss off and fly it. Do not come back down here again.' I whispered to Pete he could wake up now but he was in a coma and it took some work to get him off the plane when we finally landed.

Our final stop was Gan, a small uninhabited island in the Maldives manned by the RAF just to refuel RAF planes. This time we were led to our hut by a pleasant RAF corporal. His first words were, 'This is the worst flight for weeks.' 'What's wrong with it'? I asked. 'There are only old women on this flight, we only volunteer for this duty to chat to the wives and daughters going to live with their husbands and fathers in Hong Kong or Singapore. It's the only chance we get to see a woman in the 12 months we have to stay here. When a plane has a problem and gets stuck here everyone has to stay overnight. We then open all the booze we have and arrange a BBQ and dance. You would be amazed how accommodating the wives can be when filled with booze and a chance to let their hair down. Especially when they can quietly fly off in the morning knowing what happens in Gan stays in Gan. When we get really down we often think of finding a small

187

fault in the aircraft just to keep it here for the night.'

'Well we should be OK,' I say, 'as it's just full of hunky men.'

Old wise Pete whispered, 'I would not hold your breath, these crab-fats have some very strange habits.' However, they obviously did not know a good thing when they saw it as we were soon herded back on board. After the mandatory 30-minute wait for our drunken and rowdy officer class to board we were off to Hong Kong. As this was my first flight in any aircraft the last three landings were fine but Kai Tak was a very frightening surprise. I was sat by the window and suddenly we were flying through the skyscrapers and you could see the washing hanging out and people holding their ears. Finally we were rushing down the runway in the middle of the harbour.

Stonecutters Island (Ngong Shuen Chau)

The island is about three miles long and one-and-a half miles wide and stands in Hong Kong harbour approximately four miles to Hong Kong and the Kowloon ferry. At the time, the island was only habituated by the Army and Navy. The Army had a prison, a firing range and stored all the territory's ammunition. The Navy had a radio station. There were two bungalows near the beach for service families to get away from the pollution and bustle of Hong Kong.

Previously, during the Second World War, the Japanese used the island for rest and recuperation for its officers including a geisha house. They also had a snake farm where they milked all types of snakes found in the Far East. They used the venom to treat their troops in all the many jungles they fought in across the Far East. Unfortunately, when they left they let the snakes go free. Needless to say, after rain when the sun came out, walking the pathways around the island became very dangerous. Snakes asleep on the pathways get very angry when disturbed.

The whole coastline around the island was guarded by Indian Sikhs. They manned posts all along the shore, usually out on pontoons where there were very large searchlights and guns. They are protecting a one mile no-go zone from the shore out to sea.

The Navy radio station consisted of a series of single-storey buildings. One long hangar-type building held 20 large long-range radio transmitters and another smaller one with ten transmitters. One other building housed the single ratings living accommodation complete with dining room and kitchen. There were two large houses, one for the Navy officer in charge, the other was the Chiefs and Petty Officers' mess. Finally there were lots of bungalows for the married Chiefs, Petty Officers and Leading Hands and their families.

After travelling halfway across the world, I finally saw my home for the next 12 months. As we rounded the headland in the small Navy launch manned by Chinese sailors in uniforms, all I could see was a few buildings and before that, a very impressive Indian Sikh on the jetty welcoming us with gun in hand. Over the next few months we would get to know each other and become friends.

Up from the jetty and through the widely open gates into a nicely kept garden area surrounded by bright white buildings. I was shown around the ratings' long bungalow by a small cheerful Chinese mess boy (called a mess boy but must be over 30), another guy who would become a good friend. There were three bedrooms with four beds and wardrobes in each. A dining room, bathroom and lounge and apart from the kitchen that was it. Apparently there were 11 other single guys in the building, but they were down at the bar which was at the firing range.

In addition, the manpower was the Officer in Command who was a Lieutenant, a Chief Petty Officer, five Petty Officers and five Leading Hands, all married and living down the road in their bungalows.

I sat on my bed and thought I had fallen on my feet here. After living with 250 and sleeping in a small mess with 27 sweaty sailors and sleeping in a hammock; jumping out of the hammock in the morning and trying to avoid sticking my foot in someone's bacon and egg on the table below. Instead, I have a posh bed, matching walnut bedside table and wardrobe.

Apparently the 11 of us share three mess boys and four chefs and we can discuss the menu for the week every Monday! It was very hot and the rooms had no air conditioning, only large fans whirling round extremely fast and noisy. After a while, you forgot they were there and just talked louder.

Now I have to wander down to the beach bar and find my new partners in crime (this is what I'm talking about!).

Just a short walk down the path along the beach you came to a gunnery range. At the end of the bay, rocks rise up 30 feet where the targets were. To the right and above the range was a pleasant building with a veranda. Outside a few tables were filled with 20 people. Just as I start to wander down to meet my new friends, the Sikh guy runs over and tells me to wear shoes or the snakes may get me. Apparently, my joining meeting in the morning would include a snake awareness and a first aid course.

I finally reached the bar and was greeted by all the lads and the Leading Hands and their wives and it could not have been a nicer evening. I had a choice between San Miguel and Tiger beer, both served iced cold. Everyone was giving me far too much information to take in, especially after two days flying and four pints of lager.

Next morning I report to the Chief Petty Officer. I would have to spend two weeks training on radio transmitters before I started watchkeeping. One Petty Officer and a Radio Electrical Mechanic (REM) manned the main transmitter station with one Leading Hand and a REM in the substation. That was it, just four men manning the whole station operation 24 hours a day. I was told the man I had come to replace would be going home in two weeks so best I got my finger out and be ready by then.

The next stop was a visit to the snake man. His room contained pictures of snakes and also stuffed versions. Stonecutters Island has banded kraits (broad yellow stripes), bamboo (bright green) and the brown cobra. All very nasty and to be avoided at all costs. The bites of the remaining snakes on the island would be serious but not deadly. After going through a long lecture, I left with pictures of all the different types of snakes on the island. 'Learn and recognise' were my last warnings. This is what I was to do if I got bitten by a snake. Stay very calm and still, do not shout and run about. Quietly call for help and if possible, catch the snake! Failing that, make sure you recognise it. Getting the correct antidote for each type of venom will save your life; get it wrong and the cure can kill you. Apart from boots and leggings, the best protection was to get a dog. Within a few weeks, I had 'Sippers', a white-coated chow who became the love of my life.

Tim Collins, the guy I was relieving, was in charge of the catering in our junior rates mess. As there was no Leading

Hand who was single, one of us REMs had to do it. The Chief selected me because I had 12 months left and at 19 was one of the older guys. I was then introduced to the Commanding Officer (CO) Lieutenant Peter Bush. I was surprised to be greeted pleasantly and told his door was always open, not a welcome I had experienced before. In the two years I spent on Folkestone, I rarely ever spoke to the Captain or any of the senior officers. The CO was in his early forties, short and chubby. A small radio station was probably a nice comfortable posting before he leaves the Navy.

Next day, Tim and I jumped on the small Navy launch called a T boat that travelled back and forth throughout the day between HMS Tamar, Kowloon Ferry Terminal and the island.

HMS Tamar

This Naval base on Hong Kong island provides jetties for all the Royal Navy's visiting ships and submarines. A minesweeper flotilla is permanently stationed at the base. The new buildings were completed in 1962 and provided docking and stores facilities for all incoming ships. Close by is the China Fleet Club which provided the Navy with bars, restaurants and duty-free shopping and from 1961 it looked after the American forces on R and R from the Vietnam war.

As we on the island belonged to HMS Tamar, I had to complete a joining routine. Tim did the rounds with me to register in the sickbay, dentist, pay office and clothes store. He then took me to the food stores to introduce me to the Chief Chef and PO Caterer. They would sign off all my food orders when we sent them over each week. I would be back next week to find all the goodies available to us. As we were only 11 men, all the products were available at a special price.

Once back at our accommodation, with Tim Collins away packing, I met up with all the boys. I started by asking what they thought needed changing in meals. Immediately the main complaint came up that Tim insisted on using the Navy rations to make the chefs cook typical Navy and English dishes. They all raved about the Chinese restaurants ashore in Kowloon. 'We have Chinese chefs, let us have some of their food,' they demanded. I agreed to check with Chief Cook in HMS Tamar whether that would be a problem. I also suggested when we go on pub crawls we get the waiters in the restaurants to write in Chinese the meals we had eaten. It was 1963 and Chinese food had yet to reach UK on mass. I certainly had never eaten it. Not just for financial gain but the buzz of changing things. After a few weeks I had cleared with the Chief Cook that we could try a Chinese menu. So I had the daily ration money of 11 guys to spend in HMS Tamar stores at specially reduced prices. The store contained all the products of a UK supermarket. A couple of the married Petty Officers had approached me to see if I could get them meat, tinned products and eggs from the Naval stores. Apparently, Tim did them a few favours.

The transmitter room

After completing my training, I began working in the main transmitter room which was a large, long hall with a very high ceiling. As you entered the hall, the control desk with all the electronic monitoring devices was spread along the desk with teleprinters banked on each end. The control desk spanned the entrance and the Petty Officer and REM sat behind it looking down the hall. The room had ten transmitters each side off the walkway that ran down the middle. Each transmitter consisted of a metal cage the size of a garden shed. We worked an eight-hour afternoon shift starting at 12.00 then a six-hour morning shift from 6.00 followed by a ten-hour night starting at 20.00. Then we had two days off.

The Petty Officer in Charge of my shift was called Blood Reid. I never knew his real first name. Blood was the only single PO and he lived up the hill in the Chief and Petty Officers' mess on his own. Obviously our only CPO and all the married POs used the building socially. The high-power high-frequency (HF) transmitters send the military communications all over the world. The radio waves go up to the ionosphere and are then refracted back to Earth. The ionosphere changes between the day and night and, in order to provide 24-hour communication, we have to quickly change the transmitters' frequencies. As there are 20 of them, the two of us would sometimes be running back and forth up and down the big hall. The transmissions left each transmitter on two thick bare wires through the roof. Then up to each of their aerials. These were wires strung between 100-foot masts spread across the island.

Blood was great and very knowledgeable, he taught me how to tune and fix the machines as and when they broke down. He said his plan was to get me in a position where he was not needed and could then sleep the night away. I soon discovered he was quite a celebrity. He would come back from Hong Kong after his two-day break in such a state the Chinese boat crew would have to carry him up the hill and put him to bed. Sometimes he would get the midday boat back which was usually full of wives coming back from the shops. Blood, very drunk, would try to get the ladies to join him in a sing-song or tell them jokes. His personality would allow him to get away with some fairly disgusting ones. He would be dressed in torn shirt and trousers with the knees ripped. Grinning they would ask, 'Blood, why are your knees grazed and bleeding?' thinking they already knew the answer. Then they would try to find out who he was with and where he had been.

Next day he would arrive on shift immaculately dressed in uniform as if nothing had happened. His knees would have plasters on. I asked where he went and sometimes he said he would take me, but he never did! If he had made one of his usual arrivals back on the island, then word would spread and at the start of our afternoon shift the CPO would stick his head round the door and shout, 'Blood, I need a word.' I would be the only one in the hall and could hear the Chief shouting at the top of his voice outside. I was expected to rush out after a few minutes and say, 'PO we need to change frequency,' and Blood would rush back to the control desk. One day he was much angrier than usual. I asked why. Apparently the Commanding Officer's wife was on the boat with the wives. 'Next time I see her I will ask her if she could see her way clear not to discuss my boat antics with her husband over dinner,' he said.

Blood was the station boffin. If any other shift had a major problem, they would call Blood out to help. Any new equipment that arrived on the island he would be part of the design team. So, the station needed him and he was a nice guy. He got away with murder. Well, got away with disappearing into a nest of Chinese people and doing god knows what then return to a very secure secret island.

Eating like the locals

Three of us junior REMs began to execute the plan to make our dining room and kitchen into a top Chinese eatery. First we started going ashore, moving from pubs to an evening in local restaurants. We got the waiters to write down each dish we liked. Then we got together with our chefs and they were very pleased to cook their own food instead of steak and kidney pudding and all the UK standards. Our mess boy Mickey, so named as we could not pronounce his real name, agreed to buy all the ingredients ashore in Kowloon. The next day he came with king prawns, fish, meat and Chinese vegetables. We had never heard of king prawns and our idea of rice was just a pudding our mothers and school dinners put in front of us. Mickey was a little 30-year-old wheeler dealer. He had all the patter that streamed out of him in high-speed English, Chinese style! So, I was pleasantly surprised when he gave me the bill, it was just pennies. The plan now was to order food from HMS Tamar and sell it to the married couples who could get good-quality English food. For example, eggs and meat. The Chinese feed their poultry on rice which make meat, and especially eggs, taste very different. Cans of corned beef, baked beans, peas, tomatoes and soup were also very popular. In 1963, the naval stores charged me 1 shilling and 3 pence for an 8 inch x 6-inch tin of baked beans.

Once this plan was running smoothly, the 11 of us began living in style. Most of our food was now Chinese except for dessert. The Chinese never did master custard with spotted dick, bread pud, and the other puds mummy used to make. Mickey was now in his element. Once all the families learnt of the goods he was supplying to us, they were keen to join the club. As Mickey worked for us all, orders had to come via me. I had already agreed a small mark-up for Mickey so we added ours to their prices. To keep Mickey honest, I would quite often join him in the Kowloon markets. With thousands of communist Chinese streaming across the border into Hong Kong, the markets were manic, full of beggars and people selling just a handful of veg, eggs or cabbages, anything they could get their hands on.

As his orders grew, Mickey became an important man to some stall holders. I would be introduced to them and they would bow, smile and give me gifts. The orders got so big that Mickey and the chefs could not just bring a few bags over on the naval launch when they came to work each morning. I had to have a word with the Sikh guard to allow Mickey to come in his hired sampan. Our chefs would be aboard the boat as well to help load and unload.

All it took was a word from me saying it was our food, and Mickey telling him in Chinese that he would be rewarded with a bag of food each time they landed.

The sampan was also paid for with food. The family lived on the little boat and they relied on catching fish to live so they were very happy to chug the four-mile trip out to the island. We got to know the family when we staggered back from Kowloon after lots of beer. The last Navy boat was at 11 pm. Having missed that, we would go down in the walled sampan harbour and find their boat in its usual mooring amongst hundreds of other boats. We would wake them up and jump in the boat, often buying chips and beer on a stall at the jetty. The mum, dad and three kids would be really pleased to see us. We called the dad Sam which was what his name sounded like in Chinese. Sam would have a beer and the kids some chips. We would sing all the way back to the island and then give all our spare change to the mother.

So life was good. I would often sit on a rock and shake my head. After the experience of living on a Navy ship, here I am still in the Navy living in paradise. I have been two months organising the victuals and setting up a nice little earner, my life was now easy. I enjoyed working days and nights in the transmitting hall learning more and more of my trade. On the island, we organised tennis competitions. If we stayed on the island during the evening, Sippers and I would wander round the beach path to the NAAFI bar and there socialise with the Army and Navy families. Sippers was no longer my dog, he wandered all over the camp. Sometimes when I was on watch he would disappear. The first time I searched all over the camp for him. In desperation, I put my head round the boss's door and asked if he had seen Sippers. Lt Bush pointed down and there was my dog snoring beneath his desk. He liked air conditioning!

Between our buildings and the camp, there was the gunnery range. Our army was on the Chinese border in great numbers and different regiments would suddenly arrive at the firing range and camp beside it. Over the next three days they would be firing all day and night. When they were resting, they were in the bar getting very drunk. We stayed well away, especially after dark. Night firing and beer did not seem to be a combination that would work well. When units left, we would go and inspect the bar. Usually the Chinese bar staff would jump out from the back of the building shouting, 'They gone? They gone now?' Once they had calmed down they kept saying, 'When they come back? When they come back?'

Then the Gurkha regiment came. I was really impressed. We got to know them well, they were always laughing. We played them at hockey, tennis and football. After a match, we would sit on the beach in a big circle and they would place dustbin lids with rice around the edge and the middle filled with lamb curry. We supplied the beer, and we drank and sang long into the night. They took me down to the range to show me their firing exercises. They had one Bren gun between two and ran 50 metres and dived to the ground. The one with the

Bren began firing as soon as he hit the ground. The other laid beside him with an ammunition horn in his hand. Then the guy firing grabbed the ammunition horn off the gun. As he rolled away the other guy rolled over snapping the new ammunition onto the gun and the firing did not stop. They seemed to be firing continuously, jumping over each other to snap the new ammunition onto the gun. Then they ran on another 50 metres and started again. From then on, every time they came, I joined in a few of their Bren gun exercises and became quite the expert.

The Chinese border

My next adventure was to be the start of a monthly five-day visit to the Chinese border. I went with a Scottish L/H called Jock. He was married and even his wife called him Jock! On the island, Jock was very prim and proper. He would come down to the beach bar with his wife and daughter., chatting about the political situation and weather. After a few beers, he and his wife would put their daughter in the pushchair and head off for an early night. I was glad to have an experienced engineer and someone who had been doing the five-day stint on the border for over a year.

As we set off on the boat to Kowloon early one morning, Jock was looking serious and checking all our gear for the trip. The lads had told me he became a completely different bloke once he got to the border. We reached HMS Tamar and were taken by jeep to the Police Headquarters. Then into a police lorry for the long trip to the border.

During 1962 to 1964, over two hundred thousand refugees crossed the border. The main reason for their plight was poverty and hunger. The Chinese government used Hong Kong to export all their products to the USA and Europe. The American government had an embargo on Chinese goods. The Chinese answer was to stamp 'Made in Hong Kong' on all its products and deliver them in large junks to Hong Kong harbour. There they were loaded in the hundreds of ships to be spread around the world. It seemed to suit everyone. They all turned a blind eye and everyone seemed happy. The Chinese were desperate for foreign currency and it assumed the world was in need of very cheap goods. During this time, Hong Kong had a very urgent need for water and the Brits bought shiploads of it from China. Once again, we needed water and China needed money. It is because we all needed each other the UK remained confident that the massive Chinese army surrounding Hong Kong would not be used. The refugees were slowly integrated into Hong Kong; although they lived in terrible conditions, they were fed daily.

Then there was the fact that the US were fighting in Vietnam. The Vietnamese were supported by the Chinese and Hong Kong was used by the US Navy to bring their forces to rest and recuperate. So a few miles from China, on a daily basis, Hong Kong entertained and refuelled the American Fleet. Once again it seemed to suit everybody!

It was amongst all this strange diplomacy that the British armed forces, diplomats and police officers manned the borders. The refugees on the whole were accepted and sorted with compassion. At the time, it was thought that at least 20 per cent of them were sent as communist spies. For those on the borders, there was nothing they could do apart from moving them on, and assume someone down the line would look after the problem. The Chinese did not care as they had millions more available. Also flooding Hong Kong with a few million of its peasants was probably amusing to its hierarchy. No doubt their spies reported back saying they are coping, send some more! The mass of cheap labour now fuelled the industrial Chinese. Hong

Kong set up factories and their exports soon gave Hong Kong a healthy economy. In the end, when customers in the UK or the US saw 'Made in Hong Kong' on their products, about 25% probably was actually made in Hong Kong. Again, it seemed to suit everyone.

Once you zoom into the border area around Lo Wu, you assume there must have been a plan, and a supposed infrastructure, to cope with the defence of the border. On top of that, the day-to-day management of police, diplomats and troops. Then the organisation of coping with families with children arriving. This plan, however, was not obvious to those on the ground, with no idea how many or when the refugees would be thrust upon them. As they had no papers and were usually illiterate, what could be gained by trying to interview them? The normal rules of receiving illegal immigrants made no sense. In the early days, the troops tried to round them up and send them back. The Chinese government's answer to that was not to repatriate the people fleeing their country but to turn them round and mix them with three times as many and send them back again.

The Army manned the border but the troops themselves knew that if China came they would be overrun in minutes. Their invasion plans, military exercises and discussions were in fact futile. However, to the senior officers this is what they had always done for centuries. I think the troops were fine with just helping the refugees. That and enjoying time off tasting the delights of downtown Kowloon.

The police were a powerful force around the border. Very much a combination of British, Pakistanis and Chinese. They were well established and had been doing the job of controlling the border for a long time. The refugees were gathered by police, embassy and medical staff. They had never seen white people and thus were confused. Doctors sorted their health out, and they were fed with good food and tea. They were peasants who had never experienced the outside world, but were better off here than in China. It would take time, but they would have a better standard of living eventually.

We finally reached our destination which was a large white colonial house on top of a hill. It had great views of the surrounding areas. We were shown to separate spacious bedrooms with en-suite bathrooms. Our task was to update some communication systems, fix all faults and monitor any transmissions from across the border.

The Police Officer in Charge was a Superintendent Harold Hunter. We were taken down to a balcony with more fantastic views of the border area. Harry, as he liked to be called, was a massive figure of a man and very well spoken. He tended to shout, especially when he felt strongly about a subject. He jumped up out of a large armchair and grasped our hands. 'Great to have you here!' he shouted. 'I am the only Brit in the house until you Navy chaps arrive.' Two large gin and tonics were delivered. It was very hot on the balcony, even with the massive fan blades going hell for leather overhead. So I took a big gulp of the large cold drink. Never having had a gin and tonic before (it is still the strongest I have ever drunk) I only just managed to keep it down. 'Steady on old chap!' shouts Harry. 'Us police like them strong.' I noticed Jock had no problem handling his drink. Sitting either side of Harry were two very large white chows. 'These two never leave my side and frighten a lot of the locals. Be warned putting up your arm to me, they will have you on the ground in seconds deciding whether you are breakfast or not.'

'Do you need that sort of protection?' I ask.

'We are less than a mile from the border and this is a completely lawless area. Anyone with contacts in China can commit a crime and cross over to the other side in minutes. In circumstances like these, no man can be completely trustworthy, your family can be put in danger then you will do what you are told.

'The reason we can manage this situation is not because we are in control of it. No – it is because we know that the people who are in control of it want it to happen. However, the day-to-day crimes are of little consequence to the Chinese, so they let me handle them. I am very fair, but brutal if the crime is brutal. The Chinese understand this and they like me for it. At this time, what is happening here is part of a plan that no decision in the UK parliament will change. It will change when something at the top of the Chinese government changes.'

I find out Harry is married with kids but the family are in the UK. The beautiful Chinese lady who is serving our drinks seems to be familiar with him. 'Right!' shouts Harry, 'time for a spot of supper!' Harry strides out of the drive and gets in his Land Rover. Jock as the senior between us, was about to jump in the front, but a simultaneous growl from our furry friends had him quickly jumping in the back with me and the two chows take their rightful place on the front seat.

Harry drives us around showing us points of interest. Jock points out various communication masts and antennas we will be visiting over the next few days. We finally arrive next to a large Chinese building with sloping roofs and curly decorations on top. We walk down past the building to the water's edge of a small river. There are buildings down into the water on stilts running each side of the river.

'Those buildings over there are on the Chinese side,' Harry explains.

'Where is the Chinese army?' I ask.

'They are a mile back and leave us alone and them [pointing to the people in and about the houses on the other side], there is a rope across the river at about head height and a man standing in a boat is pulling on the rope hand over hand to drag himself to our bank.' Harry introduces us to the village boss who runs everything on the Chinese side of the border. They gabble away in Chinese for quite a while whilst I take in the amazing sights around me. People bustling about on both sides of the river, they all look the same and are shouting greetings to each other over the water. I assume they can go over and back whenever they like. I was expecting machine gun posts with each side growling at each other. I later found out that the official border is miles away and run properly with each army in uniform lifting barriers and inspecting documentation.

When Harry had finished it was time for 'a spot of supper' as promised. As we left his friend, Harry said, 'Whatever you want, just call me before you arrive and they [pointing across the river] will get it for you. They supply all my food and beer.'

I wonder what he supplies in return?

As we enter the large restaurant, we are greeted by four Chinese and Pakistan police officers. They were all heavily armed. Harry introduced us and they went to a table downstairs. We were escorted upstairs where five more guys were already sat at a large table. They were all Army Intelligence. It seems the group all gather at this place every evening. Harry said they had to have an armed escort downstairs as this eatery was so good it was used by every organisation that enjoyed the fruits that were available in the border situation. 'Be careful when you go downstairs to the toilet,' he warned. 'The officers have a table by the toilet and they will only let you use it if there is no one inside. Also they will prevent anyone coming in with you.'

I am amazed Jock has not told me all this before we got here. When questioned, he whispered back, 'You would have only told everyone and my missus would be worried. More to the point, she would give me hell. We all keep this quiet as we are not sure whether our bosses send us out here and don't care or they have no idea that this place is completely out of control. At our low level, trying to explain it will not help, they would not believe us. Just keep close to Harry and all will be well.'

The food was fantastic, the boys were hilarious and some of the tales had me literally crying with laughter. Towards the end, Harry introduced his singing game. The Scottish lads on my ship had played the same game. Harry would start to sing a song, we would all join in the chorus at the end of the song. Harry would empty his glass down in one and point to the next singer. All the songs were rugby-type songs. As I did not play rugby, I did not have any to choose from. When my turn came, I just about got through three verses of that Wiltshire favourite, 'I ad her, I ad her, the West Country way'. Harry went over to a cupboard in the corner and came out with a very mouldy torn set of bagpipes and threw them over to Jock who started playing them brilliantly.

Time to go down to the toilet. Quite drunk, I slowly slide down the steep staircase to arrive in the dark dusty restaurant downstairs. It was quite full and most of the people at the tables were leaning forward over their bowls, heads nearly touching over the tables. The noise from above was horrendous, bagpipes blaring the song sung at the top of their voices. This was not the problem, the stamping to the beat was bringing dust in large clouds from the rotten wooden floorboards above. When I first saw all the diners leaning over, I naively thought they were nodding to me out of respect! But no! They were protecting their food from the dust!

I walked over to the police by the toilet and said, 'Is it always like this?'

'Every night,' was the reply.

'What do all the locals drink,' I asked.

They said something in Chinese.

'What would it cost to put a bottle on each table?' I asked. I could easily afford the price quoted so I gave them the money and said, 'Please tell them I am solly [my Chinese for sorry].'

I went back up and Harry was still thumping his legs into the floor. I would estimate 80% of the noise was generated by Harry's enthusiasm. Next time I went down, most of the guys at the tables lifted their glasses as I passed. Maybe I would be safe now without Harry and the dogs, but I doubt it.

The police guards had told Harry I paid for a round so at breakfast he thanked me. Feeling chuffed I said, 'That's the least I could do, it was a great night.' Harry just smiled and said he enjoys the evenings there but would not rob them of their restaurant. That's why he sits upstairs and pays for everybody's food and drink upstairs and down! I nod feeling foolish as apparently the restaurant was full because all the food was free and they did not care if it was covered in dust. Harry is a one-off, there cannot be many men who could successfully handle this situation and survive it. Not only that, but he thrives on it and enjoys every minute.

We travelled around the border for five days, fixing communication equipment. Using special equipment we set up in different locations where we monitored all the transmissions. The sight of the poor families shuffling along in queues everywhere we went was heart-breaking. We could not help, in fact no one could, only time and care would cure their mental scars.

Each evening we reported our findings to Harry. However, as soon as his dark maiden with the very high split skirt brought the large gin and tonics we knew it was time to stop the boring report. Another five nights with Harry meant during the day I had to write new verses of my disgusting song. I also knew I would have to learn a few more songs when it was my turn to do another stint. Even Jock, who could keep up with Harry, looked ready to get back to the missus and kid. No doubt he would be looking forward to his return in a few weeks. We were both glad of a quiet journey back to our seemingly safe little island.

After my border adventure, I often sat at the beach bar watching the big junks passing the island, slowly going into the harbour to deliver communist cargo stamped with 'Made in Hong. Kong' You could hear the big throbbing engines grinding away and even slowing down as they slid under the cranes of the waiting cargo ships. The ship would then up anchor and leave with the cargo, having never been on land in Hong Kong. Those first five days at the border taught me all was not as it seems in this strange land far away from deepest Wiltshire.

A strange kind of charity

I settled down to normal times on the island. The food delivery was almost happening on its own. Mickey and the chefs did most of the work and I just interfaced with the married guys and HMS Tamar Victualling Office (food store). I got along well with the ten lads. We were all doing shift work, either in the large transmitting room with a PO or with a L/H in the smaller transmitting room. So we never worked together and our time off would mean three different lads would be able to go ashore together. It was just ten of us mucking in together with no special friendships.

Then a ridiculous and unbelievable event happened to us all. Sippers and I were relaxing in our lounge, feet up reading a book, when the CPO knocked and said, 'Dave can I come in?' Trust me, this would never have happened in the real Navy. The door would have been kicked in with a shout of 'Get your bloody feet off the table you ignorant shit!'. He sat down and said, 'We have been contacted by a tri service charity, they provide amenities to troops who are on an island with no civilian population. Apparently, we pass the test as we can only get ashore by a naval vessel and the island is guarded by the army with searchlights and machine guns. He will be here tomorrow and would like to talk to the guys who live in station accommodation. That is the eleven of you junior rates and PO Reid. I suggest you pick two other lads, I will inform PO Reid and you all meet here at 11. After you finish, PO Reid will bring him up to our mess to have lunch with Lt Bush (our Officer in Charge).'

I rang Blood to discuss and he said we had to play it by ear and see what the guy has to say. I repeat my concern that this guy must know we are only a 20-minute boat ride to Kowloon and the best run ashore in the world. As Blood uses our sampan to sneak back when he misses the last Navy boat, he agrees it is bizarre. I chose John a cockney guy with a quick mind and the gift of the gab. The other guy I chose to join the 'get some free goodies team' was Scouse, who spent a lot of his time looking in the mirror playing with his face and hair. He would also disappear off the island on his own (perhaps he went to Blood's venues). Scouse was very streetwise and would have strange ideas that could well be used.

At 11 am on the dot, the CPO brings the civilian guy to our lounge and introduces us to Derek and the CPO leaves. Derek explains that, 'They have discovered a fund that has not been used for quite some time. It was formed when the British Empire was a lot bigger than it is now. It is an island fund to help troops with home comforts, in order to prevent mental problems when they are stuck on an unmanned island. The problem is that, as it is a charity, we can only dispose of the funds to troops on islands that meet the mandate. The other problem is that at this time you can only just count the islands that qualify on one hand. What I need from you is a list of all things we could provide to you to make your lives easier and less stressful.' Finally he said, 'This should be a one-off as the plan is to close the fund as soon as possible.'

'Before the UK has run out of islands,' says John.

'Quite,' says Derek.

Blood then says, 'In order to make a sensible list, can we have some idea of the budget?'

'Better you tell me your ideas,' was the reply.

'Would a speedboat and sets of water skis be out of the question?' asked Blood.

'No,' he says.

'We have a large hut by the beach that could be turned into a snooker room,' says John.

'OK,' was the reply. He ended the meeting by saying he would be flying to Singapore in three days so would be back here before then to agree a list which he would take back. After he leaves, we would have to cost the agreed items and send the details to him. He would expect to quickly get a yes or no on each item from the fund chairman. Finally, Derek said at the next meeting the Station CO would have to attend and sanction each purchase as they would be assets to be managed on his station. As Blood left, he pulled me to one side and said, 'Get the lads together and start producing a list. After lunch I will take him back to his hotel in Kowloon and see if he would like to visit a few of my favourite haunts.' Blood's leaving wink was followed by a thumbs-up from me.

So that evening, with two guys on shift, that left eight of us huddled on the balcony of the beach bar, away from prying eyes and ears. With a speed boat and a snooker hall to start, we began small, with a combined record player with radio, one of the new types on legs with 30 new LPs.

Scouse spent a lot of time growing things in the garden at the back of our rooms. He wanted a gardener to grow UK vegetables, especially potatoes and corn on the cob. We would buy 20 chickens which the new gardener would look after and feed with grain instead of rice. He also asked for some pigs and a cow! He suggested that we could sell the veg and eggs to all the families on the island.

Tom the petrol head amongst us came up with two go-karts. A ten-foot-wide concrete path went all round the island so we could have races. Sprints down to the beach bar and back and Grand Prix round the island on special days.

The more we drank, the more stupid the ideas became and the louder the arguments went across the table. We finally agreed to meet the next day and give the two working guys a chance to input their thoughts. With no increases after our meeting next day we arranged to meet Blood at the same spot that night. We all agreed to try for the lot except the cow! In order to get the agreement of the boss and the CPO we planned to let all the families on the island share the use of the boat and go-karts. Blood suggested we offer that HMS Tamar could also hire the boats and we would have go-kart days with the Army. This would allow Lt Smith to get it passed by the CO of HMS Tamar. The CPO and PO mess already had a snooker table so this new one would be ours. If we were successful with the garden and the chickens, we would offer low prices for the products.
We were not invited to the meeting but all were accepted. Three months later we had our boat, go-karts, snooker

hall, gardener, chickens and pigs! On shift with Blood, we discussed the progress daily. The fact is that these items were free, and if any objections or caveats were put in the way, we could lose them all. The CO of Tamar appreciates this and agrees not to interfere. The hardest part for them to accept was that the gifts were for us lower ranks and we would be looking after them. Each charity gift had its merits. The record player with all the LPs, one of the records was 'Love me Do' by The Beatles and this was played over and over again by all the lads. You could lower the long side windows of the snooker hut near the beach and play with a cool breeze flowing across the table. The speed boat was an instant hit for trips round the island and water skiing. However, in a few months it would prove to be a fantastic money earner.

The go-karts were a slow mover. The problem was the wide concrete path went past the family bungalows and then the CO's house. Permission for the road to be shut was not easy. Still, when everyone was allowed to have a go it became quite popular.

Scouse soon had the garden up and running. The new gardener was a short squat man with legs and arms like tree trunks. He worked from dawn to dusk in bare feet under a big round rattan hat. The chickens were providing plenty of eggs and it was not long before rows of spuds, salad, veg and corn were rising from the ground. The pigs were apparently provided by a mistake, someone ticked when they should have crossed. However, they were fattened by all the food waste provided by everyone, including the married quarters. We were all saddened when one had to be slaughtered but had no qualms about attending the camp pig roasts.

Gone fishing

Stonecutters Island had a one mile 'no-go area' for shipping all around its coast. Around the island there were lookout posts on jetties or old gun platforms. These were spaced so that each post could see the ones either side of them. They were manned by experienced Sikhs who communicated with each other by phone. Each post had a searchlight on a pillar that could be swung round to identify any ship encroaching into military waters. I would often wander down on to our jetty on the way back from the evening bar session and chat to the Sikh on duty.

All around the island the waters were full of fantastic blue crabs and lobsters with which the fisherman could make lots of money. They used very fast sampans and would come in at top speed, drop their nets and run out of the protected area. The Sikhs would mark the position of the nets using the bearing on the telescope, then call for the police gun boat. These gun boats had far too much to do around the Hong Kong waters. They were always chasing large junks bringing in illegal goods from China. Illegal fishing offshore was not considered to be important. Listening to the Sikhs, they believed the fishermen were paying the water police to stay away. They are a very proud and correct race and were not happy that they could not protect their waters. However, we now had a speed boat!

Over coffee with three of the Sikhs, Scouse and I said

what if you lock your telescope and searchlight onto where the fisherman lay their nets. We then go out and pull in the nets and bring them back to shore? The problem was the fishermen were heavily armed and the nets were very expensive, so they would come in and stop us taking them. However, normally they do not wait and don't come back for two or three hours, why would they change? So the plan was we would head out with the light searching far out to sea, as normal. Then using portable radios, shout and move the light onto the bearing of the nets and switch it out to sea again. Do this until we get to the nets. Come back in with the lights searching way out to sea over the top of our little boat. Our boat is much faster, so any sign of the fishing boats we could come into the jetty at top speed.

Obviously, we would need a reason to use the boat at night. Mickey the mess man said the best time for fishing was at night, so I got permission to fish at night. There were rules, three in the boat, one with portable radio at the Sikhs' post, the ring of police posts all informed we are out fishing.

We were fishing well inshore when we got the call. We got out to the nets without much of a problem. Getting them into a reasonably sized speed boat was not so easy but the nets were not massive. Scouse and I then stayed until the fishermen came back, the Sikhs shone the light right at them and warned them away.

The next day we took an age to untangle the nets. Then, under Mickey's guidance, we took them out and laid them along the shore about 200 yards out to sea. Early next morning we moved along the nets lifting them as we went. The result was a good haul of crabs and fish. We shared the catch with the Sikhs and set up a system of a team of three men checking the nets every morning.

Over the next few weeks, we captured a few more nets until we had all we could handle. The fishermen were warned to stay out of the military waters and, if not, their nets would be confiscated. So we then went out to pick up nets whenever the Sikhs called us. There were some dodgy moments, as the fishermen now dropped their nets and waited on the edge of the no go area, watching to see if we came out to get them. When we were successful, we gave the nets to the Sikhs who sold them back to the fishermen. We did not get involved in the politics or the cash. By this time, we were catching a lot of crabs, so much so that Mickey was now taking most of them to the Kowloon fish market. Our sampan family were now ferrying Mickey back and forth to Kowloon with crabs out and food in.

Day to day we were now living a pleasant life. Two days on watch in the transmitter room keeping Hong Kong in contact with the outside world. Then off watch, water skiing and fishing with lots of trips to Kowloon to the shops and bars. The snooker hall was a great place to socialise with many a boozy night of competitions. The gardens, fishing and food purchases from the Navy store were making us enough money to enjoy ourselves and spread our wings into Kowloon.

The rise and fall of Johnny Chan

Hong Kong was becoming a favourite place to visit for all the famous stars. The prices of duty-free goods were the best in the world and its clothing became a must for all the tourists that were flocking into the new hotels. With a background of squalor and thousands of refugees living in disgusting conditions, Hong Kong was prospering. The cheap labour gave the shops a fantastic range of jewellery and clothes. You could wander into a tourist shop and ship a complete Chinese tea set to the family for less than $10HK. Quite often we would get a letter from the family thanking us for the gift we sent and we were so drunk we didn't even know we had sent it.

Hong Kong was now the place to come to get a suit made of the finest English wool. USA and UK stars would come in for a show at the theatre, stay three days and order enough suits to last the year. We used our kitty to buy tickets to see all the stars – Frank Sinatra, Sammy Davis Junior and Ella Fitzgerald.

We were recommended Johnny Chan Tailors for a good suit. It soon became a favourite part of our night out. Straight off the ferry and into Johnny's for beers and snacks whilst we picked material for a suit, trousers or shirt. He would measure us and ask us where we would be in two hours. He and his boy would then arrive at the bar or restaurant we had picked with our garment half made. We would have a fitting check and pick buttons and other adjustments. The clothes would then be delivered to our sampan. When we arrived for the trip back to the island, the boy would be there for the cash.

My friendship with Johnny developed when one day I suggested that he come over on the island and bring the suit as I could not stay for a fitting. I arranged for the sampan to pick him up and he arrived with two suitcases full of material. After the backstreets of Kowloon, Johnny was completely mesmerised by the beach and jungle. He kept looking around saying, 'Best place ever.' We went to the snooker hall and Johnny set up his wares. I had sent the word out to anyone who wanted anything made. After he had taken a few orders and the others had left, I arranged for food and drink to be brought over from the galley. I then introduced Johnny to snooker. He did not have a clue but the excitement on his face was a joy to see.

Johnny then visited every week and word soon got out. All the Brits and their wives on the island were ordering suits, dresses and other clothes. We were all given 40% off from prices on the mainland. Johnny's brother was a jeweller and he was soon making custom jewellery with genuine stones. He developed a line in leather shoes after giving three refugees a job in his factory. They were cobblers and soon he had enough of them to increase his range to make American custom-built cowboy boots. The American fleet had begun to come to Hong Kong from Vietnam to rest and recuperate. There were now thousands of US Navy and marines coming ashore complete with their war bonus to spend. Johnny was about to make his fortune. I would often have to leave Johnny for a few hours but, if so, one of the other boys would have to play snooker with him before he would leave. He told me his greatest pleasure was playing snooker. As he got better at it, the gambling bug meant he had to play us for money. We played every day and were pretty good; Johnny always lost but did not care. We had a rule all the beer and food was free.

He invited us to his flat in Kowloon for dinner. Apparently, it was an up-market apartment but to me it was a tiny rabbit hutch of a place that was not much larger than our snooker hall. He had a lovely little wife and two gorgeous children. A great night with great food and Johnny trying to get us drunk by playing their version of depth charges. Dropping small glasses of whisky in a glass of beer and drinking the lot in one go. We left when Johnny collapsed!

Within the six months I had known him, Johnny's turnover had increased to unbelievable levels. As he explained, all the refugees need work and so there is an unlimited supply of cheap labour. The last time I saw him on the island, he said he was going to Vietnam to open a large shop on an American base.

Before I left Hong Kong, I went to his shop to find out when he would be back, and was told by his brother that he had been killed by the Vietnamese. We went round to his apartment with flowers and presents for the children. Lots of bowing and tears but we could not communicate with Johnny's wife with our limited Chinese. Johnny was determined to come to UK to purchase the English materials he used to build his business. We had lost a good friend who took one too many risks.

The Beatles visit

We heard on the forces radio that The Beatles were coming to Hong Kong. Their two LPs *Please Please Me* and *With The Beatles* were played over and over on our new gramophone. We would sit around the mess singing along to all the tunes. We had only seen newsreels of them getting on planes, or going into concerts with thousands of girls screaming their heads off. Tickets were easy to get and ours were near the front. As they were due to arrive, all the newspapers were writing about was the screaming kids and the arrangements being made to control the unruly crowds. The posh English radio programmes were not only discussing why they were coming, but suggesting they should be stopped. The Chinese had far too many problems to bother. In the sixties, the Chinese youth had only just begun to listen to UK music. Before The Beatles arrived, we were told that Ringo Starr was not well enough to travel and a guy named Jimmie Nicol was going to be playing the drums.

I had never been to a theatre to watch and listen to pop music. It was just over half full, and as luck would have it there were not many excited European girls. The first act was Sounds Incorporated who were absolutely amazing. There were lots of them and they really lived up to their name, the quality of their music left me stunned. Then The Beatles arrived on stage with just their equipment. Dressed in suits and ties like the rest of us, they burst into song and although some girls were screaming, we could hear the music. At the end of the song the applause was mostly clapping. I could hear John and Paul talking and it was basically, 'These people are listening to us, let's rearrange the playlist and rock at the end.' So as far as I remember, John said to the audience, 'It's great to have an audience that want to hear us play.' They then played all their slow stuff with the fantastic harmonies. It wasn't just like the records, it was far better. Halfway through, Paul said, 'We are now going to play rock and roll so can you please all clap your hands and sing or shout along.' They started 'Twist and Shout' and ran through their repertoire of fast rock songs, finishing with 'Roll Over Beethoven'. The audience obeyed Paul and started clapping, soon they were up on their feet. Although most of the noise came from the armed forces, the Chinese were stood up clapping to the beat and smiling, some even laughing!

After the show, the newspapers said it lost money and those that went could not hear anything for the shouting and bad behaviour of the youngsters. This was just not true, everyone had a great time. Shame the reporters had not bothered to attend as they would have enjoyed themselves and been able to tell the truth.

The swimming competition

Our next escapade brought unwanted publicity to our idyllic way of life and threatened a stop to all of our dodgy activities. It all started on a Sunday morning when we quite often gathered in a small room to drink our rum ration. I was now old enough to receive my daily ration. I have described the rules and regulations of the rum issue previously. However, you will not be surprised to hear that this is not the way we chose to enact this ancient daily ceremony on our island paradise. Once a week, a sealed jar was sent from HMS Tamar containing a week's supply for the five junior ratings who were old enough, and one PO (Blood). This added up to 42 neat tots of rum. The small room is where we kept our rum locked away.

The agreement was if you were in your shift cycle during those three days you would not drink your rum. When off watch, you could have it when you like. Normally, those who are not on watch would gather at about 11.00 on a Sunday. We would share the rum out to any of the lads and we would invite married POs, who were not entitled to a tot as they had their family down the road. Sometimes even the Lt or CPO would be invited. It was a great morale booster where rank disappeared, and we all sat around getting mildly drunk, whiling the day away. We still called the Lt 'Sir' but he called us by our first names.

This particular Sunday we were mob handed and it was 'Shady's' birthday. Shady was a quiet, pleasant guy who was a loner. He preferred his own company and spent his days off exploring Hong Kong and the New Territories. If we were going ashore, we always said which bar we would be in, and asked him to join us, but he rarely turned up. He spent a lot of time studying the Hong Kong stock market, which trust me none of us even knew what it was.

Apparently he was Jewish, but at that time I did not know what that meant either. After we convinced Shady to join us to drink his rum, that meant we had about nine of us in the hut including the boss and Blood.

That morning, at the control station the lad on watch got a message over the teleprinter from the Captain of HMS Tamar's office. The message read, 'Please confirm your swimming team of ten is as per the list you sent.' The lad went to the noticeboard and checked the two lists were the same and sent a confirmation. The event was the highlight of the year and the Admiral had invited all the important diplomats and wives.

We had selected our team during a meeting with Lt Bush who was keen for us to put on 'a damned good show'. Apparently, he was invited with his wife and every officer at the do would outrank him. Blood and Lt Bush were former shipmates and he said Peter would not care a fig, but his wife would. The problem was, although we could all swim, none of us were particularly good at it and we would be against some Navy ships, HMS Tamar and the bloody Royal Marines! Lt Bush suggested that we spend the week getting fit and have practice races! As he was quite a rotund chap, he did not offer to attend the sessions, so guess what? They did not happen. We even discussed that we should all have the same swimming costumes and we were tasked to go ashore next week and get them. That we could manage. Even the colour and style was discussed at great length.

We were well into our session and the rum was getting low. We are now deciding whether anyone would make it down to the beach bar or just go to bed. Something I have never heard before was Shady talking loudly and joining all the debates, roaring with laughter at all the ditties and jokes being passed across the room. It was good to see him enjoying himself.

Back in the transmitting room, PO Strange who had just come on watch at 13.00, was wandering around with nothing to do. He looked at the teleprinter and read all the messages from this morning. Something was not right about the message from the Captain of HMS Tamar. Why would he send it on a Sunday? He went to the list on the board and the event was listed as next Sunday. Not happy, he rang the PO in charge of HMS Tamar main gate and said, 'When is the swimming gala?' The PO laughed and said, 'Today! I have organised your tender to pick you all up at 16.00.'

PO Strange had popped into the rum room for a wee snifter before he came on watch so he knew where the rest of the camp was. He shouted to his lad to hold the fort. He then sprinted across the gardens to the rum room. When he burst into the room, he could barely see anyone through the smoke. Finally he spotted Lt Bush sitting in the corner, cigarette in one hand a glass of rum in the other. 'Sir, the fucking swimming Gala is on today and the boat will pick up you, and the team in two hours!'

'Impossible,' replies Lt Bush, 'just look at the diary and noticeboard.'

'I am correct Sir,' replied PO Strange. 'Someone has made a mistake here. HMS Tamar's captain's office sent a signal this morning asking for conformation of our list of competitors. I read it when I came on watch and checked our board and it said it was next week. However, I thought why send a signal a week before, so I phoned the PO on watch at the main gate in Tamar – he said today. I double-checked with the Chief PTI [Physical Training Instructor] who is in charge of the event. He was not happy with my question.'

'Why do you ask?' he said.

I replied, 'What I meant to say is what time is our boat?'

'Right,' said Lt Bush. 'PO Reid, you organise the swim team, I will go and get changed into my ceremonial uniform and see if I can persuade the captain to let us miss the event.'

After he left Blood was smiling. He asked, 'How many do we need for a team?'

'Ten,' came the answer from us. We all looked around

counting each other and came up with nine. Blood sent me to the control room to ring all the houses of the married Leading Hands and Petty Officers to find who was available to join us. He told all the rest of the lads to get into their uniforms and return with their swimming trunks and towels. He said, 'Hopefully we will find enough men to get us out of this. If not, you are the team. When you return, we will discuss tactics over a glass of rum!'

In the control room PO Strange had already found the whereabouts of all the guys available. The answer was not good. The CPO has taken everyone and their family away for the day! It's called a banyan and they had hired a junk to take them to a remote island where they had organised a BBQ on the beach. The only guy still at his home was Jock. Apparently, his child was sick so he had to cancel. 'I have told Jock to report to the rum room in his uniform with his swimsuit,' the PO informed me.

With no word from Lt Bush, there were now ten of us gathered in the rum room with glass in hand. Blood cleared his throat, lit a cigarette and said, 'This is not our fault, so rather than moan about it we should have some fun. We are all pissed and all of us are crap at racing in a swimming pool. So let's take the ten races and pick who will do what and how we can have a laugh doing it.'

Backstroke 50 metres, 100 metres, crawl 50 metres, 100 metres, breaststroke 50 metres, 100 metres, butterfly 50 metres, 100 metres, underwater distance, diving. John was a strong lad so we gave him the 100 backstroke. Scouse was given the 100 front crawl. I got the 100 breaststroke. Jock was the last competent swimmer so he volunteered

231

for the 100 butterfly. The rest only had to swim one 50-metre length which we deemed manageable, even if they all came last.

Blood said, 'As all our fast swimmers have chosen to go on a banyan what can we do?' With a big grin on his face he followed this comment by adding, 'As I hate swimming I will enter the diving comp.'

Shady, who was so pissed he could hardly speak, put his hand up and said, 'As I can hardly swim a stroke, I will do the underwater race.' The whole room collapsed in laughter which went on for at least five minutes.

Finally drying his eyes, Blood asked, 'How will that work?'

Shady looked at him with a very serious expression on his face and mumbled, 'I will jump in and walk very quickly!' The room roared with more laughter with some of us rolling on the floor holding bellies.

At this moment, Lt Bush in full ceremonial dress walked in and held up his hand for silence. However, he had to wait ten minutes before he could be heard. Even then Blood beat him to it, and quickly told him the situation. 'Sir, the rest of the station have gone on a private banyan organised by the CPO. All we could add to the numbers is Jock. However we now have all ten races covered and we will do our best. Would you like to join us in the pool as we are weak in a few races, and very weak in one of them?'

The nine men who had stood up straight on the arrival of the CO were now turning away holding their mouths and failing badly to stop the laughter bursting through their hands.

'I am glad to see you are all in good spirits before we face this disaster,' he began.

'He should have said full of good spirits,' someone whispered.

'I have been told by a very angry Captain I will be sitting with the top brass, as Liaison Officer, to explain the teams and who is who during the racing.'

The CO went on to explain that he had contacted the Captain of HMS Tamar to explain his impossible situation and that he could not muster a competitive set of swimmers due to an unfortunate administrative error and would he mind if the transmitting station did not attend? The Captain was not interested in excuses. 'Lt Bush, you will bring a full team even if it's full of Chinese chefs and mess boys and you lose every race!' he screamed.

Lt Bush finished with a limp shout of, 'The race is on, guys.' Blood tried to help the situation by stating, 'At least your wife will not have to witness the fiasco.' He answered with a tired groan, 'I went to great lengths to persuade her but despite my pleas she is insisting on coming, unfortunately!' With the CO thinking it would be better for him and his dear wife not to join us on our boat, he left us to go over earlier, getting as much distance from us as possible.

Blood was now in his element and thoroughly enjoying himself. He rang the beach bar and told them to deliver a crate of beer to our boat and put it on his tab. Spending the long hours through the night with him on shift meant I have got to know the man. He hated the upper crust of British society. He was a genius at his job and could not stand the ignorance of his peers. This gala was a chance to make a mockery of all the pomp of such an event. When he first saw it on the noticeboard, his comment was 'The only difference to this and the Roman games is the lords and ladies cannot put us to death. All they can do is look down and laugh at us before they trot off to their cocktail party. I will not be attending that event,' he shouted. Now he was, and we were happy to dance to his tune.

On the boat, we drank our beer and sang 'Row, row, row the boat ashore'. Jock suggested I sing, 'I adder I adder the West Country way' and followed with one of his disgustingly rude Scottish aires before we all finished with 'Roll out the Barrel'.

Once on the jetty at HMS Tamar, we marched to the team changing rooms where we were suddenly presented with the reality of what we were facing. The other groups were all putting on their matching swimming trunks and had matching towels across their shoulders. We, unfortunately, all had different coloured trunks. Most of us had the new-style American ones that nearly reached our knees. Our beach towel colours were even more outrageous. This was the first time Shady told us he didn't have any trunks. 'What are you going to wear?' we asked and he showed us a pair of white Navy-issue underpants! Luckily, Big John had a spare pair of trunks. They were much too big, but with the drawstring pulled in tightly, they would just about do the job. Shady was also one of those fortunate – or unfortunate – people whose whole body was covered with very thick dark matted hair. I forgot to mention the reason we called him Shady was that he always wore sunglasses. He had some sort of eye condition that was affected by strong sunlight and had permission to wear them all the time in Hong Kong. So please imagine Shady with a GI haircut, standing in line with us wearing a baggy pair of bright green trunks, his body covered in black fur, wearing large sunglasses. This look he topped off with a dirty towel he'd been using for three days and pink flip-flops on his feet. We were all assembled in groups behind a large screen at the end of the pool.

The Chief PTI came over to us and began with lots of 'what the fucking this and what the fucking that', finishing with 'who is in charge of this fucking rabble?'. Blood stepped forward and said, 'PO Reid reporting, Chief. We were ordered to attend with only 30 minutes to get on the boat. There was some misunderstanding by the admin office, they thought it was next week. These lads, being off duty, were having their Sunday dinner and a few jars at the bar. I was in the POs' mess doing something similar when the CO came knocking at my door. He had tried to persuade your Captain to let his station miss the gala but his reply was to get a team at the start line on time, or else heads would roll. So here we are, the only ten that were on the camp. I cannot be responsible for their individual performances as I have never seen any of them swim. I cannot even guarantee they are medically fit to race. There are nine junior rates, one Leading Hand

and my good self. We would be happy and relieved to step down from the event if you can get the Captain's permission?' The Chief marched away shouting over his shoulder, 'It starts in 15 minutes, so OK you go ahead, but I am not happy.'

Our plea would probably have been more successful if we had stepped aside and showed him Shady lying on a bench snoring, with his gigantic todger flopping out of one of the legs of his oversized trunks.

The large pool at HMS Tamar had tiers of seats rising either side of it. I peeped round the corner to see it in all its splendour, the crystal-clear water showed reflections of the very impressive seating rising high. The dignitaries were taking their seats, the men wearing uniforms of all the different services. The ladies competing with each other with fine dresses and hats. There were PTIs spread evenly round the pool with large varnished poles. There must be a better explanation of their use than shoving the swimmers back in if they try to escape! They certainly looked impressive with tight white T-shirts stretched across their six packs. Also they had very tight shorts that locked around their 'to die for' buttocks. As they were facing away from the audience it is no wonder all the ladies' hand fans were going at ten to the dozen.

When I saw how high the boxes were that we had to clamber up to start our race, I became a bit concerned. I am not sure all the guys would be able to manage them. I thought we had to just dive in from the side of the pool. Jumping in off the box and then waiting to come up and start swimming would certainly give all the smart arses something to laugh about. Then I saw how high the diving board was; I did not think telling Blood would help.

For each race, the ten competitors were assembled in a line ready to march out. We had the lane farthest away, which meant we would swim nearest to the important guests. It also meant, for each race, the line would be led out by one of our drunken men. The CPO should have had the sense to put us at the back.

The first four races were the 50-metre sprints. These we just about survived, apart from our drunken boys tripping over and struggling to get on the box. Also, two of them, not hearing the CPO's shout of 'halt', went marching past the last box leaving all the competitors to march into each other and scrabble about working out which was their box. We lost all four races and our plan to dive into the pool and swim away obviously needed practise. When our lot dived in and came to the surface, the other nine were halfway up the pool. The crowd were great. As the winner was being congratulated at the far end, they cheered loudly when we finally finished. I thought it was a nice gesture of the other swimmers to stay in the pool and wait to see if our guys would actually reach the wall.

The first of the 100-metre races saw Big John representing us in the backstroke. We had high hopes for John, probably our only chance of a few points. John was in the lead at the turn, unfortunately he had no idea how to turn and came out in the wrong lane. The guy in the next lane threw himself off the wall during his turn and became entangled with John. A drunken John is not to be messed with, so as soon as the guy's head rose out of the water, John hit it in the face. Royal Marines are trained in underwater combat! For me and the spectators, all we could see was what looked like a gigantic splashing competition which went on for a long time. The PTIs clenched their buttocks and ran to the scene waving their long poles. They stabbed at the melee, however it did not occur to them to jump in the pool and stop the fight. Imagine what it would have done to their immaculate crisp white outfits! Eventually, a body was floating face down in the pool and we could tell it was John because Royal Marines don't wear bright orange shorts! The marine pulled John to the side of the pool and threw him onto the poolside tiles. He then literally jumped out of the pool, picked John up like a sack of spuds, tossed him over his shoulder and carried him round the pool and behind the large screen. He walked past us and laid John on the bench next to the sleeping Shady. He looked at Blood and said, 'Yours I believe?' and sauntered off to join his muscly mates.

With medics attending to John, Scouse, Jock and I completed the remaining 100-metre races without any trouble, telling each other we came last because we held back to avoid any more incidents. Now came the underwater distance competition with our entrant Shady still sleeping on the bench. The CPO was forming the line ready for the march out.

'Where are Stonecutters Island he shouted?'

Blood pointed to Shady on the bench and said, 'He is not very well, can one of us do the race'?

The CPO marched over to the bench lent over Shady and

shouted, 'Wake up! Are you ready to race?'

Shady jumped straight up and said, 'Yes Sir.'

'It's Chief, not Sir, are you sure you are well enough?'

'Yes Sir,' Shady replied.

'Have you ever been in an underwater distance race?' he asked.

'No' said Shady.

'How are you planning your race?' asked the Chief.

Blood and I stood very still, a reply of 'jump in and when I get on the bottom start walking quickly' would be very funny but would get him thrown out. Shady looked determinedly at the Chief and said, 'Get in and go like hell Sir.'

The CPO sighed and just pointed over to the line of racers. 'Get over there and out of my sight.'

Blood looked at us and said, 'There is no way this is going to end well.' We all nodded in agreement.

On the shout of 'left turn quick march!' Shady wandered out in front of the marching line, tripping up a few times in his pink flip-flops and holding his hand above his head to shield the sun from his eyes. When he finally managed to get on the box, there was a murmur from the crowd. What could they be saying as they witnessed a six-foot bean pole covered in black fur wearing long bright green trunks and pink flip-flops? Just before the starter said 'on your marks' a PTI stood behind Shady and took his glasses off him. These were not just sunglasses, without them in the sun, Shady would be nearly blind.

The whistle went and Shady jumped in, we could not see him and began to worry.

'Where is he?' I cried.

'Same place as the rest, underwater,' was the reply.

We could see most of the contestants underwater halfway down the pool. What seemed like minutes later, there was an eruption of Shady rising out of the water! As he rose he spewed lumps of food and slosh into the air. Unfortunately, he spewed and spewed and no end of the PTIs prodding him with their poles could make him stop. He made it to the side of the pool and there, with his arms and head over the tiles, he continued to spew. To his credit, he looked up to the Admiral and his wife sitting within five feet of him and whispered 'Sorry' and, after a long pause, 'Sir.'

The PTIs now saw a chance to help the situation and grabbed his arms and pulled him out. As they dragged him, the inevitable happened. Shady's shorts snagged on the pool's edge and, by continuing to pull hard, they left the shorts in the pool. Then lifted him to full height by his armpits not realising the unfortunate display Shady was providing to the astonished crowd. Displayed before the Admiral and all his ladies was now a man covered in black hair that contained large sections of repulsive vomit topped off by an incredibly large member flopped between his legs.

The PTIs now had a decision to make. Carry him out displaying him in all his glory or leave him there and cover him up. Eventually they found him a robe, and once again a member (no pun intended) of our team was delivered to us and dumped on the bench. The CPO strode over only to be stopped in his tracks by Blood who said, 'I told you he was not well!'

With lumps of sick now floating all over the pool's surface the volunteer ladies' synchronised swimming had to be put on hold! The men were no doubt disappointed as they were looking forward to seeing the officers' wives' bums (sorry bottoms) sticking out of the water. 'That's a pity,' said the guy next to me. 'I have been pool guard all week whilst the ladies practised. They end their routine by joining hands underwater forming a large circle with their legs in the air. They then raise up their legs together. Just as their legs are completely out of the water, they spread them to a maximum to touch each other's toes. It's called forming a daisy. There was much talk by the trainer about the exposure of their crotches! They had a photographer up on the top diving board and his photos were going to be part of the adverts for the show. They are now on sale in selected bars.'

With their poles useless at collecting sick, the PTIs had to change them for fishing nets. They were now the main entertainment for the crowd. Shouting 'there's a bit, there's some more, over there, more over here' were the cries.

In order to move the attention away from the pool cleaning, it was decided to begin the diving competition. Blood had, by now, obviously seen the diving board. We asked if he had ever dived before and he replied, 'No but it cannot be that hard.' Not the reply you would expect from a well-educated person. 'What's the plan?' we asked and he just laughed and said, 'You'll see.' The board was down the other end of the pool. The spectators were a bit close to the edge but far enough away from the middle where the divers should enter the water.

The standard was nothing like the Olympics on the telly so our thoughts were Blood shouldn't make too much of a fool of himself. We had all been drinking beer after we had finished our races, but Blood had been drinking solidly all through the competition.

We were surprised to see Blood on the top board, as most of the other competitors had been using a board below. Blood stood up at the back of the board with his legs closed and slowly rose onto tiptoes with his arms over his head. He looked very professional as he lightly stepped with pointed toes across the board. One knee came up and he jumped on the board. Now in the air, feet together, toes pointed down and still having his arms above his head, he had jumped up at an angle so was descending towards one side of the pool. As he came down, his arms slowly lowered and his knees came up into his chest. The arms then wrapped round his knees, and he entered the water at top speed making the biggest 'bomb' I have ever seen. He completely soaked a large section of the crowd, luckily not in range of the Admiral. Perhaps Blood thought that Shady had already sorted that section.

'That must have hurt,' someone murmured. Blood was disqualified, and now walking bow-legged headed back to us. The CPO was back striding towards us once again. Blood got in first, 'I missed the jump off point and had to bail out of the dive to miss the crowd. I had no other choice.

242

Do you mind if we go now as we are not interested in the serious competition later and the synchronised swimming might be a while?'

'Yes, piss off. I expect there will be an inquiry on all the cock-ups, and you will definitely be required to attend.'

We set off into Hong Kong, all of us asking Blood if we can go to one of his favourite haunts. Two bars later Blood suddenly disappeared, and later we got our sampan back to the island. Sat in the boat watching the lights of Hong Kong disappear in the distance, Scouse said, 'Did that just happen?' 'Ask them,' we said, pointing to Shady asleep on the floor and John next to him with his arm in a sling and a bandage round his head.

There were no repercussions at our level after the gala. Blood went to the wash-up but escaped without any punishment. We never heard about why the office got the dates wrong. Lt Bush implemented a stricter routine on the issue of rum, but within a few weeks all was back to normal with him, on the odd Sunday morning, slipping into the rum room for a wee snifter. When we asked him if he enjoyed the gala he said the foreign guests that he was chaperoning seemed to find the whole event very amusing.

Lt Bush called Shady into his office to discuss his party piece. Apparently, the Lt could not help laughing as he lectured him on the wrongs of drinking. It's a shame, but Shady is back to being teetotal and is very careful to avoid any attempt we make to get him to join with us socially.

The days passed pleasantly by. After completing our shift in the transmitter rooms, we took turns collecting the crabs in the nets. The garden and the grocery shop continued to thrive. There were a few minor incidents that caused amusement.

The wife of the army officer in charge of the prison was chased into the sea by a brown cobra snake. She was in the water for a couple of hours. When someone finally found her, they asked her why she was standing in the sea. 'So it cannot get me,' she replied. 'But they are good swimmers,' the chap kindly replied.

The situation was thought so serious by the powers that be, that we were called out and issued with 303 rifles and sent into the jungle to shoot it! Lt Bush had been replaced by Lt Strank and he liked to think he was a tough disciplinarian, so he gathered us to shout orders. We fell in, and our new officer stared at Sippers sitting to attention next to me.

'Form a line and go through the jungle and find that cobra,' he shouted.

'How do we know which one committed the crime?' someone asked. It was ridiculous, the snake being an expert in disguise. The only way we could catch him was to step on him or leave it to Sippers as he liked eating snakes. Someone had the bright idea to fire our rifles into the air to make it sound like we were being successful. When we got back, the CPO asked how many we had shot as it sounded like a hell of a battle. We told him none, but those snakes would think very carefully before attacking our women again.

We were asked nicely to be waiters at the CPO and POs' ball (bribed was nearer the truth). Blood was not happy about having to attend, and made sure there were drinks strategically placed for us to pop behind a screen or tree and snatch a few gulps. Sippers and our chefs had been in the garden since dawn cooking and basting a large pig (not one of ours) which was about ready to eat. All of us spent the night nipping over to it and pinching the crackling. Scouse went too far when goaded on by Blood, who said that the best crackling on a pig was the ears. Scouse borrowed a knife from the chef and ate one and gave the other to me. Blood was right, they were very tasty.

An hour later, the traditional knockout dance was announced. This started during the first ball when the Brits got back, after the Japanese departed. Getting on the dance floor was compulsory and the rules were basic. The dancers had to stop when the music stopped and not move. The MC would then run around trying to make them laugh, and subsequently move. Earlier, Blood said the prize was five days in Macau which was pretty impressive; there was also a forfeit that the winners have to complete as part of the prize. 'What's the forfeit?' I asked I witnessed another one of Blood's grins and thought whatever it is, we are not going to like it.

The dancers were finally whittled down to the winning

pair. They were then led over to the pig. The MC announced, 'To receive the holiday you have to complete the forfeit and both of you have to eat one of the ears!' He then shouted, 'Chef, cut off the ears!' It was our Chinese CPO Chef, looking at the pig's head, he spluttered in his Chinese English, 'No possible, no possibility.' The MC looked at the pig and shouted, 'What the fuck!' Scouse rushed across the dance floor and snapped two big bits of crackling off the pig's bum and dropped to the floor. Raising the crackling up in the air he said, 'Here are the ears, they must have dropped off.' The MC was not fooled but went with it, giving the crackling to the winning couple and he started the countdown. They both ate their pieces before the count of ten. With the forfeit completed and the evidence destroyed we could all relax.

All the CPOs and POs were gathered at the bar and the wives were dancing with themselves. Scouse, with his looks, was grabbed by one of them and pulled to the dance floor. Not to be out done, the rest of the wives came over to us and we were all dragged onto the floor. We and the wives were having a great time, jiving to all the new records of the day. Even Sippers and one of the PO's dogs were chasing each other between the dancers.

Before we knew it, the music was stopped, the CPO was on the microphone and telling us to all go back to our barracks and he would see us tomorrow. As we staggered back home, the music started back up and I expect the POs had been forced to get back on the dance floor. On the way back, Sippers was very sick. It seems there is a limit to the amount of pig a dog can eat.

Gino and Mick arrive with a sitrep

I have a phone call from the CPO Chef from HMS Tamar. He said I have a guy called Gino who wants to talk to you.

'Dave,' says Gino. 'Can Mick and I come to your island for a visit?'

'Is it just you and Mick, no Danny or Robbie?'

He laughs and says, 'No, we are all alone.'

I agree to meet them but on my terms. I send them to the boat harbour and tell them where to wait. Mickey will pick them up in the sampan and bring them over to the island. I tell Mickey to watch them for an hour before approaching them. If he sees anyone with them, leave them be. Also make sure that no boat follows. Mickey asks, 'These people are enemy?'

I reply, 'I hope not but you cannot be too careful.'

'I take Big Chef just in case.' Big Chef is one of ours and lives up to his name. I see the boat coming round the headland. Mick and Gino see me and wave.

They have not changed. Sippers and I greet them and we head down the path to the beach bar. I turn round to see Mickey and Big Chef following us. I shout it's OK and they head back to the mess.

'I see you have your own protection in place,' says Mick looking back.

I point to the armed Sikhs on their pontoons and say, 'That's my protection, those guys do not miss anything and they are my friends.' As I indicate the table to sit at they look out along the beach and into the jungle and both whistle and say, 'Jesus you have fallen on your feet here Dave.'

I grin and reply, 'I bloody deserve it after all the shite you lot got me into.' The beers arrive with Chinese snacks and I say, 'Tell me everything, I will ask questions at the end.'

Mick starts with saying Robbie has disappeared and is probably dead. 'We do not know everything but our parents have told us that he was climbing up the ranks of our East End crowd. His job was to organise smuggling routes from the Med to the UK, mainly using Navy vessels. He was controlling the NAAFI Canteen Managers [Can Men]. It all went wrong in Portsmouth harbour when all the ships coming in from Gibraltar were raided at the same time. Before any stores were unloaded, they arrested all the Can Men, Robbie and a CPO. Teams from the Provost Marshal in Portsmouth then flew to Malta and Gibraltar, most of the ships were found to have smuggled goods in them. The whole exercise has been kept under wraps so none of this is common knowledge. Apparently, the Maltese guys in London have been kicking up a stink as the Brits are all over their organisation in Malta. Whether Albert (Al) or the Maltese have sorted Robbie we don't know but he is no longer around. Danny has a new minder and has left the Navy on mental grounds, he is now back in the East End living with his mother next door to Al the boss.

'Robbie's other task was as a minder for Danny. It was his idea to get him away from temptation and into the Navy. So here's the truth. Danny was sexually abused by his father (who at the time was head of the East End mob). When he was 16 and his sister was 14, he opened a door and found his father having sex with his sister. Danny closed the door, got a gun went back and shot his father.

'The whole thing was covered up and rival gangs were blamed. You couldn't have a boss as a nonce [child molester]. Danny's sister lives with her mum and is rarely seen. The question is, has Danny hurt those girls, and we do not know the answer to that. Danny is weird, everything has to be clean, he has a lot of strange habits. However, on the plus side he is funny, good company and very generous. When it comes to sex, we believe he has a problem. If forced or laughed at during the messing about stage with girls he gets violent. The only time we have witnessed this is when I pulled him off the Cypriot girl. That's when Robbie made us all join the Navy. We cannot imagine Danny cleaning up and hiding bodies or any of that stuff. If he hurt those girls, Robbie or someone else would have to fix it for him. Our gut feeling is that he is innocent, but we have no idea who if not him. The London crowd were all over Robbie for all the problems and us three are not in the frame for any of it. We do not think they even know you exist.'

I look at them both and ask, 'Why me? How did I get involved?'

'Danny,' they said. 'He always gets what he wants. On the train going to Raleigh you came up to us and chatted like we were old friends. You were funny and a smart guy like us. Danny liked the vibe you added to our crew, you were a nice change from us Londoners. He enjoyed showing you around and told Robbie you were staying as part of his crowd.'

I then remembered the advice from the guy in Raleigh, that you would never become firm friends with the first group you meet.

We had a long session and they left long after the sun sank over the mountains. Finally I delivered them to the jetty, and the Sikh called our sampan. Sam pulled up his fishing lines and chugged over.

They are on different ships but are due to sail in the morning. We agreed to have another session in London but I thought as I waved them off that this might be the last I saw of them.

Three months left in paradise

Nine months of my stay was completed. Blood had done his stint and was back home, likewise Scouse, John and all the others from our original gang. With new boys seeming to be joining daily Shady and I had now been on the island the longest. Jock was still here and we were about to go to the border together for my last time. Sippers has now joined Jock's family, as the married men do two years on station. Jock, with a year left, has promised to hand Sippers over to another loving family when he leaves. It's not the ideal situation as no one wants their dog to learn to bark in a Scottish accent.

When I get back from the border, I will be working days, instead of doing shifts, in the transmitting stations. It was the routine for a guy about to depart, to go over to Tamar and complete his leaving checklist, visiting all the departments and getting his flight details and medicals sorted. It was also considered that by now I would have obtained enough knowledge to perform the service routines of the 30 transmitters.

Back on the border, all seemed the same as previous trips at first, but security had been increased and we had armed police with us wherever we went. Three days ago there had been a vicious gun battle between the police and a group of Chinese. They were drug smugglers using the refugees to bring in the drugs. The police found the location where the smugglers stopped the refugees to take the drugs back off them. They watched the operation for a few days and then decided to raid the buildings. The smugglers were tipped off and were ready. They were heavily armed and three police officers were killed, half the smugglers were either shot or captured. The ring leaders escaped across the border. Harry wanted them back.

When we arrived at the Colonial House of Superintendent Harold Hunter, we were soon sat on his veranda in the large chairs, with equally large gin and tonics. Harry was fuming. He had spent three days demanding, discussing and begging the Chinese top man in the border town for the return of the smugglers. 'They are Hong Kong citizens but members of the Chinese mafia called Triads. The Hong Kong Triad is different from the mainland Triad so they should be sent back to us. We do not know who has them in China. Which is ridiculous, we want them in our jail as they are from Hong Kong.'

As we drive to the same restaurant by the river, I doubt we will be singing and throwing beer and wine down our throats like last time. Harry had arranged to meet the headman from across the river. He went to the waterside and led him into the restaurant. They sat at a table downstairs whilst we went upstairs to our normal table. Harry sat discussing the problem with six policemen looking on from the next table. After three hours, Harry climbed the stairs with a huge grin on his face. 'The deal was done with two lorry loads of scotch whisky, which the police had captured on a ship from Triad smugglers. I have got them back using their own whisky,' roared Harry. 'The Chinese Army had them, and would have killed them but everyone in China is bribable,' said Harry. I was wrong, we did sing and drink the night away.

In the morning, I felt very privileged to witness all the high-level shenanigans of a story the whole world was tuned into. We were checking that the Chief of Police Communications was secure and was recording transmissions from Hong Kong to China, so we were required. Jock was 28 and I was only 20, it seemed strange to be put in that position. I remembered Blood saying never get pissed with your own importance. The truth is, they should have sent someone of a higher grade, perhaps Jock was right and they sent us because we were expendable. Cannon fodder as Blood would say.

Back on the island, starting my day job I was told to go to a meeting. Gathered were the boss, CPO, two POs and Jock. Also in the room were Mr Chan the head of the Chinese riggers that climb the 100-foot masts and fix all the antennas. At the head of the table were three Americans. The boss introduced them and said we have to install two transmitters and a giant antenna in two weeks. The American navy will assist us and train us to maintain and service the transmitters. This is an emergency as the system will link the US embassy and the fleet to Guam. The HF multi-frequency antenna was like a gigantic TV aerial. It came on a barge and with a work force of twenty or more. We were very impressed. It was up and running in about three weeks. The new transmitters made our 30 look very ancient, the American engineers did not know whether to laugh or cry when they saw all the cages with massive glass valves humming away. 'Jesus,' said the guy I was chaperoning, 'you guys must have your work cut out keeping them on the air. How long have these been in service?' I had no idea so I replied, 'Too long!'

Typhoon Ruby

I now had two months to go before flying home and then Ruby hit us.

Typhoon Ruby was a strong tropical cyclone that struck Hong Kong, Macau and southern China in early September 1964. The precursor disturbance that led to Ruby was first identified on August 29 over the Philippine Sea, and this system organised into a tropical cyclone by September 1. Ruby intensified as it moved west, becoming a typhoon the next day and subsequently passing over the Babuyan Islands of the Philippines. After reaching the South China Sea, Ruby turned northwest and intensified further, attaining peak ten-minute sustained winds of 195 km/h (140 mph) before making landfall with that intensity near Hong Kong and Macau on September 5.

Ruby was one of the strongest typhoons in Hong Kong's history. The storm produced a peak wind gust of 268 km/h (166 mph) at Tate's Cairn and a gust of 230 km/h (143 mph) on Waglan Island; the latter was the fastest gust observed for that site. A total of 38 fatalities were attributed to Ruby, though another 14 people remained unaccounted for. The storm sank 314 fishing vessels and destroyed or damaged thousands of homes. Rain-triggered landslides and wind-blown debris caused 300 injuries. Among locations in Hong

Kong, Tai Po was most seriously affected. A wind gust of 211 km/h (131 mph) generated by Ruby in Macau was the strongest gust measured there on record; at least 20 fatalities were reported in Macau. The typhoon caused serious flooding along the mouth of the Pearl River in Guangdong Province in South China, where at least 700 people were killed. A total of 8,500 people were classified by the Royal Observatory as 'disaster victims'. Numerous injuries were caused by sheet metal torn from buildings under construction in downtown Hong Kong. Fifty thousand refugees from the People's Republic of China were rendered homeless. The typhoon destroyed 20 ships capable of oceanic travel throughout the Hong Kong area.

At least ten ships ran aground. Nine people were lost after a Panamanian freighter, the Dorar, sank in Victoria harbour; 14 others were rescued. Kai Tak International Airport, ferry service, and other transportation systems were brought to a standstill throughout Hong Kong, in addition to the Hong Kong Stock Exchange. Roads were blocked by toppled trees and overturned cars. One road was obstructed by cranes that fell from a 20-storey building. Heavy rainfall caused by Ruby led to floods, landslides, and razed homes. High voltage electrical wires torn by the winds caused hundreds of fires before the power service was terminated.

Tai Po was the hardest-hit area in Hong Kong; there, the storm destroyed thousands of village homes and temporary shelters. In Kowloon and Tsuen Wan, 1,368 houses were affected. A loosened bolder in Kowloon trapped ten people. At Mui Wo, 30 homes were destroyed and 180 others were unroofed. High waves pushed water into the Hong Kong City Hall, causing a delay in the 1964 Summer Olympics torch relay. Following the passage of Ruby, hundreds of workers cleared and repaired streets most seriously impacted in Hong Kong. The colonial government appealed for public donations for victims of Ruby on September 6. Hot meals and cash assistance were prepared for the displaced Chinese refugees in Hong Kong by government welfare groups

Ruby hits the island

We have been having lots of mini typhoons over the last few months. So we were well practised and getting bored of standing by and ready, then standing down when the typhoon changed direction or blew itself out. Ruby however decided to smash straight into us. Stonecutters was a very exposed little island in the middle of Hong Kong harbour with only a small hill; the rest of the land was barely above sea level. Very large waves would reduce the size of the island considerably.

The problem for the transmitting station was the aerial field. The four 100-foot masts had cables strung between them and over these cables were thick wires. These were the aerials that were required to keep us in contact with the rest of the world. Wires ran from the transmitter rooms to the bottom of the aerials via telegraph poles with insulators to keep the wires separated. Travelling through the wires were high-frequency transmissions; if you touched the wires they would burn your fingers off. The system was not sophisticated enough to stop transmitting if the aerials were blown down in the gales. If the two wires that travelled up to the aerial touched they would spark and catch fire. If the lines fell and lay separated and the engineer touched them then he would be seriously burnt. There was much discussion about whether the aerials would survive in 100- or 120-mile hour winds. We were about to be hit by 140 miles an hour.

As the storm increased, our team of the Officer in Charge, one1 CPO, five POs, five Leading Hands and 12 junior rates gathered at the control desk. We also had Mr Chan and two of his Chinese riggers. Ruby was going to come straight at us so we would have six or seven hours of increasing winds, a lull as the centre goes over head and back to the ferocious winds. As a day worker, I would be part of the eight-man outside crew. It would be our job to patrol along the aerial runs and free any branches or trees that fell and fouled the wires. We split into two teams, my team was PO Tony Hall and the Leading Hand was Jock, also with us was a very sober Shady. Tony was a bull of a man who I often played tennis with and Jock and I knew each other well. Ben seemed a good guy, but was looking around in a daze. After two years on a destroyer, then a two-day flight across the world, who could blame him.

As the wind began to increase, armed with axes and machetes we began our patrols. We were in radio contact with the control room and if any transmitter went down we would be sent to check its aerial. We could also check if lines were live by hanging a lamp on the line. We had them on long wooden sticks. If the lamp lit then the line would have dangerous RF transmissions going down it.

When the wind increased to nearly 100 miles an hour we were in trouble. Dustbins and debris were being hurled around and if it hit us we could be badly injured. It was now difficult to stay together as it was almost impossible to stay on our feet. We went back to the control room for a sitrep and discussion.

The next plan was that each team would use a small four-wheeled flatbed truck. These trucks were normally used by the gardeners and pulled by a small three-wheeled moped. One man up front pulling the truck with one on either side and the fourth member pushing. By putting all the tools in the truck we kept our hands free. Shady lashed his glasses to his face and we were all roped to the truck to keep us all together. Four powerful large battery lights were placed back, front and to the sides. Once outside on the concrete paths with jungle each side, it was very frightening, the wind was really howling and we could hardly hear each other. Any communication had to be done by shouting loudly in each other's ear. The radio was almost useless. We could just about hear the control centre if we got on our hands and knees on the ground down beside the truck. The lights gave us about 20 feet of vision up the road and into the trees.

In any other situation we should all be locked and battened down in one of the stone buildings. However, the mission statement for the transmitter station in a hurricane was to keep Hong Kong in touch with the outside world. The Officer in Charge would be expected to take controlled risks to ensure we were still in contact by the time it passed over. We were military and, even if the enemy was a typhoon, we were expected to step up! That's what we were told over and over in our typhoon planning meetings.

Moving slowly along the path through the trees, we turned a corner and up the road were three people in full foul weather gear. Two were leaning over another guy who was lying on the road. Shouting was a waste of time so we pushed as fast as we could to reach them. It should have been obvious as they were all very small, it was Mr Chan and his two riggers. I am afraid it is typical of the British and their Chinese workers. The management had ignored

259

the aerial expert who had been working in the field since it was built and left him to his own devices. Apparently, they had been out on their own fixing an aerial and another one next to it had fallen on them. The guy on the ground had serious burns so we laid him in the truck and roped Mr Chan and his assistant to it and headed back.

Once we handed over our casualty, we added Mr Chan to our team and headed back out. His assistant would join the other team when they got back. The situation we found at the control centre was pretty grim. Out of 30 transmitters we were down to ten working. We now had a list of priorities, with our expert Mr Chan it should be possible to fix one or two, even in these conditions. Also if the storm kept to its current course, the centre of the storm would come over us and give us a lull for an hour or two to get enough transmitters up and running to survive the next onslaught.

Unfortunately, after managing to jury rig three antennas, the rest of them fell down and we were left with those three working at 75% power. Whilst reporting in for them to use these antennas, we were told to go down to the two holiday cottages near the beach. HMS Tamar had called to say that the two service families staying in them should have left before the storm stopped the ferry. However, the two husbands had been called back on duty earlier and left their wives to pack up. Now it would seem they had not arrived back to their flats in Hong Kong. We had to go and see if two women and three children were still in the cottages. The phones to the houses were down so we had no idea what we were faced with. As we approached, we could see the massive waves hitting the beach but the houses, although surrounded by swirling water, were still intact.

The houses were not on the beach but about 20 yards away, even so the sea was now on their walls. With our truck 50 yards away, we roped ourselves together and tried to make our way to the water's edge. It was into the wind and almost impossible. Once we were at the water's edge we shouted pointlessly at the buildings. By the look of it, the water at the building was about four-feet high and we had about 25 yards to get to it. What to do? Suddenly we saw a movement and then someone waving!

We got in a huddle and a plan was hatched with Tony in charge. The problem was with the water still coming up the beach, we did not know how much time we had. We radioed for the other team and any spare men to come to the houses with long ropes and dry clothing, hot soup, blankets, etc. Mr Chan would wait by the truck with one radio. Tony, Shady, Jock and I held a long rope that would be fed out to us from the large coil by Mr Chan. We looped ourselves round the long rope with individual ties. I looked at Shady before we set off into the swirling sea, his government-issue glasses were clamped flat against his face. He seemed in a determined trance and was gripping his rope very tightly, staring out to the bungalows. If I was frightened before looking at Shady, I was now terrified. We would try to walk carefully to the bungalow with the aim of getting one person inside with the spare radio. We walked slowly out and did not find it too difficult as the water behind the bungalow was somewhat calmer than the stuff hitting the front. With about ten yards to go, Tony undid his rope and wrapped the long rope round his waist and headed to the bungalow on his own. Still looped round the long rope, we fed it through slowly, giving Tony enough slack to keep walking to the building. He reached a shuttered window and banged on it. A woman opened the window and shutter and Tony pulled himself up and in. He tied the rope inside and waved us back to the water's edge. Tony called us on the radio and it was copied to the control centre. He said the two women were there with two girls and a boy. They were soaking wet, cold and in shock. The children had gone through the screaming phase and were now quietly sobbing. They were on a table but that was now floating. So he lifted them onto two chest of drawers which were only just keeping them above water. He finished by saying we need to get these people out of here within an hour if not sooner.

We had a good strong rope secured both on the shore and on the bungalow. It really was just a matter of who, and in what order, we would escort/carry them to safety. The other crew arrived and the six largest were picked to loop a rope over the joining rope and go over two at a time and bring a child ashore. Shady and I got out easily enough and Tony passed the boy out. I strapped him to my chest within my foul weather jacket and with Shady making sure I did not stumble, we got the boy back safely. It did not prove to be a difficult task. We decided to get the two girls out in a similar fashion. Two other lads took out foul weather gear and boots for the women and they walked ashore with them. Tony came back with another one of the lads carrying the women's valuables. No point in leaving them there as the bungalows looked like they would not survive another three or four hours with the wind still rising. The boss and HMS Tamar made a big thing of it, but by keeping it simple and not making it more complicated than it was, we got them out quickly and safely. Much better than overreacting and playing it too safe. Tony's decisiveness to go for it proved correct as the water round the bungalows was soon up to roof level.

As the storm started to ease, we were told the centre was passing through and we had about an hour before it began to build up again. Once we could walk unaided, we formed eight teams to try and repair as many aerials as possible. We had finished up with only one transmitter working into an intact aerial. As we were down to just one aerial, there was much debate at the control centre who was the most important service between the government, Navy, Army or RAF.

Back with the same team, Tony led us along the beach, passing the bungalows towards the jungle beyond the firing range. As the rain eased and the visibility increased, we were amazed at the sight of a large cargo vessel on the beach. The bow of the ship was up on the beach and, apart from a slight list, it seemed to be staying upright. Tony said, 'When the waters drop back to normal that ship will be stuck forever.' The sea was still furious and crashing onto land with the beach completely underwater. We approached the bow and a few men leaned out and were shouting at us in Chinese. Mr Chan had left us to continue fixing aerials so we had a Sikh policeman to translate, but it was useless as the sound of the waves were much too strong. We contacted the control centre and reported the ship. They said they would get Harbour Control to contact the ship.

The boss arrived at the scene and said the Harbour Control had scores of ships in distress so could not send a tug to assist and could not get in contact with the ship. The ship fired two lines onto the land and we looped them together and tied a radio onto one line which they pulled up. Once the ship's staff had figured out how to use the radio, our Sikh friend stepped in and we began discussing what could be done before the second phase hit us. They had lost power so there was no chance of powering astern when the waves come bounding in and lifted the ship higher up the bank. Lowering men into the swirling waters around the bows was very risky. It was decided that it was safest for them to stay on board the ship until the storm passed. We would keep in contact with the ship but once the winds got up again we would be back fighting to keep the aerials up so would not be able to help. We would be back to them when the sea calmed down.

The high winds returned, things got very bad and soon the last transmitter had to be shut down when it lost its aerial. This meant we lost contact with the outside world. It was now too dangerous to go out as all the paths were blocked with trees and branches and we could not get to the antennas without the truck. So, we all huddled down in our quarters and most of the married men got back to where the families were sheltering.

Calm after the storm and damage report

When I finally got to walk around the island, I could not get the last 48 hours out of my mind. To be outside for hours in the anger and the hostility of the wind, rain and sea was a million miles away from anything I had ever experienced. During that storm this planet was in charge of our lives and there was nothing man could do. I was 20 and since joining the Navy I had had nearly three years of experiencing all sorts of emotions – anger, fear, happiness and regret – but this one has left me stunned. I wander on towards the beach and there was Shady sitting on a rock looking out to the sea and Hong Kong beyond. Sippers trotted over and sat close to Shady who put his arm round him. This was strange. Shady was frightened of dogs, it had taken a typhoon to make him human.

'Are we having fun yet?' I asked.

Shady looked at me and murmured, 'How did we survive that?'

'Was it your god or mine that could walk on water?' I asked.

'I think you'll find we have the same god,' he said.

'I wouldn't know, I have never heard of Jews before I met you.'

'Don't they have them in your village?'

'If they did, they kept it quiet.'

'Anyway, you don't seem to bother with yours and I certainly stay the hell away from mine,' said Shady making it very plain that subject was finished.

'Whoever helped us get out to those bungalows should be thanked next time one of us chats to a god,' I finished.

Shady looked over to Hong Kong and said, 'If half the rumours are true, the Chinese over there are suffering greatly.'

'We will find out how all our friends have managed to survive when they all come back to work,' I said.

Eventually the typhoon passed through and the great clean-up began. It took weeks to get up and running. The sea remained very rough for days so the guys on the cargo ship had to wait before they were eventually taken off and taken to Hong Kong. The ship would be part of Stonecutters Island for quite some time.

Whilst we waited for normality, Shady and I spent time calculating the financial state of our business. As and when the 12 original shareholders left, we would calculate the monies at their time of leaving and pay each holder his share. With only two of us left, we had over the last three months made a tidy sum. We put aside a lump sum for emergencies and divided the rest by two. Then we decided to shut the business down and pretend it never happened. I would hand over to the new guy the job of catering for the 12 junior rates. I told him the married guys would pester him to get them UK foodstuffs from the Navy stores and if he liked he could charge them extra to subsidise the food bought in the Chinese markets.

The rest of the business was in chaos. All our nets disappeared in the storm. The speedboat was damaged but repairable. The garden was destroyed and the chickens and pigs were nowhere to be seen. The snooker room was hit by 30-foot waves. The shed with the go-karts collapsed, though the carts were probably repairable. Business, what business?

As we were going home in four weeks we had a meeting with the new guys, told them what we had planned to do but never did! I finished by saying I wished we had got it going and made a success of it. Of course, Shady did not say a word but agreed with the plan to sneak out quietly.

Two of our cooks finally arrived back into the camp; we had spent two weeks fending for ourselves. They came to see me and told how badly Mickey had been hit by the typhoon. He had lost his flat and all his possessions and his family were homeless. Shady and I decided to go and see him and asked the chef where he lived. The chef suggested we met Mickey in a bar as he would lose face if we saw his family huddled in a charity tent. We discussed how we could help and the chef said he needed to rent accommodation until they repaired the government flats. So we met Mickey in a bar and gave him 500 HK dollars out of our kitty, that amount would allow him to get an apartment for six months. He got very emotional but we said without him we would never have made all this money. It was a thank you for being a man we could trust. He already knew the state of our island and said, once he had settled his family, he would be back next week. I told him Shady and I had handed over the reins to the new guys and we were not sure they were up to sneaking out to sea at night and stealing the fishermen's nets. Mickey grinned and said, 'Better to discuss with fishermen that they give me nets. Then we fish our waters and share the catch with them. Everybody happy.' I wish I had thought of that nine months ago, better than all the underhand stuff we did to make our money. Mickey also told us that Sam and his family were in trouble as his sampan had been badly damaged and sunk.

The walled harbour was filled with hundreds of boats and most of them were destroyed. Mickey took us there and the scene was very sad, we just looked around at the devastation as we stood waiting for Mickey to find Sam. The thought of that lovely family being left with nothing was heart-breaking. They have had to live in an open boat with just an awning over them and were happy. We spotted Sam and Mickey in the distance and went over to them. Shady said, 'Let's give Sam the rest of the kitty. We have our cut.' I agreed. Sam would lose face if we had to see his family sitting on the jetty looking at his capsized sampan. Rather than going to see his boat and family, we just gave him 400 HK dollars and told Mickey to tell Sam we were going home to the UK and we felt we owed him this money for helping us. We left him staring at the money in his hands. That was the kitty all gone. Time to go home.

Homeward? Er no, Singapore

I had mixed feelings about leaving. With Christmas on the horizon and the prospect of being in the UK to enjoy it with my family, who I had not seen in a long time, I was not totally miserable. What could possibility go wrong?

I shed buckets of tears saying goodbye to Sippers and was still blubbering as the boat rounded the headland and headed for Hong Kong.

Shady and I boarded a RAF Britannia heading for Singapore. At the last minute, our flight was changed and we were told, because of the increased tension between Indonesia and Malaysia, the plane was going to be used to fly the wives and children back to UK from Singapore. What they did not tell us was that we would not be on it! As we climbed into the clouds we said our last goodbyes to Hong Kong. After previously being rammed into a Navy frigate, the last year was so different, we both knew we were going back to the sad reality of being in the real Navy again.

During the flight we discussed what we were going to do as soon as we arrived in the UK.

Shady said, 'My family are Orthodox Jews which makes it very difficult for me as I gave up my faith to join the Navy. I plan to stay in a hotel near my home in

North London and meet my father or mother and see if we can then work out a way of getting together as a family. Both my sisters are married and I doubt that the husbands would let me see them.' He slowly described his life as a child and what it was like to be brought up in the Jewish community. This sounded like some sort of cult to me. Shady said, 'I planned my exit from my family very carefully and chose the Navy because I would be in the Navy's charge and my family could not contact me. I waited until I was 18 so I would not need parental permission. I felt safe inside a Navy camp and even better on a ship. Also the Navy paid me and fed me, I did not need any other support. Finally they would give him the chance to see the world and learn about all the different people and customs. Before, I could not even read books about the world because my reading material was censored,' he said.

He continued, 'The reason I seem quiet and find it difficult to join in conversations is probably because I have never been allowed to express an opinion. The Jewish way to bring up children is under a strict disciplinary code. Leaving was a momentous decision and I am amazed I had the strength to go through with it. I still cannot believe I actually did it.' I now looked at Shady in a different light. Underneath those hours of lying on his bed reading and walking for miles on his own discovering Hong Kong was a man discovering himself and planning a new life.

I said, 'We should get together when we get home. If it did not work out with your family, rather than stay in a hotel you can come down and stay with my family in Wiltshire.' I was about to say the nightlife would not be as good as

London but then realised that Shady had probably not experienced any.

We bumped down in Singapore and all the single men were ushered off the flight towards a large hangar-type building. A stern looking CPO greeted us and was not very apologetic. He said, 'Right, there is a fucking war on between us and the fucking Indonesians but in order to keep the fucking press under fucking control they are calling it a fucking emergency. It is however a fucking war! We are very short of men so all the RAF planes are flying families out and coming back from the UK with more troops. Until we get our numbers up to the required amount no one is going home. Before you ask, it is estimated that we should be up to strength in two months but I would not hold your breath.'

Shady and I looked at each other in shock but managed to keep our mouths shut. One of the other lads on the flight muttered about not making it home for Christmas.

The veins in the CPO's neck started throbbing. 'Your fucking Crimbo is fucked mate,' retorted the CPO. 'You will all muster here at 07.00 tomorrow in working clothes and boots, carrying your gas masks to start weapon training. As some of you may go to the front line in Borneo you will spend the next four days firing all of the Army's small arms including machine guns and 303 rifles just in case.'
'What a charmer,' whispered Shady out of the side of his mouth.

'I am guessing his own Crimbo was also fucking fucked,' I said.

My first problem was I had sent all uniforms and my working clothes, boots, hats and gas mask in my kitbag which was at this time going back to the UK by sea. My suitcases were full of presents for everybody back home. The rules were that we had to travel with our uniform and send all other personal effects back by sea. Once we had been shown to our accommodation with about 50 beds spaced down a long room, all I could do is leave Shady to look after my luggage. Then I had to quickly go in search of all the Navy kit I needed to keep me out of jail. Shady of course had read the rules and was now laying his uniform out, no doubt preparing to iron his clothes and shine his boots. HMS Terror was a very large barracks and it took me time to find the clothing stores. Once there, I decided as I had cash, the best plan was to tell the truth and see if I can talk my way into getting the kit without being put on a charge. Maybe I was being a bit melodramatic but my thoughts were, if I get sent to the regulators on a charge, I would be the first into a lorry heading for Borneo. We have always been warned not having a working gas mask available was a serious offence.

At the store was a friendly Leading Hand who listened to my tale of woe. To be fair, spending 12 months away and being dumped off your flight home so the families can escape and you can keep the enemy at bay until the reinforcements arrive, is a very sad tale! So he said, 'Have you the cash to buy the Navy kit?' I got out my wad that I had changed at the airport and he was suitably impressed. He supplied two sets of light blue shirts and dark blue shorts. Followed by long socks, boots, shoes and a hat. He gave me a set of overalls for free. The gas mask was a problem. The only solution he could think of was for me go to the dump and persuade the Chinese guy to give me a defective one. Apparently, the insurgents were suspected of having chemical weapons so everyone in HMS Terror had to have their masks checked. If defective, they were changed in the naval stores. It was agreed that he would keep the store open to change my defective mask until I got back. I suggested that Shady and I would meet him later in the NAAFI where the beers would be on me.

I took directions and rushed out towards the rubbish dump. I reached the playing fields and the dump was at the other end of them. The problem was twofold, first there were about eight soccer fields and six rugby pitches, not to mention the cricket pitches to cross. Secondly, it began to rain and there is a reason Singapore has six-foot wide and eight-foot ditches along all roads and pathways. They are called monsoon ditches and they collect the raging torrents of rain during the daily storms. Within seconds I was absolutely drenched, but I had to get me a gas mask so I ran and ran until I finally staggered into the dump. There were three guys huddled in a hut and I am not sure if they were frightened or amazed at this sodden white guy staggering towards them. I stood outside as I would have drenched them if I got too close and proceeded with hand signals saying can I have a second-hand gas mask please? I found it hard to believe after five minutes of pretending to put a mask over my head and breathing through it, they still just sat there in amazement. I finally looked round and over the other side of the compound was a large area covered by a tin roof, under it were piles of gas masks. I rushed past them, ran across and grabbed one and came back over to where they still sat unmoved, with the same quizzical look on their faces. I got out my sodden wad, stripped a Singapore ten dollar note out and handed it to the oldest guy. He looked up at me and said 'OK.' The three of them turned their heads and watched as I ran back across the playing fields. Probably thinking, did that just happen?

Halfway back, the rain stopped and the sun blazed down. By the time I reached the naval stores I was almost dry. Leading Hand Steven Moat was there to greet me and changed the very wet gas mask for a new one. He also handed me a pile of trade badges I would have to sew on the left sleeve of my new shirts. 'You should also buy work clothes from the tailor, those naval issue ones are far too thick and clammy for this climate. If they check your kit you have to have them but we all wear these,' he indicated. 'The tailor is at the row of shops down beside the NAAFI. I can take you down there if you like?'

'You have already saved me from getting into serious trouble, I can find the place,' I said.

'Not a problem,' said Steven. 'My missus and two kids went home last week and I could do with a few pints and a laugh.'

'OK, we will pick up my mate Shady on the way, we have just spent a year together.' He got out more trade badges for Shady's new shirts and locked up the stores.

At the tailors, Shady and I bought the two sets of work shirts and left them and the badges to be collected next day. Today they would bring me one shirt to the NAAFI with the badges sewn on. Next door we bought two loud shirts, beach shorts and flip-flops. At the bar, Steven asked how easy it was to get the gas mask.

'No problem,' I replied. 'I just waved ten dollars at him and he said OK.'

Steven fell about laughing and cried, 'You could have got 50 for that.' I had forgotten that Singapore dollars were worth three times more than Hong Kong dollars.

The three of us sank many pints of our new-found Tiger beer and finished the night at a circle of outdoor stalls just outside the barracks. There were at least 20 stalls, you just found a table and walked round the stalls, pointing at dishes which were then delivered to your table. Singapore chilli crab was to die for. The place was heaving with a lot of men enjoying the night, not knowing what was going to happen in the future.

We reported next morning outside the hangar building with about forty other sailors. We were then put into groups of six. Our job, until we were up to speed, would be on night patrols around Singapore in trucks keeping the peace. We would be trained on crowd control and management. The trucks could be shot at so we would also be taught how to protect ourselves and the truck. Also each truck would have a PO and LH. Shady and I were in the same truck so at the first tea break we discussed the delights of sitting in a slow-moving open truck waiting for someone to shoot at us. 'Have they thought this through?' I kept hearing.

I suddenly heard a loud voice from the past that made a chill run down my spine. I turned in the direction of the voice and there standing high above a pile of Petty Officers was Screech! Big fat Screech! Shady said, 'Dave what's up?' I turned to him and he indicated towards his arm that I was squeezing as hard as I could. I dropped my hand and nodded over to Screech and said, 'An evil bastard from my past has finally reappeared. When we have a few hours I will tell you the messy story I was mixed up in before I came to the island.' After a few minutes I added, 'Time on the island was living in a bubble that just got well and truly burst. Right now, I need to think and plan and carefully work out what my next moves are.' I watch him closely and see he is now a Regulating Petty Officer so I assume he will be one of the POs that will be in charge of a truck.

Typically, even after having a word with myself, without planning anything I promptly get up and start to stride over to demand he tells me what has happened to Patty. Luckily, I am stopped in my tracks by the CPO shouting for us all to gather in our sixes. We were all stood at ease in two rows of three. Then all the POs and L/Hs marched over to their men and yes, you guessed it, Screech marches over to our six. He introduced the Leading Hand and himself and then looked us over.

He stared at me and said, 'Where do I know you from?'

'Basic training HMS Raleigh,' I state.
'What's your name?' he asks.

'David Samson.'

'Yes, you were with those London boys, right?'

'Yes PO,' I growl.

'Let's have a chat when we fall out, there are a few things about your lot's Passing Out Parade that have always puzzled me,' he finished.

I now have a revised plan. I will just listen to his questions before asking mine. We spend the next few hours playing soldiers and finally break up for lunch. Screech beckons me over. I wave at Shady and say I will see him later at the canteen. We sit on a wall and Screech tells me his story.

Screech says, 'At the end of the Parade I was dragged away to the main gate and asked lots of questions by an angry Regulator. First I had to go into great detail about my whereabouts the previous night. Then he asked me about a young NAAFI girl who worked in the bar. When I heard the description, I said I had seen her in the bar that night. I said she was with the blond London boy from my class. His name was Danny, I forget his last name but I told them at the time. First they were sitting at a table holding hands, just before we left they were in a passageway kissing. I remember tapping my mate Terry on the arm and saying that git is going to get more than we are tonight.

'Then I was asked about some pictures and paperwork hidden under the floorboards in my cabin. I could not believe it, he described the goods and asked where they were. Apparently, I was supposed to have put them in a hole and dug them back up again. After all this madness, I said I was going to the Commanding Officer about my treatment. This Lieutenant Regulator then said not to worry, just provide a written statement and he would leave it at that. I insisted that Terry Cotton did the same, confirming and countersigning my statement as well. This we did.'

I sat there stunned. His account sounded genuine. If he was telling the truth, all this time we had him completely wrong. Well not completely, he had still made our lives miserable and was still a bully. But we had nearly stitched him up with a crime that he had not done. How had we read it so wrong? I couldn't tell him our part in leading the Regulator to him. I explained there was something about the London lads which might suggest an involvement with abusing girls. I left out the mob stuff and potential smuggling ring with all the subsequent actions of Robbie.

I asked, 'Are you sure you are totally in the clear?'

'I still have a copy of our statement,' he said. I ask to see it and he suggested we meet early evening in a bar just outside camp.

At the bar, I read the statement and guess who had signed it, none other than Lieutenant Robert Appleton (Robbie). I told Adam (forget Screech!) that his statement had never been filed with the police or the Navy. I then added I knew people who could use the statement to get some justice for Patty. If he could investigate it from his end that would help as well. After all, he was now a member of the naval police. He agreed that, when I go home in a couple of months, I could take a copy with me. I was so keen I asked the bar if I could get a copy made and he pointed down the road. I told Adam about Petra and said I would give the statement to her dad, as his wife was a lawyer she might be able to find out more about these girls. I suggested that we get the copying done and I treated him to a plate of chilli crab. We had an enjoyable evening, Adam was soon pissed and shouting at the top of his voice. Strange that I enjoyed the screeching after hating this man for over two years.

We spent four weeks driving round Singapore, rifles between our knees. Bums bruising on the seats of our very ancient trucks, moaning constantly. Then good news, Shady and I were taken off patrols. Followed by bad news, we were sent to the jungle.

On arrival, we were told our task was to fix the radios on the patrol boats and vehicles. There were machine guns mounted on the roof of all the trucks and the front of the boats. When asked what experience we had on fixing these small radios, Shady gave his normal non-bullshit answer.

'We have been trained to fix transmitters the size of a garden shed,' he told the Sergeant.

'Well these little ones should be easy for you then,' was his reply. They were easy, as most of the faults were ripped-out handsets and headphones.

Every now and again we were taken to the sharp end. At one post we were working as the patrols came staggering back in from fighting the enemy. One crowd came in and slumped next to us in the canteen. A guy, seeing we were Navy, said, 'Shit, that rum of yours is strong, do you get used to it?'

'No,' I reply, 'we get addicted to it.'

'Yeh, one of our guys could be up for a medal and the rum helped. We were going to flush out a small compound and just before we began, we lined up and were given a tot of rum each. When we found the enemy, a machine gun opened up and pinned us to the ground. After an age, Gordy just got up and ran at them tossing grenades firing from the hip. The firing stopped and Gordy was lying on the ground. They took him away and said he was suffering from shell shock.

'When we visited him, he whispered that he was as pissed as a fart and what the fuck happened? "How did you get pissed?" we asked. "When the Sergeant passed us the rum both the guys either side of me asked if I wanted their tots, so I had theirs." "Jesus," I said, "three tots can have disastrous effects." The guy laughs and said, "It gets worse, the Sergeant came back and asked if anyone wanted seconds?"' Shady was turning a darker shade of pale remembering his pool antics. I look up at the sky and think of Punchy.

As we while away the weeks in the jungle, I tell Shady all about the three girls. We agree I will come up to London after a week at home and he will help me find Danny.

Finally leave Singapore for home

Eventually, the guy in charge of Indonesia decides not to invade and we are all finally sent back to Singapore. We spend three days in the barracks before our flight. Every night I go to the stall, put on my plastic pinny, and wrestle with a chilli crab. Not really recommended just before a two-day flight back to the UK.

This is my first return to England after a time in the tropics and the gloom and rain that appears as we come down through the clouds is not a very cheerful welcome. Not having any way to contact Arthur, I had no milk van to get me home. So I talked the RAF bus driver to make a detour through my village on the way to Swindon station. As Shady looked through the gloom at my village, I wished I had not exaggerated the splendour of the place.

Neither of us had the wherewithal to contact each other by phone so the arrangement was to be under the clock at Paddington station at 11.00 on the allotted day. Arriving two hours early, I sat at a cafe within sight of the clock. Dressed in one of Johnny Chan's up-market suits, and his very posh shoes, I felt comfortable. Flicking sausage roll pastry desperately off my trousers brought me back down to earth. At 10.50, Shady approached wearing one of Johnny's more conservative numbers and ordered coffee. He said he had used his wad and investments to buy a two-bed flat so I could stay with him. He had also got a phone installed in the flat. We headed to North London. He had only just got the flat so there was just two beds, table and settee. That meant we would be eating out in the pub down the road. Shady had got out all the London phonebooks ready and we began. Hours later, still trying to find the number of Danny in London, it seemed impossible. Shady kept saying the guy is probably ex-directory and not in these books.

So I ring the number the Coxswain gave me and as soon as it was answered I ask to speak to CPO Henshaw and tell them my name. The lady answering asks for my number and says she will get him to ring me. I explain it is a bit delicate and would it be possible to give me a number to ring. She told me to ring back in one hour. I ring back and the Coxswain answers, 'Dave Samson are you ready to speak to me?' I ask if Petra has recovered. 'I am not sure how she is now, but six months ago she still wasn't talking about her ordeal.' I explain to the Coxswain that I met RPO Yelton (Screech) in Singapore. I told him about the witness statement and that Danny has been lying to me from the start. He told me to report to him in Portsmouth after the meeting.

Sitting on Shady's lonely settee with my head in my hands, I listen to him begging his sister to come and visit. He puts the phone down smiling and said both his sister and mother are coming round in two days' time.

'Right,' I said, 'we need to decorate and buy stuff to make this flat something for you to be proud of.'

'What about the young girls and all the other things you are trying to solve?' he asked.

'Danny can wait, I need to decide how to approach him.'

In London you only have to walk out of the flat and down the road and you will find an upmarket second-hand furniture shop. In the shop that we found, there was a guy who was about thirty and once we told him our problem, he suggested he came back to the flat to survey Shady's needs. I assumed he supported the same god as Shady as he had a round piece of black cloth on his head which failed to come off, even when he had to run across the road. The two Jewish lads seem to enjoy each other's company so the plan was I would stay in the flat and paint all the rooms whilst they ran around North London buying stuff. This suited me perfectly as I had some serious thinking and reflecting to do.

Everything kept coming back to Danny and Robbie. I was trying to remember who led the campaign against Screech to fit him up with abduction. Did Mick just come over to the island to tell me everything was rosy and to let things lie? What about the other girl in Gosport? Is that real or just fiction made up by Robbie?

Adam Yelton's signed statement says Danny was with Patty the night she died. I thought Danny was getting his kit ready for our marching out parade and with us in the mess. Since reading the statement, try as I might, I cannot place him in the mess. However, it was chaos with everyone waiting for an ironing board, cleaning webbing and shoes. We were all concentrating on our stuff not on anyone else. So, it was Danny with Patty, that is a fact, forget the others, sort out Patty.

Over the next three days, I decide to go and see Danny three times and chicken out twice so at the moment I am going to see Danny.

My excuse is that Gino and Mike said you had left the Navy through ill health. As I am staying in North London with a friend, I thought I would visit you and see if you needed cheering up. We had some great times and it would be a shame not to keep in touch.

I read this out to Shady and he looked up after reading it and said, 'This is your plan to approach a mad psychopath who attacks girls?'

'Now I am back, why shouldn't we meet? I need to know what happened.'

I make up my mind to do it, and Shady and I go to the library to get the address of Albert Smith. I leave a very excited Shady at home to greet his sisters. I choose this day to risk irking Danny's ire, as it seems that us gentiles (that's what I am) are not high enough to attend this religious gathering. Shady has been perfecting making chicken soup for days and I have not been allowed to touch it.

I take a taxi and the driver asks me the address twice, then I make the mistake of saying it's OK my friend lives there. I am now addressed as 'Sir' instead of 'mate'. When we arrive, there are two very large houses built exactly the same. Through a double gate, they both have a long drive with a turnaround at a huge front door, which is under a covered canopy held up by stone pillars. 'Which one Sir?' asks the driver. I see that one has a man at the gate and a Range Rover with two men in, so I choose the other one.

I get to the door and before I knock a big man steps out and says, 'What?' I explain I have come on the off chance that my friend Danny is in, as I am in the area. 'Wait,' so I did. A very attractive women comes out smiling, she must be over fifty but still looks like a film star.

'Who wants Danny?' she asks.

'I am sorry to trouble you, my name is Dave Samson. Danny and I were good friends in the Navy and I wonder if he is in.'

She smiles and says, 'Come in Dave, I have heard a lot about you.' Then shouts, 'Danny, Dave Samson to see you.' Danny runs down a large winding staircase and greets me with a big hug (I worry about the sweat running down my armpits!). 'Dave,' he said, 'I wondered when you would have the balls to come and see me.'

He leads me into a spacious lounge that spreads through wide patio doors to a paved area with armchairs and tables spread amongst the plants. A short path leads to a large pool with a fountain on the end. Running down the path wagging their tails are two black and tan dachshunds. Danny, still laughing, sits down and indicates for me to sit down. 'Meet Bella and Daisy,' he said. 'They are little sods till they get to know you so don't get up quick or they will have your ankles.'

He asked if I wanted a drink and I answer, 'Whatever you're having,' he shouts for tea. Then he said, 'Excuse me,' and goes over and picks up the phone. 'Hey, Dave Samson is here, come over and say hello. It won't be a problem,' he said sharply. 'Just come over now and bring sis.' He looks back at me and looks serious for a moment. 'Dave, it's great to see you, I have been trying to build up the courage to get in touch but you will soon see why it has not been easy.'

It was all feeling a bit surreal. I came here wondering whether I should be in fear of my life and I am greeted like a lifelong lost friend. Was this a trap? Two beers and three glasses of wine were brought in by Danny's mother who was introduced as Dora. (Who on earth would name this gorgeous lady Dora?) OK, I have had my fair share of surprises lately but the next one takes the biscuit.

'We're here!' a girl shouted.

'Out here,' called Danny. Walking round the table in front of me are two very beautiful girls who look like twins. One does not recognise me and one does. I look up at her and ask, 'Patty?'

'Hello Dave, how are you?' she said.

'Very surprised and happy to see you,' I manage to answer and jump up and hug the life out of her. 'I can't believe it! I have spent the last two years wondering what happened to you and fearing the worst,' I said trying not to be too angry. Then I joked and said, 'I cannot believe you chose Danny over me, I thought my Wiltshire accent would have swung it, especially as you are a Janner (from Plymouth).'

Danny interrupted, 'I think Dave and I have to have a one-to-one talk. Give us a few hours and we will go find a restaurant and celebrate.' I was introduced to Debbie his sister as she left. The mother was gorgeous but when you look at Danny and Debbie they were the true stars.

Danny sat back and said, 'I have some explaining to do. First things first, has anyone told you the truth about what happened to my father?'

I nodded, 'Mick told me you killed him and why.'

Danny began his tale of woe. 'I was abused from a young boy by my dad. As I got older, he bothered me less and less. Unbeknown to me, he had then switched his attentions to Debs. When I walked in and found them at it, I totally lost it and went and got his gun and shot him. Once Debs got away from him, I, in a frenzy destroyed him. Debs and I now have mental problems that, in the beginning, included an attempt to end our lives. I will not bore you with the details. Since that day we both cannot, or to put it better, do not want or need sexual relationships with anybody. With the help of a therapist my mum found, we are now on the road to recovery. The problem is we come from a family that has strict macho rules which has brought them on top of a very successful empire. Dad obviously had problems in his youth to make him the monster he became. The reason for his killing could not be made public.

'We managed until I became involved with a little spoilt Cypriot girl who was the daughter of a top Cypriot drug baron. A girl who played the field and was used to getting what she wanted. Unfortunately, she wanted me. It was then I found out that a girl who took her clothes off and then tried to rip mine off made me very angry. The repulsion I felt made me hit out and attack her. The next thing I know is Mick holding me up and dragging my body away. She was taken to hospital and later claimed she was raped. What really happened I do not know, I could have hurt her but I certainly did not rape her. Anyway, the solution from them on high was for me to run away from London and join the Navy under the control of Robbie.

'At Raleigh when we met Patty it was not long before, listening to her story and watching her sometime stutter or flinch, I knew she was hurting. I found out by accident that the best way to spot someone abused was to say "As a little boy I was abused, is it happening to you?". She nodded and I then found out the true story. Her father had abused her for years and her mother was turning a blind eye, having none of it. He was a friend of the NAAFI manager and got Patty a job at the bar. He took her there and back. She was never allowed to be on her own. Her problem was the same as mine, she was getting older. Two problems actually. One he liked them younger and two, when she became 18, he would no longer be in control and she could run off and tell the world. Remember when someone attacked her in the woods in Raleigh? That was probably her father!

'So the night before we had our parade was our last chance to save her. In the NAAFI, I struggled to convince her that the escape plan would work. Finally, she agreed that she would leave at closing time with the other staff. I slipped off earlier and got through the perimeter fence with wire cutters. I then walked up to the father and put him down. Patty left the other staff at the end of her road. Mum drove down and was waiting a few doors from her house. Debs has a hairdresser's salon a mile from here which has a flat above. She agreed to move in and take care of Patty. Now, two years later, they are inseparable and together run a very successful business. Patty is now a qualified hairdresser but, more importantly, very happy.

'The reason we had to keep all this quiet was apart from my beating of her father, Patty was only 15 at the time. Her father had lied about her age to enable her to get a job in the NAAFI. If the police had found her, she would have been returned to him. My solicitor told me that the law would ignore his abuse even if Patty provided a written statement of his treatment. With no proof, she would be back under his control. (In 1963 this type of abuse is not mentioned in public and is almost never brought to court.) Next month Patty is 18 and we have all the legal protection in place to stop him trying anything. That's not to mention the other threats my family have at their disposal. I am not sure Patty's family deserve it but it's up to her whether she contacts her mum or not. Obviously if all this gets out, the press will have a field day. I am sure you will agree it is best to carry on as we are, until Patty is strong enough to announce she is still alive and ran away from her abusing father.'

After a few minutes getting my head round it all I began asking questions. 'When did you get all your kit ready for the parade?'

'Come on, you know me, my kit was always immaculate. It was ready before I left to see Patty. You lot were so busy panicking and rushing around you did not even know I was missing. When I slipped back in the mess just after midnight you did not even speak to me as you were all still running about like blue-arsed flies.'

'Which of you three was the expert locksmith?' I asked.
'That was Mick,' he said. 'His dad and brothers were the best in the business. He could open any lock and he did not even discuss Screech's office and bedroom with us. One day he beckoned Gino and I over and just walked into Screech's office and pulled the filing cabinet drawers out. He must have been working on them previously.'

'So the only person who could get into Screech's rooms was Mick. Could you or Gino get in without his help?'

'Not even with the key he made as he still had to use his

set of levers to get into the other doors.'

'So the photos and letters and stuff must have belonged to Mick? If not, how come they were removed once we told the Navy police about them. Screech did not know we had told the police. Why would he shift them?'

'I had forgotten all about that stuff. Where are you going with these questions?' asked Danny.

'Well, you knew what had happened to Patty. Whereas I have thought for the last two years that either one of you three or Robbie had killed Patty and attacked Petra!' I replied struggling to keep my anger in check.

'Petra?' Danny was looking really confused.

'The girl in Malta whose father I played tennis with.'

'Is she dead?'

'No, but the day after the tennis tournament she went missing. Next day she was found in a hut very disorientated and had been attacked. I have spent the last two years thinking that you were somehow involved. It was too much of a coincidence, you were there in Raleigh and you were there in Malta. Two cases of missing girls. I had been thinking somehow Screech had been posted to Malta! But that seemed unlikely. It had to have something to do with you London lads.'

Danny was scratching his head. Eventually he said, 'I got on great with that girl, we clicked like kids do.' He held his hand up and said, 'Nothing sexual, we just made each other laugh.' After a few minutes he said, 'Now I do remember, I was supposed to meet her that evening, her parents were going to some regatta and I was invited. I got ready and when I went to my locker my ID card and Leave Card were missing. The quartermaster would not let me leave the ship.'

We both looked at each other and he said, 'Are you thinking what I am thinking?'

'Was Mick in the same mess as you on your ship?' I asked.

'Yes and he was always used in the mess to open a locker if anyone had lost their key.'

'So the question is,' I say, 'was Petra attacked by Mick or a complete stranger?'

'He did go ashore that night but I cannot remember discussing Petra with him,' Danny replied.

'But wait a minute, Mick and Gino turned up in Hong Kong and Mick told me you were weird and have a lot of strange habits. He also told me about pulling you off the Cypriot girl. He said if you had hurt those girls, Robbie or someone else would have fixed it for you.'

Danny said, 'Robbie has been part of the family all my life. He was caught as one of the minions in a lorry hijack when a teenager and had a choice between borstal or the services. He chose the Navy and rose through the ranks as a Regulator. He was stationed in Malta and helped with the relationship between my dad and the London Maltese guys. Any senior Navy officers who got involved in casino money problems, Robbie would be informed. Also, if they got involved with woman or men he would be informed. He set up a successful business using the officers who had returned to the UK. He acquired companies that supplied the Navy around Portsmouth with meat and vegetables. These companies provided substandard produce at top prices and the naval supply officers and senior rates were rewarded for signing the required documentation.

'He suggested we join the Navy after our incident with the Cypriot girl. Robbie knew nothing at all about Patty, all the planning and action was carried out by my mum and I. The problem was, he thought I had killed her and then began a plan to get one of you boys to take the rap. I had to go along with it to protect Patty.

'I made a point of trying to keep Robbie out of my life. Now he was out of control running around bringing attention to Patty's disappearance rather than letting the police and the Navy slowly give up on it. After Malta, my depression came back and I got very down. I contacted Mother and she arranged for my doctor, the therapist, here to contact the Navy and explain my mental problems. Which, thanks to Robbie, seemed to be missing from my naval medical records. Once my ship got near Gibraltar, I was flown off and taken straight to hospital and from there discharged from the Navy. The Cypriot girl problem had been sorted by Al (Albert) so I was safe to come home. Robbie was told to forget about the girls.'

I asked how that was managed.

'Robbie became too big for his boots, first by thinking my mum was part of the deal. Secondly by going ahead with the Maltese guys to use Navy ships for smuggling without discussing it with Albert. I believe this smuggling deal recently went tits up and Robbie had to run. I have no idea where he is and it's best not to ask.

'Mother, Debs and I are now on reasonable terms with Al. We all agree that this side of the family now needed to separate away from here. Soon we will sell this house and move to at least the other side of town. We have all the legitimate businesses in our name, the rest are with Albert. I am planning to set up a charity to help kids like us escape from abusive families. I am also going to university to study psychology.

'I do understand you have been manipulated and lied to. What can I do to put right all the wrongs?'

I said, 'Yes, I have had to put up with some very unsettling incidents. All of them meant I had to grow up very quickly. I want us all to find out who hurt Petra. If she is still mentally scarred and not responding to treatment, I want you to help her. Also, another incident discussed over the last two years, was that Robbie interviewed both Gino and me about an attack on a girl in Gosport. Apparently, you had a girlfriend in Gosport and her mate got attacked?'

Danny said, 'I met a girl in Southsea called Sally who lived in Gosport. Mick and I went out for dinner over in Gosport with Sally and a friend whose name I cannot remember.'

'Can you get that police detective guy to find out what the present state is?' I ask. 'I think we have a problem with Mick. It must have been him who stowed the documents under Screech's room. In Malta, he must have broken into your locker and taken your ID card and Leave Pass – why? He went with you to Gosport, if you did not hurt the girl then was it Mick? Then we get to the Cypriot girl and if you flaked out before she was seriously beaten up, was she raped like she claimed and was it Mick?'

Danny took a good few minutes before replying. He has a way of seriously looking you in the eye. 'If Mick is hurting girls, we need to be very sure. His family will not take kindly to any such questions and will act violently.'

I said, 'You should also spend some time trying to remember what happened with the Cypriot girl. Then the same with Gosport. Going into fine detail of each incident should at least give us what you know. This is the first time that two separate incidents with you and Mick together have been questioned. Am I right?' I ask.

Danny said, 'Give me a day to get my head round the questions. I will ring Alan, the detective we spoke to in London, and ask about Gosport. I have to think who to ask about the Cypriot girl, whose name was Georgia by the way. She may have been a diva but she did not deserve what happened to her. I should try and get up the courage to speak to her, but don't hold your breath.'

I said, 'Why don't I contact Timothy West and see if we can help the family? You say you want to help people who have been abused. Debbie and Patty could talk to Petra or

295

alternatively your doctor lady. Even you and your mum could have a go. If it was Mick who hurt her, and she would agree to tell the police, he could be arrested without us being involved.'

We finished and called mum (Dora) and the girls back outside. The reason they reminded me of twins was because they were both in their hairdresser's outfits before. Now they both had their own style but Debbie was the talker, Patty just sat and laughed at the banter. Danny held his hand up and proceeded to explain everything we had discussed. This came as a surprise to me but at the same time I felt completely at home with it. The reason is both his mum and the girls listened intently and were nodding in agreement at all the conclusions we had just made. When the three girls were mentioned individually, our audience gasped and held hands. At the end, Dora said, 'We must help all three girls. Danny, you have to find out your involvement and make good and accept responsibility for your actions. Despite our sufferings we have to put this right.' Danny nodded.

Debbie said to me, 'Dave we must help Petra and we will, won't we Patty?' Patty stared at me and with a grown-up growl she said, 'Make it happen Dave!'

Dear me, I thought, this is a very impressive team I have just joined.

'Would you be surprised if it was Mick?' I asked.

Dora replied, 'We have ceased to be surprised about anything in our strange lives. Let's take everything very

slowly and meet that problem when we have all the facts.'
I agree and I say, 'The only guy I have not thought was
guilty of all these misdemeanours is me. Screech, Danny,
Gino, Mick and Robbie have all been guilty in my eyes at
sometime over the last two years.'

Danny invites me to stay over. I ring Shady and tell him I
am alive, then give him a quick sitrep, including Patty
is alive and sitting next to me. I managed to get him
off the phone with a promise to ring later and explain
all. I have a great evening sitting at a restaurant table
surrounded by beautiful people. Every person walking
past us, sort of stopped and studied the five of them
thinking who are they?

In the morning, I sit in their garden with a large tea, and
a hangover, feeling very pleased with myself. A weight
has been lifted; as far as I can tell, no one has died and
with the help of my new team we may get close to a
happy ending.

I ring the Coxswain to ask for Tim West's phone number. I
tell him enough facts to get a few days' grace before I have
to meet him.

Tim's telephone rings and he recognises me as soon as he
hears my name. Tim is his usual polite self but there is
a 'what the hell can he want?' in his voice. I explained
I have spoken to the Coxswain and he has told me what
happened to Petra. Quickly I explained my posting from
the ship to a remote island in Hong Kong. With no answer
from Tim, I continued and asked if it was possible to meet,
as I believe I may have some information that might help.

He was quite abrupt and told me if I had any information I should go to the police. I immediately thought that obviously as the attack was done in Malta and as far as I know not reported in UK that would be a waste of time. Instead I said, 'You and your family were very kind to me in Malta and I have a great respect for all of you. I would not waste your time if I did not think I could help. Can we please meet and discuss the time before and after the tennis match?'

'By we, who do you mean, not the Coxswain surely?'

'No, I would like to start with my friend Danny who was with us in Malta. If you are comfortable with that, then we would introduce you to Danny's sister and a girl called Patty who have both suffered severe abuse from violent men.'

'Can I bring my wife?' he asked.

'That would be perfect, I was afraid to ask but yes please she will see how desperate we are to help.'

He was reluctant for us to see him in his house and I said we would be better off somewhere private so we arranged to meet at Danny's next day.

In the meantime, Alan has got back to Danny, on Gosport. Sally's girlfriend was Margaret. She was attacked three days after the dinner with Danny. The attack was in a lane near her house and she does not want to talk about it. Danny rang Sally and she said Margaret did not see Mick after the dinner because he scared her. Creepy was how

Margaret described him.

Dora has phoned Georgia's mother to see if they can meet up and talk about that night. She has said Danny is full of remorse and would be happy to meet up with Georgia and her mother.

Timothy and Fiona arrive and I can see they are suitably impressed. We introduce them to Dora and the girls and then lead them out onto the terrace. They make their apologies and then just the four of us sit down to three beers and a glass of red wine. Once again, we do not hold anything back. First Danny tells his tale including his dad, Debbie, Georgia, Patty and Mick. Then I tell my story leaving nothing out. Both Tim and Fiona look stunned.

I say, 'It is a lot to take in, and most of it has nothing to do with you, but if we are right about Mick we must stop him. Until the girls are happy and progressing, Mick will not be mentioned. Rest assured we will be watching him.'

Danny said, 'Tim, Fiona can you tell us exactly what happened in Malta? Can I also ask that Dora and the girls join us? As you have heard, they have come a long way since their trauma and if we are to get anywhere, Debbie and Patty are probably the best chance of success.'

Fiona said, 'Yes let's do it.' Tim nodded in agreement.

Dora returns and reinforces our message. 'We have three girls who are all struggling with themselves and they are more important than Mick. It would be great if Debs and Patty could meet and hangout with Petra just to see where that takes us. As a fall back, we have the best doctor in the country who fixed Danny, Debbie and Patty. She is a close friend of the family and is willing to help. She is on the board of our charity and does it all for free. The other two girls we mentioned hopefully will accept our help and get free of their depression.'

Danny says 'Tell us what you know about Malta.'

Tim started, 'The evening began with Petra's disappointment of you not turning up. She sulked most of the evening. A whole group of us walked back to our friend's house and there was a bar and pool in the garden. I saw Petra sitting by the pool with a crowd of teenagers. Later, Fiona saw her on some seats in the garden with what we think was the same crowd. It was not before everyone started thinking of retiring that we began looking for Petra. We, the staff and the remaining drinkers searched everywhere and in the end we brought in the Naval Patrol. It was extended when the local police were brought in and we searched all night. In the morning, all the previous night's partygoers were questioned, lots of them remember her, but no one could remember any strangers, or seeing her walking away from the crowd.

'Late the next day, a gardener was watering the plants after the sun went down and he heard a very quiet knocking sound coming from an old hut amongst the trees. The door was barred from the outside, he removed the wood that was jamming the door and he found her lying inside. She was covered in bruises with a broken arm and fingers. We first saw her in the hospital and she was so traumatised she could not speak and just lay there not moving. Within a week, her wounds were well on the mend and she could walk. Whether it was correct or not, we decided to get her back to London, where we believed expert help would bring her back to us.

'I insisted the Naval Provost Marshal shut down the investigation and remove our names from it. They had not found a scrap of evidence on her clothes or from the hut and its surrounding land. I agreed to provide any clues or any description of the attacker that Petra remembered when she got better. The press were never informed and the word was put out that she returned to the house the next day and was in a lot of trouble with her parents. The family had all returned to the UK as planned. Obviously, I had to inform the Captain. It is a pity you only got half the story from my Yeoman on the Folkestone.

'Petra over the last year now talks to us. She lives a very sheltered life. We have tried three different schools and two of the best doctors London can provide. The problem is, the consultants know what is wrong with her but have not yet found a way to improve her condition.'

Debbie sitting next to Fiona reaches out and holds her hand and there are tears in her eyes. 'I understand, please let us help. Our nasty clouds still hang over us but we have learned to live with them and be happy.'

We leave the girls arranging a visit and days aimed at getting Petra involved. My ears popped when I heard them talking about tennis. Tim, Danny and I had moved away from the girls.

'Tennis?' I ask.

'Yeah,' says Danny, 'those three play twice a week and I hear they are very good.'

'Fiona is a good player and Petra would have been even better if Malta had not happened,' adds Tim.

'Let's hope they manage to get her playing again. Then we can step in and show them how it's played,' I say.

With the girls out of earshot, we begin discussing Mick. I suggest we contact the Coxswain and put a case for him to find Mick and then see if he thinks putting surveillance in place is possible. Tim says he will look at the legal issues with his father.

Danny says, 'Let's all have a few days as I have to get some progress on the other two girls.' We agree to meet here at Danny's in three days.

Shady is happy for me to stay with him so I grab a lift with Tim. The flat is now fully furnished. As I walk round admiring it, Shady explains where some more improvements are required. Scratching my head and looking around I say, 'Shady, it's finished you need to stop.'

'You could be right, Dave.'

We then catch up on my visit to Danny which leaves Shady shaking his head. 'You are either in a nightmare or a movie' was his only comment.

Shady is back in touch with his family so when we go to the pub for supper he only goes and orders steak and kidney pie! 'You back with the family but not eating their stuff?' I say.

'There is only so much chicken soup a man can take,' was the answer.

Next morning, I ring the Coxswain. I get halfway through my story and he asks me to jump on a train to Portsmouth. There is lots to talk about, including Lt Appleton (Robbie). I tell Shady that I will be in Pompey for a couple of days and will be staying in the Fleet Club and to leave a message if I am needed. I also ring Danny with the same info.

The Coxswain's office is in HMS Excellent. So it's a taxi from Portsmouth Harbour Station to Whale Island. Finally, I find his department. I am taken into a large office and led to a smaller one in the corner. I'm greeted with a smile (didn't get many of them on the ship) and he then pointed to a chair on the other side of his desk. Before we start our chat, he hands me three railway warrants and chit for a two-day stay at the Fleet Club with meals. Then he counts out my expenses in cash and gives me a form to sign.

The Chief said, 'I am off the ship so you call me Chief now.' Then he began. 'Let's split this discussion into two cases. The first case being Lt Appleton and the second case Able Seaman Michael McDonald.'

'Do you know where Robbie Appleton is?' I ask.

The Chief replies, 'No, do you?'

'No, I have been told not to ask.' I reply.

303

The Chief says, 'So tell me what you know about him.'

I explain all my meetings with Robbie and why he joined the Navy, in fact the whole story. I then add some new information. 'When Robbie was stationed in Malta he became a go-between for the Maltese guys and his London mob. During that time, he was given a list of senior officers who got into trouble with money, girls or boys. When he got back to Portsmouth he used this information to set up businesses supplying inferior meat and veg to the Portsmouth command at top prices. He bribed Senior Store Officers that had served in Malta with cash and threats. I believe this scam is still in operation now. It's so successful that most Chief and Petty Officer Caterers are also getting a piece of the action.

'I assume you know that I put the smuggling plan into Punchy's possessions? [Chief nodded.]. Robbie was convinced that Danny was committing the crimes on the four girls. He thought he had to save Danny from prosecution, so he proceeded to invent a case for the three of us. How could that happen? I wanted to hurt the bastard, that's why I gave you the info through Punchy. Why didn't you guys catch him?' I ask.

'We did,' replied the Chief, 'but as a Naval Officer he was confined to the wardroom and he just jumped out of the window and that's the last we have seen of him. Did your London friends get him?'

'So I am told but it's only second hand. I cannot believe you lot let him go, he was mister big!'

What happened was way above my pay grade,' the Chief

muttered. He followed with, 'Try and confirm that if you can so we can stop looking for the bastard. Now.' The Chief paused, 'Michael McDonald. What exactly has he done?'

'First I have a question, in Gib when Robbie was questioning me, you knew that Petra was alive and safe in UK. Why did you let him ask me all those questions and not tell me until we got outside?'

'Because you were not telling me the truth about him. My fellow officers knew he was bent but he was too powerful. A team above my head were watching him and they were informed about Danny's family connections. I kept telling you to talk to me and here you are, finally talking. Your message in Punchy's letter was perfect and everything we needed to get him. The powers that be are very pleased and your efforts are noted. However, it is best we now let you slip quietly back to making your way to being an electronics engineer in our Navy. So Michael McDonald?'

I started, 'Danny my friend in London is hoping to get any one of the three girls we believe he attacked and raped to make a statement. After chasing lost causes and red herrings we are now certain Mick is attacking girls. How often and why, we do not know. Even if we convince one of them to say it was him, we still need them to agree to go to court and convict him. One of the girls is a Cypriot and if she fingers Mick he will disappear like Robbie.

'I have just left Tim West and his wife and they are working with Danny and his sister to help Petra. However, even if she were to get to the stage of telling them who attacked her, would Tim want it acted out in court? Danny knows the third girl's best friend and she could be our only chance. We do not know if the victim is angry and seeking revenge or is denying it ever happened. Hopefully we should have a better idea of what to do in a few days. The problem we are facing is in the three cases it would seem better for Mick to just disappear.

'As he is a naval rating, would you be able to put a team together to investigate him? As I described earlier, he can open any lock and has spent his youth avoiding getting caught. Following him would be almost impossible. We now believe the stash we found under the hut was Mick's.'

I remind the Coxswain of all the items we found in Screech's cabin.

'These items must be important to him, or why would he have risked removing them at the last minute at Raleigh? We think he will have them hidden close to him. Finding them might be all the proof you need.'

The Chief said, 'He is back here in this establishment halfway through a Leading Patrolman's course. Leave it with me, we may be able to put a stop to his antics. The fact that we are on Whale Island will help us monitor his movements. I want to know straightaway if any of those girls confirm he was responsible. We can't do anything without credible evidence'

I return to Shady's flat and ring Danny daily to get an update. Petra is playing tennis again and has spent two days in the hair salon. Danny is going down to Gosport tomorrow and his mum is meeting Georgia and her mother at the same time. We agree a meeting at his house the day after.

Sat around in Danny's house, everyone reports back.

I tell of my meeting with the Coxswain, including the fact that Mick is on a patrolman's course.

Dora explained, 'Mick's parents think Mick is still abroad and don't know when he is back. She says, 'I have been to see Georgia and her mother. Georgia said they were taking drugs and she remembers Danny flaking out first and soon after she must have drifted off as well. When she awoke, Mick was pulling Danny off her but he was still out of it. She was badly bruised with her clothes ripped off and could not stand up. Danny was dressed with not a mark on him. She thinks Mick was wearing different clothes but cannot swear to that. The reason Danny was told that it was OK to come back home was she had told all this to her dad a few months ago.'

Danny said, 'I went to see Sally and Margaret. Margaret is not at all traumatised, she is very angry and wants to catch the bastard. Her words. However, he attacked her from behind and did not speak so she cannot help us.'

Debbie said, 'Petra is coming along fine. Patty and I have explained in detail our living hell of being forced by our fathers. Slowly she is talking about what happened to her that night. We are waiting for the mention of the man who attacked her. Until she gets to that point, we cannot show her a picture of Mick or even talk about him. She is starting to laugh and she enjoys helping in the salon. Tim, I think we will be playing mixed doubles before we hear what happened to her. It is going to take time.'

With no real progress I ask if I can ring the Coxswain. When he answers, I explain what we know.

The Coxswain said, 'We have made considerable progress. When you left I selected two of his classmates to get close to him. Over the past few days, Mick has been for walks over the playing fields. We have only followed him from long distance. Then we had stationed people on the route. Yesterday, after getting out of sight from the main buildings, he went round the back of a small maintenance building. Today, whilst he was in the classroom we got the specialist police unit to help. The door was locked by key and padlock. We had the key but the high-end padlock must be his. It took half the day to find his stash underground covered by a steel plate. It is in a large holdall suitable for a quick escape. The contents are overalls, woolly hat, boots and gloves. A flick knife, truncheon and gun with ammunition. All the pictures and letters you described. Finally there are objects which could be from his victims. Clothing, necklaces, bracelets. The experts have photographed all the contents and put them back as they found them. Tomorrow we will fingerprint everything and decide whether to wait for him to revisit or arrest him. He is now being watched 24 hours a day. I will bring the pictures to you in the morning and send a man to Gosport this afternoon. In the meantime, can you get all concerned to think back to what was worn and if any objects were missing.'

I agreed, put the phone down and gave a deep sigh and stood amongst them all, holding my hands up to get their attention. When I began relaying everything the Coxswain told me, I soon had silence in the room.

'You were right, Dave,' Danny said in my ear as he gave me a big hug.

Dora got on the phone to Georgia to find out if she could help. Tim and Fiona were trying to remember what jewellery Petra was wearing that evening. Fiona, putting her lawyer hat on, said it's a pity none of these crimes had any police statements attached to them with the missing objects described. We will have to prove any item was owned by the girls.

At this moment in time I don't care, all I can think of is that we were right. It all started when we found the stuff under Screech's cabin and now it all ends with it being found again. The picture and letters being in a bag attached to Mick means I can think of something else and get on with my life.

The professionals were then in complete charge and responsible for the case. I am irrelevant and now free! In two weeks I am to start my Leading Hands course at HMS Collingwood. Shady is on the same course which is good news. The bad news is that no matter how much I try, the bastard will be top of the class!

As I march up and down to my classes in HMS Collingwood I often think of my first three years in the Navy. Never anything to do with the poor girls but always Punchy's runs ashore or Shady's underwater marching.

'Get that fucking grin off your face, Samson,' shouts the PO. 'What the fuck have you got to laugh about on this cold and frosty morning?'

I feel like putting my hand up and describing Shady shooting out of the water projecting chips and pie in the air then vomiting rum all over the Admiral and his lady.

Unfortunately I have never managed to finish the ditty. Halfway through I always drop to my knees in convulsions of laughter. Then I think of Sippers and the smile disappears.

To finish the Mike saga, all of the girls recognised some of their clothing and jewellery. Unfortunately, there were more objects in the holdall and other girls came forward. Mick was arrested and eventually transferred from the naval prison to a civilian prison. It only took a week before Mick hung himself in his cell. We all individually feared this would happen but never discussed it out loud. You do not, as part of Danny's and Mick's family group, commit multiple rapes, do your time and come out and live happily ever after. No – instead, someone enters your cell and hangs you.

On a lighter note, all the girls are recovering the best they can. Petra is now working in the very successful salon. It must be very confusing for anyone (especially men) entering to be met by three beautiful blonde girls all dressed the same. Gino is training to be a caterer, no doubt planning to feather his own nest, as well as feed us good scran. Danny is in university studying madness. Screech will soon be a Coxswain, hopefully his 'screeches' will become more refined. Blood? God knows where Blood is, he does not seem to need other human beings in his life. I am told Sippers is happy on the island and barking in Scottish.

Shady? I am stuck with Shady. I just wish I had a film of our swimming gala.

I am back to being a matelot and looking forward to when I can head back out in the world on one of Her Majesty's warships. I have been selected to complete a two-year electronics course and when I finish that I will be a Petty Officer.

Imagine the chaos that can be created as a Petty Officer? If I survive, I might even come back and tell you. Punchy, if you are looking down, I intend to impress you!